Luke Spade

A Secret Enemy for the Cowboy Billionaire

by **Sophie Devon**

Chapter One

A pretty, but red-nosed brunette sat huddled up on a couch in the cozy living room and rolled brimming eyes to her friend's face.

"I had to break it off with Luke. I just couldn't take it any more," she sobbed. "I woke up on my birthday and realized I was middle-aged, and no closer to my wedding day." She shook her head bitterly. "I'm thirty, I've sunk years of my life into Luke Spade—and he's never going to ask me to marry him!"

Julie Parker raised her brows sadly and slipped an arm around her best friend's shoulder. "I'm so sorry, Trina," she murmured. "I wish this hadn't happened."

"I wish it hadn't, either!" Trina agreed indignantly. "Breaking up with Luke was the last thing in this world I wanted. I've loved

Luke Spade from the first day I set eyes on him." She sniffed and smiled weakly, and her eyes got that faraway look that twisted Julie's heart. She'd seen that wistful look since the first day she and Trina had put their heads together and whispered about boys.

"Luke was busting broncs at the rodeo," Trina breathed, "and he was so handsome in his plaid shirt and jeans, Julie, you just don't know. He was riding a big palomino horse, and when the spotlight fell on him he lifted his Stetson and—his blonde hair was so beautiful," she murmured in a faraway voice. "Like wheat, or gold or something. His face was so brown," she whispered. "And when he stared up into the crowd, he looked right at me and smiled so handsome that I..."

Trina wiped her eyes with her hand and laughed weakly. "I couldn't believe it when we started to go out. I never dreamed such a handsome man would be seen with an ordinary girl like me."

Julie's eyes slid to the coffee table, where a big portrait of Luke still enjoyed a prominent place in Trina's house. Trina had always claimed Luke was to die for, but to Julie's eye, Luke wasn't what she'd call drop-dead gorgeous. She tilted her head. He was cute as a button, and he looked fun and laid back and—she narrowed her eyes—*possibly,* a little rascally.

If she had to guess, she'd say that Trina had fallen more for his charm than his looks. True, Luke had glorious wheat-blonde hair and long bangs that almost covered his brows. He had bright blue eyes glinting with mischief, high, proud cheekbones, a straight nose, and a wide, smiling mouth.

But there was something in that grin that suggested Trina's praise owed to something besides his boyish good looks.

Julie stifled a sigh. She could see why Trina had loved him, and why she was brokenhearted to have to give up on him.

Still, she couldn't allow Trina to see herself as less important than Luke, no matter how handsome or rich he might be.

Her heart melted in sympathy. "Don't sell yourself short, Trina," she objected. "You're a wonderful person. And you're very pretty."

"No I'm not," Trina sniffed. "I'm just average. I'm short and pudgy, not tall and leggy like you. The kids at our school used to call you Wonder Woman because of that long, pretty dark hair of yours, and your blue eyes. They called me the Pillsbury Dough girl, remember?"

Julie gave her friend a sympathetic look and said nothing, and Trina hiccuped, "But Luke was so sweet, he never made me feel plain. I began to hope. After our second anniversary I got brave enough to pick out a wedding dress!"

Julie frowned and tightened her grip on her friend's arm. Trina's anguish wrung her heart, because Trina was family. The two of them had been best friends since kindergarten.

Her mind flicked back to her childhood. She and Trina had shared their clothes and makeup and childish dreams, they'd lived at each other's houses. They'd had no secrets from one another, even when they began to date. Not even boys had come between them.

When they graduated from high school, and she moved away to Los Angeles, they'd talked to each other every week. Julie looked down at Trina's dear, familiar face, twisted in grief, and felt her own heart contract in sympathetic pain.

Trina was the sweetest, kindest person in the world. She didn't deserve a broken heart.

Trina shook her head and sniffed, "You were always the pretty one, Julie. You never had any trouble getting dates. But Luke was just about the only steady boyfriend I ever had." She pulled her mouth down. "I don't know if I'll ever find anybody else that I'll love as much as I loved him." She convulsed in a new wave of tears.

Julie pulled her closer and murmured, "Trina, are you—are you sure that this isn't just a big misunderstanding? You were the one to break up with Luke, remember," she added gently. "Maybe he isn't as reluctant as you think. He's dated you for years, after all," she smiled. "He must love you."

Trina slowly raised her head, and despair settled over her flushed face. "No," she replied in a small voice. "No, Julie. I know him, and he just...doesn't. Not really."

Julie stared at her. She'd never met Luke Spade, but she still couldn't quite believe that. Trina had filled her ears with Luke's praises for the last two years, had gushed about his handsome looks, his sweet personality, his successful family, their huge ranch. Her friend had painted Luke Spade as such a paragon of virtue that she couldn't believe Trina had just...dreamed all of that. Julie took a new grip on her resolve and tried again.

"That surely can't be true, Trina," she soothed. "A man doesn't spend that much time on a woman he doesn't love!"

"Luke did," Trina replied faintly, and the hopelessness in her voice pierced Julie's heart. Still, she couldn't believe that any decent man would use a woman so heartlessly; and least of all a sweetheart like Trina. She shook her head and pulled her friend closer.

"Trina, why don't you call him, *hm*? Couples say all kinds of things when they're mad, but they don't really mean them. Maybe you overreacted to think that Luke doesn't love you, or, or that he doesn't mean to marry you," she stammered.

Trina looked down at her hands. "I'm not freaking out, Julie," she insisted. "And I'm not making it up in my head. I told him the reason I was upset. I told him I wanted us to get married."

Julie raised her brows in pained sympathy as Trina shrugged, "Luke did what he always does when I mention it. He said he didn't want to get married, and—he ran away."

A frown dawned over Julie's face and slowly deepened. If that was right, then there really was no excuse she could offer for Luke.

If Trina had laid it all out for him, and he'd still turned his back on her, then it meant that he really didn't love her.

A man in love didn't have to be begged to commit. He did it gladly.

But Luke had walked out after he'd kept Trina dangling on a string for years. Julie's frown deepened. Luke had kept Trina waiting and hoping for a commitment he knew he was never going to make. He'd probably known that pretty soon after they started dating, what was more.

He *had* used her.

It was cruel.

Anger blossomed in Julie's heart, slow and dark, like a tropical flower unfurling its blood-red petals. It bloomed wide in her chest, coiled its tendrils all through her, released its opium deep into her blood. Her pupils contracted, and she glanced down at Trina in burning indignation.

Luke had committed an unforgivable betrayal of her friend's trust. Trina was such an honest person that she couldn't imagine dishonesty in a person she loved. Luke had seen that in her, and taken a cold, heartless advantage of it.

And even that wasn't all. Luke had wasted the years that Trina could've spent looking for a man who'd really love her.

It was incredibly selfish of him.

Her friend's voice brought Julie's attention back to the present. Trina twisted her tissue in her hands and stammered, "I just took a job in Oklahoma. I have to get away from here, Julie, I can't face all my friends any more. I know what people are saying behind my back, how they're laughing that I wasn't able to get Luke to marry me." She shook her head. "And now they'll be saying that I wasted all that time. It's humiliating!"

Julie stared at her in dismay. "But—you're surely not leaving home, Trina?" she wailed softly. "You've lived here all your life, all your family and friends are here. I'm back here now," she added earnestly. "There are so many things we were going to do together!"

Trina glanced up at her and smiled bravely, but shook her head. "You're sweet, Julie, but I've already put the house up for sale," she sniffed. "It's for the best. I couldn't live here, knowing that I could bump into Luke any day. It would be torture. No, I have to start over. Build a new life somewhere else."

A wave of shock slapped Julie. "But—I just got back from LA," she stammered. "What happened to that dress shop you've been talking about—the one you were going to open?"

Trina smiled at the reminder, but shook her head sadly. "I know, Jules. I'm so sorry. But I just can't be here any more. I've taken a job teaching in Oklahoma City." She glanced up at her appealingly.

"I hope you can understand."

"Of course I do, Trina," she stammered, and watched in frowning concern as her friend stood up, wiped her cheek with the back of her hand, and shuffled to the doorway.

"Look, I can go into the kitchen and whip something up for dinner," Julie suggested; but Trina just glanced at her sadly over her shoulder.

"You go ahead if you want," she murmured, with a crooked smile. "But I'm not very hungry. I think I'm going to go lie down."

Julie kept her expression calm and smiling until Trina left; but as soon as she disappeared, Julie put a hand to her eyes and choked back the big lump in her throat. *I can't believe she's selling her family home,* Julie thought numbly. *She's lived in it all her life!*

Slowly the yellow-orange of her shock deepened to the dark red of anger.

Luke Spade has ruined Trina's life, Julie fumed; then crossed her arms.

It'll be a cold day in Laredo before I let any man do that to me!

Chapter Two

"That's much better. Rest for a minute, and we'll move on to the next exercise."

Julie took a few steps back from her patient and gave her a minute to breathe. The girl who climbed down off the big treadmill was named Penny Baker. She was a willowy, fresh-faced blonde, barely out of her teens; but she'd suffered a concussion that hadn't resolved in the usual time. She needed a combination of aerobic and cognitive exercises to get her brain pathways working again.

Julie tossed her long ponytail back over her shoulder and checked her watch. She'd let Penny rest for five minutes, then she'd present her with a puzzle challenge that would help rebuild her visual function and memory.

Julie walked over to a big table to prepare a puzzle tray and its brightly-colored plastic pieces. She'd just started working as a part-time physical therapist at the local hospital, and she was doing what she loved: helping injured people get better.

But this particular morning had proven a real challenge. Julie glanced over her shoulder, met her patient's eye, and smiled.

Penny had gotten the concussion from a nasty blunt force blow to her skull. Her chart reported that she'd also presented with a black eye and three broken fingers. Julie glanced at her patient again. One of her hands was still bandaged up.

Julie frowned and rubbed a little spot between her eyes. There was a note in Penny's file that the ER physician had suspected domestic abuse; that he asked Penny if she'd been abused; that she'd said she had not.

She'd claimed she'd fallen down the stairs in her house.

Julie tried not to let her anger get the best of her. For the sake of her patient she needed to project smiling confidence, and so she put on her brightest expression, arranged the puzzle pieces on the desk, and beckoned the young woman over.

"Now that you're all warmed up, it's time to give your brain a workout," she smiled. "Sit down here and we'll get you started on this puzzle. The goal is to get all the pieces back into the tray the same way they're pictured on this sheet." She slid a picture of the completed puzzle toward the tray, and stepped back to let her patient settle in.

Julie let Penny sit down and get comfortable, then checked her watch again. "I'll set my watch. You'll have five minutes. And—go."

Julie stepped to one side and crossed her arms, watching her patient's hand-eye coordination as she began to pick up the plastic pieces and arrange them in the tray. Penny had been in therapy for almost a week, and she'd made moderate improvements. But she was still a bit slow to sort out the puzzle pieces, and Julie watched her pause over them, as if she couldn't quite process the bright colors and shapes.

Julie watched her hesitation and stifled the impulse to give her more time. She glanced at her watch as the minutes flew by, then looked up and called, "And...stop. Let's see how you did."

She walked over to the desk and leaned over Penny's shoulder. The girl looked up at her apologetically and murmured, "I still can't seem to get them all. I'm dumb, I guess."

Julie put a reassuring hand on her arm. "You're not dumb at all," she replied firmly. "You got three more pieces this time than last time. You're making gains." She paused, then added evenly: "You've suffered a serious head injury. It's going to take some time for you to come back from that."

The girl tucked a sprig of hair behind her ear, looked down and said nothing, and Julie's heart hurt for her.

"If there's anything you need from me, you only have to ask," she added slowly. "And if there's anything you want to tell me, I'm here for you. Ready to help."

She stood there, waiting, and her heartbeat quickened in the heavy silence that followed; but to her disappointment, Penny only shrugged and asked:

"Is that it for today?"

Julie took a deep, painful breath. "That's it for today." She mustered a smile. "Another day, another step forward. Be patient."

To Julie's gratification, her patient looked up at her and smiled. "I will. Thank you, Julie."

"You're more than welcome. Next session on Monday. I'll see you then."

Julie watched as Penny gathered up her purse, slung it over her shoulder, and walked out into the waiting room of the office. She drifted to the doorway and saw a pale, thin man with a frowning expression rise from a chair to meet her. Julie watched him walk the girl out with narrowed eyes and a heart burning with indignation.

She didn't know who that man was, or if he'd raised a hand to her patient; but the suspicious circumstances cast a dark cloud over the rest of her work day. She caught herself muttering under her breath, and more than once she slapped something down harder than she had to.

By the time she got off work, she was more than ready for a change of scene.

At five-thirty Julie stepped out of the physical therapy building and out into the spring sunshine. It was early May, and the sky was a pale, sunny blue, having just been washed with rain. She closed her eyes, took a deep breath of the clean, rain-scented air, and let it drive the dark clouds out of her heart.

She skipped across the wet street to the lot where her car was parked. Every tree on the street was bursting with green buds, and as she watched, a pair of birds flitted over, circled each other in the air, and darted off.

Spring, the time of love, Julie thought wistfully; and her mood darkened again as she opened the door of her pale blue VW Beetle.

But she hadn't witnessed much love since she'd gotten back home to Green Oak. Her best friend had been played by her boyfriend and her current patient was likely being beaten by her husband.

Julie caught herself growling under her breath as she pulled out into the street. It was enough to make her fantasize about slapping people; but it wasn't her place to do that.

And that made the abuse twice as frustrating to witness.

Sometimes I wish I could be a huge man just for a day, Julie thought angrily. *There are people I'd like to beat up.*

She switched on the radio impatiently as she drove the VW out of the hospital complex and out into the main artery through town. Soothing music flowed out into the car, and she sighed in relief. She always set the radio to the soft jazz station. It helped keep her calm and relaxed.

Julie's eyes flicked to the big white arches of the Fast Fatty's as she drove past. On an impulse, she suddenly yanked the car into the lot. Fast food was desperately unhealthy, she knew, but she'd spent five years in LA starving herself and obsessing over every detail of her appearance as a model.

Then, she'd gone to school to be a physical therapist and had the importance of good nutrition drummed into her head every day.

A juicy, meat-crammed hamburger would be a real comfort, especially since she was upset.

She pulled up to the red-and-white checkered speaker, and a gravelly voice barked, "What'll ya have?"

Julie bit her lip and glanced up at the menu. "I'll have the double Fatburger combo with a large sweet tea," she replied, with a flick of guilty zest. She couldn't remember the last time she'd had a burger stacked high with cheese and pickles and bacon.

"Drive around."

Julie nudged the Beetle around the building in rising anticipation. When she rolled her window down, the aroma of hamburgers and fries floated in on the breeze, and she inhaled gratefully. There was nothing that told her she was back home in Texas like the mouthwatering scent of frying meat.

She pulled up to the window, flashed her card, and grabbed the paper sack and cup a uniformed teenager thrust at her. She nudged the car out of the drive thru, paused just inside the exit, and fished a couple of french fries out of the bag.

Mmmm. Oh my gosh, she thought, and rolled her eyes up in delight. She licked the salt off her fingers and shook her head wordlessly.

She'd been good for a long, long time. So long that she'd forgotten how much fun it was to cheat on a diet. She jammed the cup into the holder at her elbow and stuck the straw in her mouth as she waited for traffic to clear.

Why am I still on a diet? she wondered suddenly. She wasn't trying to lose weight, or even maintain a size-7 figure anymore.

Force of habit, I guess.

She grabbed another fry, then pulled her little car out into the street and down a mile to the beautiful condo she'd just bought. It was in a brand new, mixed-use development not far from the hospital. Three-story colonial condos, upscale cafes, and one-story, painted-brick doctor's offices shared the same elegantly-landscaped neighborhood.

She turned right at the fourth light, continued straight a block down, and turned right again into The Glades. There was a big black wrought iron gate at the entrance, and Julie rolled down her window to tap out her entry code, then waited for the gates to swing open.

As Julie rolled in past the tiny guard house, and the row of ornamental trees beyond, she was reminded of how lucky she was. There was no way her part-time salary would pay for the place she was living in. Her modest paycheck was just about enough to pay her monthly expenses.

Julie pulled into her tiny drive and flicked the remote. As soon as the garage door opened she nudged her little car down the sloping drive and inside. The beautiful, elegant condo was her reward for five long years of dieting and deprivation as a model. Her career had been short, but successful enough to pay for physical therapy school and a place of her own after.

She sighed and picked up her bags. *I may not be Naomi Campbell,* she thought wryly, *but I guess I did all right, considering.*

Julie juggled her keys and her bags as she slid out of the car and unlocked her kitchen door. She'd only been back home for a month, and she was still adjusting. There was a world of difference between LA's frantic pace, and the sleepy little Texas town she'd grown up in.

She smiled a bit wistfully. *Well, maybe not so sleepy anymore. Maybe I want to remember Green Oak the way it used to be.*

Julie bumped the door shut behind her and kicked off her sneakers. She padded into the huge kitchen, grabbed a plate out of the cupboard, and poured her dinner out onto it.

She breezed out into the great room, sank down onto her couch, and flicked on the t.v. Julie took a sip of tea and settled into the pillows. She had the weekend off, and she was planning to use it to go furniture shopping.

She hoped to take Trina with her. They always used to pick things out together, and maybe an outing would be good for her friend.

Julie took a bite of hamburger and glanced up at the television. The local news was on, and she was just about to change the channel when a grim-faced female reporter announced, "We have breaking news just in," She put a hand to her earpiece and added, "There's just been a fatal shooting at the Kwik Mart just outside the county hospital."

Julie stared at the screen and frowned. She'd passed that gas station on the way home. It was less than two blocks from where she worked.

The reporter's brow clouded. "We're getting reports that a man shot a woman in a convenience store, then turned the gun on other bystanders before shooting himself. The police report that the woman died on the scene, and that the man died on the way to the hospital. Two other people were shot, and they were also taken to the hospital with non life-threatening injuries."

Julie's frown deepened, and she shook her head. *What is wrong with people,* she wondered darkly. Her anger stirred again.

It seemed like everywhere she turned lately, she was seeing some poor woman being abused. Killed outright, this time.

The reporter announced, "We have Jim Hendley on the scene now. Jim, can you tell us what happened at the Kwik Mart?"

A troubled-looking man appeared on a screen behind the reporter's head, and the woman turned to glance at it. Her colleague adjusted his grip on his mic and intoned, "That's right Delia, the employees here say that at five twenty, a blue sedan pulled into the lot, and a woman jumped out and ran into the store. She rushed to the counter and asked them to call the police. She said she was afraid of her husband; but before they could help her, the man came inside waving a gun. They said he shot the woman down where she stood, then started shooting at them and the other customers.”

Julie put the burger down and stared at the screen in stricken sympathy. *That poor woman,* she thought in horror.

“Do we have any word on who the victim was, Jim?”

The man stared into the camera and nodded. “The police have released the couple’s names. The victim was Penny Baker of Green Oak, and the shooter was her husband Tom Baker, also of Green Oak.”

Julie clapped a hand to her mouth and uttered a strangled cry. The fries cascaded off her plate and fell in a heap on the floor.

"Do the police have any idea what the motive was for the murder?"

The man nodded again. "Police here say that they'd been called to the Baker home once before for a domestic dispute, and that…"

The rest of his words faded away into oblivion, and Julie reached for the remote and turned the television off. She felt as stunned as if someone had struck her.

It couldn't be true. She'd talked to Penny not an hour ago, had watched her and her husband walk out of the office together.

Tears welled in Julie's eyes as she remembered how earnestly Penny had worked to recover, how much progress she'd made. She'd tried so hard to get better, and now…

Julie's eyes squeezed shut, and her hands curled into the plush pillows, twisted them. Fury surged up in her, burned in her throat, swelled in her chest; and she pressed her face into the pillows and poured it all out in a muffled scream of protest.

Chapter Three

"What do you think of this Queen Anne chair, Trina?"

Julie glanced up at her friend's face. She and Trina were standing in an out-of-the way corner of the biggest furniture store in Green Oak.

Julie maintained a bright, pleasant expression, but it was a fragile mask. It had taken her a day to calm down from the shock of losing her patient. To accept that there was now nothing more she could do for Penny.

She'd never been very religious, but she'd said a prayer for Penny just the same. She needed to mourn, to take a deep breath. And now that she had, she was going to move on.

To focus on something she still had the power to do:

Cheer up her best friend.

Trina cocked her head to one side to consider the object in question, a lovely formal chair upholstered in a pink-and-champagne stripe.

She gave it an apathetic glance. "It's pretty." She trailed her hand along the gleaming satin arm.

Julie stifled a worried sigh and pasted what she hoped was an encouraging smile on her face. "I think it would be perfect in my front room. The one with the wine-colored drapes and the beige rug."

Trina shot her an admiring look. "You have such an eye for color, Julie," she smiled. "I wouldn't have thought of that combination. That's working in the fashion industry, I guess."

Julie repressed a snort. "There's no trick to it, I promise you," she retorted. "Most of the people I worked with had a good sense of color, but it sure wasn't a requirement. I worked with some of the tackiest designers in the world."

A flick of genuine amusement brightened her friend's eyes, and for an instant, Julie got a glimpse of the old, mischievous Trina. "Really?" she grinned.

"*Ugh*, yes. Once I had to walk out in front of a whole room of fashion writers wearing a neon orange coat and purple bell bottoms. I felt like an extra from a kid's movie."

Trina giggled, then shook her head. "I could never have done that," she confessed. "I can't keep a straight face."

Julie smiled at her friend in affection, then added, "Then it's a good thing you didn't see me go sticking out onto the runway wearing accordion pants last spring. I thought I was going to die of shame, but they turned out to be the most popular piece in the collection," she laughed. "People are crazy."

"No they're not," Trina replied softly. "You just made the accordion look good, Jules."

"Huh," Julie retorted. "You're sweet, but they were hideous. Marilyn Monroe would've waddled like a duck in them."

Trina burst out laughing, and a nearby browser turned her head to stare at them as she passed. Trina reached out and squeezed her arm affectionately.

"You always make me feel good, Jules," she smiled. "No wonder you're a nurse."

"Physical therapist," Julie corrected gently.

"Aren't they the same thing?"

"Not quite."

Trina shrugged a round shoulder. "Well, you have a knack for it, anyway," she concluded.

Julie stared at her affectionately. "So we're agreed that this chair is right for the front room?"

"Perfect," Trina echoed wistfully, and skimmed its silky surface with one hand. "I wish I could hang around to help you furnish the rest of the house, but I'm starting work Monday week. I'm going up to Oklahoma City tomorrow. I found an apartment and I've got to get my things moved in."

A pang of dismay stabbed Julie. "I didn't know you were leaving so soon," she stammered, and her friend shrugged again.

"I may as well get it done," she sighed. "The sooner I move up there, the sooner I can start over."

Julie bit her lip, then decided to make one last attempt. She reached out to rest her hand on her friend's arm. "Trina, are you sure you aren't being just a little impulsive?" she asked softly.

Trina looked up at her and smiled sadly. "I'm sure, Jules. You're sweet for asking, but I'm sure."

Julie's hand fell back to her side. "As long as you're settled in your mind," she sighed in defeat. "Can I help you move?"

Trina shook her head. "I've already got a moving company lined up. Even a realtor. She's going to sell the house for me." She shrugged. "It's kind of hard to sell it. I grew up in that house."

So did I, Julie thought with another pang of sadness; but she smiled to hide it and nodded toward the front of the store.

"Come on, let's get some lunch. My treat. Let's go to that little drug store cafe we used to haunt back in the day. Chicken salad sandwiches and tea, just like always."

Trina's freckled face brightened. "Let's go!"

Julie laughed and took her arm; but as they walked out, she was secretly shaken to think that it might be the last time they ever ate there together.

Chapter Four

"What's the matter with you, boy?"

Luke looked up through his bangs to see his brother Buck standing over him with his hands on his hips. He chucked a rock out into the cattle pond and didn't answer. The rock hit the water with a *plunk,* and Buck watched as ripples spread out across the quiet face of the lake.

He turned back to stare at Luke. "You ain't been at the house for a week and more. Hank told me you're sleeping out in the bunkhouse like a stray. Said he don't know what to do with you."

Luke hunched a shoulder and stared out into the distance, where one cow stood on a bare ridge, all lonesome and blue.

Kind of like him.

He ran a hand through his bangs. "Aw, I forgot our anniversary, and Trina—well, Trina quit me."

Buck nodded and gazed out over the pond. The silence stretched out between them, and Luke rubbed the back of his neck and finally added, "She wants to get married. She got pretty mad at me when I didn't take to the idea right off."

He glanced up at his older brother. Buck looked as if he was thinking something real strong, but to Luke's relief, he didn't say it.

He just grunted.

Luke rubbed his face with his hands. "I know we've been together a long time, but where is it written you got to decide on the spot? It's not like a race."

At that, Buck turned to look at him; and his expression made Luke go hot. "Well, if you're not sure you wanna marry your girl after all these years, I'd say that's a sign," Buck told him. "Maybe it's for the best." He clapped him on the shoulder. "Come on back up to the house. Take your mind off your troubles. We're having a barbecue tonight."

Luke glanced away. "No, you go on, Buck. I'm not hungry."

"Well, that'll make the first time ever," Buck retorted, and kicked at his boots as he sat on the ground. Luke picked up a pine cone and threw it at Buck's head.

"Come on up to the house," Buck urged. "Unless you think it's better out here with the cows." He slapped at his arm, and a fly zoomed off over the water.

"No, I told you, I'm all right," Luke insisted, and squinted up at him. "You go on."

"Well, suit yourself," Buck shrugged; "but I don't see the difference between moping here and moping at the house. At least up there, you'd have ribs and beer."

Buck punched him in the shoulder and strode back up the bank. Luke watched him go, then turned his eyes back out over the pond.

He felt as low as a catfish lying on the bottom of the pond. He couldn't remember when he'd felt so bad.

He rubbed his nose. He hated to see Trina upset. She hadn't been exactly crying when she dumped him, but her voice had got all high and trembly like it did when she was about to.

He just wished there was something he could do to make it right, without marrying her.

He'd offered her flowers; she didn't want them.

He'd promised her a big present; that was no good either.

Nothing would do for her but that he fetch a preacher, and just the thought of it made him go cold all over.

They were friends, they were comfortable together, things were going good. There was no call to fix something that wasn't broke.

Or at least, that was what he thought; but Trina didn't see it that way.

Maybe he should call her again. Trina'd had a couple of days to cool off. Maybe he could smooth her down. Maybe they could even get back together.

Luke pulled his phone out of his pocket and punched Trina's number. The phone rang once...twice...three times...four.

Come on Trina, Luke thought in exasperation. *Aren't you even gonna talk to me?*

The answering machine picked up and Trina's high, cheery voice chirped, "This is

Trina, you just missed me. Leave your name and number after the beep…"

Luke exclaimed in frustration, jerked his arm back, and lobbed the cell phone out into the air. It sailed over the length of the pond in a long, smooth arc, then plunged into the weeds on the other shore with a loud *splash*.

Luke watched it disappear, then closed his eyes and rubbed them with one brown hand. He could still hardly believe that Trina had dumped him, but it looked like their romance was over.

She did say she wanted to get married. I guess she just got tired of waiting on me, he thought despondently.

He grabbed a tree limb and pulled himself up with one hand, swiped pine needles off his jeans, and turned to climb the bank behind him. Maybe Buck was right.

It didn't much matter where he was. His butt was gonna be dragging no matter what.

Luke walked up the rise. A glorious palomino was picketed under the shade of a pine tree at the top, and he ran a hand across its fluffy white mane.

"Ready to go back to the barn, Buddy?" He smiled a bit when the palomino nodded and stomped its foot.

"All right then. Let's go." He jumped up easily into the saddle, turned the horse's head, and sent it trotting across the rolling pasture.

Luke squinted in the direction of the ranch house. He couldn't see it, it was miles away east and he'd reach their massive barn and cluster of bunkhouses first.

Luke pulled his mouth to one side. Buck was right. He was acting like a kid, running off to the bunkhouse to lick his wounds. He might as well go back up to the house, to his own apartment.

It wasn't gonna be a happy chore, to take down all his pictures of Trina, or all the reminders of them together. He'd collected a lot of them, over the years.

Luke rubbed his neck. He didn't exactly know what he'd expected Trina to do. Sooner or later she was bound to buck, because she'd told him she wanted to get married often enough.

He couldn't really blame her for getting tired of waiting on him.

He frowned. It was the same old thing with him, all the time. He could never seem to settle down. Trina was right about that. He'd never held a job for more than six months, he could never seem to finish a project. It wasn't that he didn't want to.

He just never did, somehow.

Something else always came up, and he got distracted, and before he knew it, it was a month later.

Still, he'd be lying if he said he didn't get restless. And nothing got under his skin faster than somebody trying to tie him down. It made him itch all over.

Luke glanced in the direction of the house. His brothers had gotten used to it. Buck had worked with him for months, trying to train him to stick to a long-term job, but finally had to give up. Morgan never gave him any chore around the ranch that lasted more than three weeks, and Carson had laughed when he'd asked about working with his thoroughbreds.

Jesse had told him right to his teeth that he was a flake; Will had warned him never to join the military; and Chase just stared at him.

Well, maybe I am a flake, Luke thought unhappily, and reached down to pat his horse's neck. *Maybe I'm just wired different.*

It made him feel so low that he was tempted to go back to the bunkhouse and curl up on a cot; but he wasn't going to do it. He was going to get hold of himself.

He'd broken Trina's heart. He hadn't meant to. But if there was ever a sign that he needed to start acting like a man, this was it. A flick of something almost like desperation branched through him.

I got to buckle down.

I got to!

Chapter Five

By the time Luke stabled his horse and left the barn, dusk was falling and the mouthwatering scent of barbecued ribs was curling over the lawn. Every window in the big house was blazing with golden light, and he could hear his family even from outside. His brothers' booming voices mingled with his sister-in-law's laughter and the high piping of children's giggles. That happy cacophony reached out and curled around him like welcoming arms.

Luke smiled a little in spite of himself. It was hard to feel blue at a barbecue. He hadn't eaten anything all day, and even his misery over Trina couldn't keep his stomach from rumbling.

Luke's long, jean-clad legs ate up the ground as he quickened his pace. The ribs that Buck had talked about were bobbing in his head like a restaurant commercial. They were floating just ahead of him, and when he inhaled, he could taste them in the air.

As he climbed up the last rise to the paved courtyard, the big front door of the house opened and Kit streaked out, with a laughing Molly in hot pursuit. Luke reached out and grabbed his nephew by the seat of the pants, swung him around, and dangled him on his hip. He looked down into Kit's laughing face and drawled, "Where you going so fast, buddy?"

Molly came running up, then bent over to catch her breath. "I'm it," she panted; then she slapped Kit's knee with her hand and tore off around the house, laughing.

Luke set Kit back down on the ground, then called after him, "Hey, you two slow down!" But they'd both disappeared already, and Luke shook his head and made his way inside.

It wasn't hard to tell the center of the action. Buck had set up a couple of industrial-grade grills out by the pool, and everybody in the house was out there. Buck and Morgan were grilling, Kate and Heather and Donna were lounging side by side on pool recliners, and Carson and Chase and Jesse were standing by the buffet table, beers in hand, talking about something.

Luke paused by the main stairs, gazing out on that pretty picture through the glass wall. It hit him good and bad. He was glad everybody was having a good time; but he wasn't up to going out there and joining in.

He didn't want to have to explain why Trina wasn't there with him.

His eyes moved to the groaning buffet table, and his stomach growled again. As he watched, Donna stood up, leaned down to smile at Kate, and came walking through the glass door into the house.

Luke licked his lips as she breezed in, and returned her smile. "Evening," he nodded.

She paused and tilted her head to one side. "I hope you aren't going to miss the barbecue. The ribs are delicious."

Luke's eyes rolled to the faint spiral of smoke drifting up from the two grills, and this time instead of growling, his stomach cramped.

"Can I ask you a favor?" he blurted. His new sister in law raised her brows, but looked faintly amused.

"Certainly."

"I don't much feel like a party tonight, but I sure would like some of those ribs. Would it—

would it be too much trouble for you to bring me a plate, if I just stay right here?”

Donna looked as if she was trying to swallow a bubble of laughter, but she murmured, “Of course not. But I think you’re making a mistake. It’s a beautiful evening out. The weather is perfect.”

“Thanks,” Luke told her, with a grateful look. “I sure do appreciate it, Donna.”

She acknowledged him with a nod, and turned back to the pool patio. Luke watched hungrily as she walked to the buffet and filled a plate with ribs, potato salad, grilled corn on the cob, and a huge biscuit.

He saw her lick her thumb, flick her hair over her shoulder, and bring the plate back inside. His eyes followed it as it bobbed through the air toward him.

“Here you are,” she murmured. *“Bon appetit.”*

Luke took the plate as if it was made of gold, then flashed her a smile. "Thanks again Donna."

She shook her head and continued on her way, back toward the kitchen; but Luke took the stairs two at a time, all the way up to the second floor. He tapped a code into a number pad beside the lock, and the door swung open for him to walk inside.

It was a relief to be in the privacy of his own apartment at last, and his shoulders sank a bit as he closed the door behind him. He just didn't have it in him to face the family that night.

He frowned as he shuffled down the hall and into his kitchen. The place was kind of a mess, and he made a mental note to spend some time cleaning it up. He opened the refrigerator, got a beer, and walked back out and down the hall to his living room.

He flopped down onto the beat-up leather couch, set the plate and the beer on the coffee table, and propped his boots up. He popped the top on the beer and lifted it to his lips with a sigh.

The walls of his living room were a deep green and covered in old rodeo posters and action photographs of some of his more memorable rides. Luke let his eyes linger on some of them.

He chuckled as his eyes moved to a photo of him with one hand in the air and the other on the reins of a vicious bronc named Toodle-Oo. His hat was airborne, a foot above his head, and he was leaning back so far that he was practically lying down. The bronc's hind legs were close to straight up, and its tail was flying.

But he'd managed to stay on for the full eight seconds, and he'd won twenty thousand dollars that night.

Luke closed his eyes, and instantly he was there again in the chute, waiting for the gate to open. The familiar scents of the rodeo filled his senses: leather and tobacco and beer and sweat. The horse under him snorted and tried to buck, and he tightened his grip on the reins.

A loud male voice suddenly blared over the speakers. "Folks, let's give a warm Colorado welcome to Contestant Number Three, Luke Spade. He's riding Toodle-oo tonight. Let's wish him luck!"

A roar went up from the crowd, and the spotlight swung to him as he sat there waiting to go. The light was white, practically blinding, and every eye in the stands was on him. He'd hoped the fans couldn't see that he was sweating, that his heart was going like a jackhammer.

Suddenly the gate banged open and Toodle-Ooo exploded out of the chute with a scream of rage. He'd leaned back to keep that devil from launching him into the sky, and held on for dear life with one hand while the other one waved high in the air.

Luke smiled a bit. Busting Toodle-Ooo had been the biggest rush on earth. That monster was a legend and had turned his world airborne and sideways: a spinning blur of lights and the weirdly mingled sounds of the crowd's roar, the horse's panting and his own grunts.

It was hard to believe that ride had only lasted eight seconds when it had been the longest, most hard-fought contest of his life. He'd known it was over when he looked up from the ground with dirt in his teeth and the crowd going crazy.

That win at the Greeley Stampede had been one of the high points of his twenty-year rodeo career. He'd been into it pretty strong there for awhile, but like everything else he did, he'd kind of...slacked off.

He hadn't competed in a rodeo for four years now.

Luke took another sip of beer and glanced at the wall. Morgan had convinced him to put his trophy buckles into a display frame. "You earned 'em," Morgan had rumbled. "You got busted up winning 'em. You deserve to show 'em off."

Luke stared at them. He had nine big, glittering buckles of silver and gold, some inlaid with turquoise and other stones, but he'd never worn them, in spite of his brothers' urging. It felt like bragging, and he didn't need to brag. Everybody who knew rodeo knew he'd won them.

Yeah, he had to say, the rodeo had been good to him. He'd learned, he'd had a lot of fun, and he'd made a lot of friends.

He'd even met Trina at the rodeo; but he made himself push his ex-girlfriend out of his mind.

After a solid week of misery, it was only self-defense.

His stomach rumbled again, and he reached for a rib and began to eat his dinner. He mumbled in appreciation at the succulent meat and the tangy sauce that a mesquite fire had sealed right to the bone. Buck sure knew his way around a grill.

Luke polished it off and licked his fingers, and his eyes returned to those buckles on the wall. The rodeo was the closest thing he'd ever had to a steady job, and those buckles were what he had to show for twenty years of his life.

They showed that he'd been good at something, but now that he was getting almost too old to compete, he didn't know what he was going to do with the rest of his life. He didn't need to work, but he wanted to. He just hadn't figured out what else he'd be good at.

Luke frowned and stared into space. He hated feeling like he was stuck in a boat out on the ocean going nowhere. He needed to decide what he wanted for the rest of his life, and then work out a plan to make it happen.

And he would.

Right after he watched a recap of the weekend rodeos on the sports channel. He flicked the t.v. on, took another sip of beer, and settled into the couch to enjoy the action.

Chapter Six

"Well, he may not be happy, but at least he ain't sleeping in the bunkhouse anymore," Buck grumbled.

He was leaning against a ragged wooden fence post on the edge of the barn pasture, and Morgan was standing at his side. It was a glorious spring morning, bright and fresh with a clear blue sky; but Buck's heart and his expression were dark. He and Morgan both watched as a tiny Luke rode his horse across a faraway pasture, then disappeared over a low hill.

"Hank's branding calves today," Morgan muttered. "I sent Luke out there to help. It'll keep him busy. It ain't good for him to sit up in his apartment and brood."

Buck looked down and kicked at a tuft of grass. "Well, I gotta believe it's for the best, him busting up with that girl. You know how easy-going Luke is. He really liked her, and I think he was trying to please her. Trying to convince himself. But if he'd even halfway loved her, he'd had proposed the first year."

"Yeah," Morgan sighed. "But I think his case of the blues is more than that."

Buck turned to look at him. "What do you mean?"

Morgan stared off at the horizon. "I think this bustup with Trina has got Luke asking questions about his whole life."

"*Good,*" Buck retorted, "he needs to ask questions! He needs to ask himself why he can't settle down to a steady job on this ranch."

Morgan grumbled, "Yeah, it's a shame. Luke's the best hand we got when he puts his mind to it. He can rope and ride better than anyone I've ever seen, and he can send that horse of his over a four-rail fence. He's a born cowboy." He shook his head.

"Well, Luke don't work here for a month at a time, and they ain't no ads for *born cowboys* in the paper," Buck replied. "He's got money all right, but he needs a job as much for his pride as anything. How's he gonna get a woman if he can't tell her what he does?"

Morgan's keen eyes flashed. "The Seven is a family business, after all."

"If you *do* something it is," Buck retorted, and waved an arm in the air. "What does Luke do around here? He stays gone half the time."

The defensive look faded from Morgan's eyes. "Yeah, I know," he grumbled. "Well, that's something Luke's gonna have to work out for himself. You and me both have tried to help him, but there's only so much we can do."

"That's for sure," Buck agreed. "That boy needs somebody to light a fire under him. Give him a good fast kick in the pants."

"I was gonna say he needs prayer," Morgan quipped, and shot him a laughing look from his bright eyes. He shook his head. "You've already tried giving him a fast kick in the pants, and it didn't take."

Buck grumbled under his breath and glanced over his shoulder to the far hill that Luke had crested. "Maybe one kick wasn't enough."

Morgan chuckled and clapped a hand on his shoulder. "I think I hear Big Russ now," he teased. "Be careful, Buck. You're Luke's brother, not his daddy, and not Big Russ. You lean too hard on him, he's gonna buck and gallop off."

"Somebody needs to," Buck grumbled. "Somebody needs to snatch him up by the collar, or he's gonna go on drifting all his life. I'd sure hate to see that happen."

It made Buck's heart ache, even thinking about it. He rubbed his chest, as if that would smooth it away.

Morgan sighed, "Well, we're doing some riding classes for the public this summer. It's a charity thing for the hospital. I asked Luke if he'd like to teach the classes, and he said he would. So at least that'll keep him busy doing something for the next few weeks."

Relief washed over Buck. "That's a great idea, Morg," he agreed. "Odds are, once he's out in the fresh air doing something he likes, these blues of his'll fizzle out. You know Luke–he's Mr. Sunshine. He never stays down for long."

"Yeah, we've got that in our favor, at least," Morgan nodded, and turned for the barn. Buck followed him across the bright carpet of new pasture grass and pulled his hat down low over his eyes.

He was worried about Luke. He wanted to rush in and give his younger brother a good long talking to, but maybe Morg was right. Maybe he should step back and wait for Luke to come to him.

But Luke hadn't come to him so far; or to anybody else in their family, as far as he knew. Luke was Mr. Sunshine all right, he had the happiest temperament of anybody in their family; but he was still a Spade.

That meant he was also stubborn as a mule; and Buck grumbled to himself as he followed his brother into the barn.

Chapter Seven

Julie shivered and huddled into her coat. It was only five in the morning, and the fog was so thick that Trina's car was unrecognizable–a big gray blob.

She'd stayed overnight at Trina's house to help her friend get the last odds and ends packed up into the car. Now their work was finished, the car was jam packed with boxes and clothes, and it was time for Trina to go.

She had to be in Oklahoma City that morning to move into her new apartment.

Julie glanced at the little bungalow unhappily. It, too, was a big gray shadow in the pre-dawn fog, and the light on the front porch was blurred and dim.

She stood there, waiting for Trina to say her last goodbye to the house, come outside, and drive away.

Julie closed her eyes and pictured it in her mind. Trina's footsteps would echo loud and hollow on those wooden floors. She could see the empty kitchen with the antique white porcelain sink and ceiling-high white cupboards. She'd scrawled her own name in pencil inside those cupboards when she was six, and for all she knew, her childish artwork was still there.

She could see the living room with its big bay window facing the street, and the cozy padded bench where she and Trina had spent hours curled up, reading *Pippy Longstocking* or *Anne of Green Gables*.

A gust of anger swept Julie's heart. The whole thing was surreal. Trina should've lived in that house even after she married, so she could fill it up again with children's laughter.

But now it stood dark and cold and empty in the early morning fog, and both her heart and Trina's were breaking.

And all of it—*all*—was Luke Spade's fault.

The sound of the door opening made Julie look up. She couldn't see her friend coming down the front steps and across the yard on the little brick walkway, but her footsteps sounded loud in the deep stillness.

Trina emerged from the fog a few feet away and held out her arms. Julie went into them and hugged her tight.

"Call me when you get to your place," she sniffed, and Trina nodded. Julie could tell that her friend was too overcome to reply, and when she stepped back, Trina pressed the house key into her hand and mustered a smile.

"I'll call you," she mumbled, wiped her eyes, and opened the car door. Julie walked to the door and looked down as her friend settled in and put on her seat belt.

Trina looked up at her through brimming eyes and laughed a little. She wiped her eyes. "I never thought I'd be this sentimental."

Julie summoned an answering smile. "You get to be whatever you like," she replied softly. "I'm going to miss you."

"I'll only be two hours away," Trina joked, then looked away. "Call me, Jules."

"I will."

Julie stepped back as Trina closed the car door and cranked the engine. She raised her hand in farewell as Trina backed the car out of the driveway, flashed the lights in farewell, and drove off into the fog.

Julie stood staring after her for a few moments, but the damp chilled her bones, and she hurried to her own car and shut it out as she closed the door behind her.

She cranked the motor and backed out of the driveway slowly and carefully. The fog was so thick she could hardly see the street lights, but she nosed the Beetle down the street and past the other ghostly houses. The development that had modernized other parts of town had passed the old neighborhood by, and now it was just a few quaint blocks of fifty-year-Old bungalows.

Julie paused at the train tracks as the flashers flicked on and the safety gate slowly came down. The ground beneath her car trembled and the front seats lit up with the yellow reflection of the warning lights. The train whistle blasted out, loud and eerie in the stillness, and she could dimly see the engine flash by in the fog, followed by a long gray line of phantom cars.

Julie watched it sadly. That ghostly train embodied her mood perfectly. Everything and everyone seemed to be rushing away from her into a gray and frightening future: a place where all kinds of evil surprises were possible, and nothing happened like she'd planned.

Her sadness faded, and was gradually replaced by resentment. The red flower of her anger unfurled another fiery petal.

It isn't fair.

Her fingers tightened on the wheel and she frowned at the cars flashing past. Trina was leaving her whole life behind, driving on a dark, lonely road at 5 in the morning so she could start over again in another state.

But Luke Spade was snoozing peacefully in a multi-million dollar mansion. Not a worry in the world. What did he care that Trina's heart was broken and her life was totally upended?

He was a billionaire. He was set for life. And he'd probably already moved on to the next girl.

Julie's frown deepened. She knew that life wasn't fair, she knew that she and her loved ones weren't special. Trouble came to everyone.

But it seemed that trouble came to you more often if you were a woman; and that it camped on your doorstep if you dared to trust a man.

Julie arrived at her condo a little after six. The fog was thicker than ever, and she was relieved to see her garage door close behind her. She climbed out of the car, opened her kitchen door, and flicked on the lights. She hadn't slept a wink that night, but she had to be at work at eight.

She might as well just shower and make breakfast.

Julie padded off to her bathroom for a quick shower and shampoo. Twenty minutes later she emerged with pink cheeks and her hair wrapped up in a towel.

A hot shower had made her feel better, but she still dreaded going to work that morning. It would be her first day back to work since Penny's murder, and she wasn't sure she was ready.

Julie drifted back to the kitchen and switched on the coffee maker. She was as strong as the next one, but it was going to be hard to just pick up where she'd left off. Everything in the therapy room would remind her of Penny; and the whole office would be buzzing with the terrible news of her death.

It was senseless, Julie thought angrily and slapped the coffee tin against the counter top. *Brutal. Cowardly.*

What did that poor girl ever do to deserve that?

She stopped, closed her eyes, and took a deep breath; then went on making her breakfast.

By the time Julie climbed out of her car and hurried across the road to the physical therapy building, it was almost eight. The fog had thinned somewhat, but it was still a gray, chilly spring day, and the weather only confirmed Julie's dark mood.

The office was as stirred up as she'd expected. As soon as she walked through the door, the secretary met her eyes and hissed, "Julie, have you heard about Penny?"

Julie suppressed a sigh. "Yes. I saw it on the news."

"So terrible," the girl murmured. "It just goes to show that you just never know." She shook her head.

"It goes to show that a girl needs to find a decent man, and not a snake," Julie retorted, and in an angrier tone than she'd intended. The other girl blinked at her.

"Oh–oh, yeah. So true."

Julie mustered a wan smile and thought, I need to get hold of myself.

"Who's my first patient today?" she sighed. The secretary consulted her computer screen. "Um....Mrs. Healey, in fifteen minutes."

"Thanks."

Julie moved down the hall to the physical therapy room and began to set up for the day. She had three patients that day, one knee problem, one rotator cuff, one tennis elbow. A full plate.

But she had to struggle to keep her mind on business as she set up for the day. The little puzzle tray was still in the same place Penny had left it; and her file on Penny was still in the little metal cabinet next to the door.

Her cell phone trilled suddenly, and Julie reached for it anxiously. When she picked up, Trina's voice jumped out at her on the other end.

"Jules?"

Julie tucked a sprig of hair behind one ear. "Hi Trina. Did you get to Oklahoma City okay?"

To her dismay, her friend's voice sounded upset. "Not exactly."

Julie straightened up in alarm. "What's wrong?"

"My car died on the road," Trina confessed, in a shamefaced tone. "And I couldn't call for help because I forgot to charge my phone. I'm calling you from a gas station outside of Ardmore."

"Oh, Trina!" Julie gasped. She couldn't keep her mind from replaying the terrible news report about Penny's death at a gas station, and her heart jerked in her chest. "Are you safe?"

"I guess," Trina replied.

Julie licked her lips. "Which gas station are you in, and on what road? I'll call a wrecker for you. And a car rental, if you want one."

Trina's voice was thick with relief. "Thanks, Jules," she quavered, and Julie's ear was quick to hear tears in it. She scribbled down the information her friend gave her and replied, "I'm going to call them right now, Trina. Your car should be in the shop within an hour, and I'll find a car rental place so you can make your appointment in Oklahoma City."

"You're a lifesaver," Trina murmured. "I don't know what I'd do without you, Jules."

"You don't have to thank me," Julie told her. "I'm hanging up now, but I'll call you when I've got the wrecker on the way."

"Okay. Bye Jules."

She'd no sooner hung up than the office phone buzzed. She hurried over to the little desk to pick up, and the receptionist greeted her with: "Mrs. Healey is here, Julie."

Julie fumbled with her cell phone and muttered, "Give me about ten minutes, and then send her back."

"Okay."

Julie hung up, opened her cell phone search bar and tapped "wrecker+Ardmore Oklahoma." She frowned as she perused the different wrecker services listed. Her day had hardly started, and she was already flustered and off-balance.

The office phone rang again, and Julie sighed and picked it up. The secretary's voice sounded a bit harassed.

"Julie, Mrs. Healey says she has an appointment after this one and she has to be on time."

Julie stifled an exclamation and barked, "Tell her I can see her in ten."

The secretary's voice sounded doubtful. "All right, then."

Julie hung up the office phone and turned her attention back to her cell phone. She glanced down at the list of wrecker services and punched the phone number of the first one on the list.

By the time five o'clock rolled around, Julie was tired and ready to go home. She'd managed to get a wrecker out to Trina, and had found a car rental company not far from the wrecker service. She was secure in the knowledge that Trina had gotten a replacement car and had arrived safely at her new apartment in Oklahoma City.

But her own day had gotten off on the wrong foot, and she'd felt flustered, distracted and about ten minutes behind schedule all day long. When she reached for her bag and slung it over her shoulder to leave the office, she was more than ready to go home, put her feet up, and do nothing else for at least two hours.

She walked out through the big, open lobby of the therapy building but paused momentarily to read a neon-yellow flyer tacked to the announcement board near the elevator. There, in a big cowboy-style font, was the headline:

RIDING LESSONS AT THE SEVEN SPADES RANCH!

Help the hospital charity drive and learn to ride at the same time! Lessons for all ages taught by Luke Spade, former rodeo star and winner of nine champion buckles.

Registration $45 for a week of adult lessons, $2o for kids. All proceeds go to the hospital's charity drive for the new children's wing.

Julie's eyes narrowed and her lip curled in disgust. *Well, old Luke is sure prostrate with grief,* she thought angrily. *I'm glad he was able to move right on!*

She pushed out through the revolving doors and into the landscaped grounds of the complex. The therapy building faced the main artery through town, and her car was parked in a lot across the street.

Julie stumped to the crosswalk and waited for the light to change. While she was waiting, her cell phone vibrated; and when she looked, she saw that she had a missed call and a message. Julie pressed the little red square on the screen and waited.

To her shock, Penny's voice greeted her.

"Hi, Julie. I just wanted to see if I can reschedule our appointment for Monday. My husband wants me to come with him on a company event, and it's the same time as our appointment. I'm sorry to change on such late notice. I hope it's okay."

There was a short pause, then she went on in a shy tone: "I really appreciate what you're doing for me, Julie. I've improved so much since I first came to therapy. I know that's because of you."

Julie's eyes welled with tears and she clapped a hand to her trembling mouth to stifle the sob that was building in her chest. The grief she'd pushed down came roaring back, and with it, her anger at the injustice.

She stood there on the sidewalk, trying to get control of herself, and as she waited a sleek, mostly silent motorcycle came gliding up to the light. She glanced up at it, then glanced again.

To her amazement, it was Luke Spade.

Well speak of the devil, she gasped inwardly. She'd seen his photo a hundred times, and it was unmistakably the same wild shock of blonde hair, the same wide, smiling mouth, the same brown face. Luke was taller and lankier than she'd imagined, but she didn't dwell on his looks; because to her outrage, a pretty young blonde was sitting behind him and had both arms twined around his chest.

It was plain as print that poor Trina was right. Luke hadn't cared a rip for her. He hadn't even waited a week after their breakup to hook up with some random blonde.

Julie stared at them in a mixture of amazement and rising fury. Everything that had happened—the night she'd spent talking Trina through her grief, her own grief at Penny's tragic and senseless death, Trina's abandonment of her own home—united in one big tangled knot of rage in her heart. That knot had been red, but now it was purple, and it was quickly darkening to black. She glared at Luke's smiling face in fury. In that moment, for her, he symbolized all that was wrong with the world.

Everything Trina's been through is your fault, Luke Spade, she fumed. *But you don't even have the decency to feel bad about it. Trina's alone in a strange place tonight, probably crying, and look at you. You're having a high old time.*

You're just going on with your life like nothing happened. You're young and rich and good-looking.What do you care if Trina's life is ruined? You've already found somebody else to take her place.

Men like you don't know what consequences are.

The light changed, Luke lifted his feet, and the motorcycle glided off into the distance; but Julie watched it go through narrowed eyes. Slowly her fury and frustration made way for a new feeling, a feeling that grew stronger as she watched the motorcycle fade into the distance.

Men like you don't know what consequences are.

Until somebody teaches you!

Chapter Eight

Luke pulled up into the driveway of a small ranch-style house on the outskirts of town. He braced the bike against one foot and turned around to smile, "Well, here you are, Lucille. I hope it wasn't too scary a ride."

His passenger climbed off the motorcycle, slowly and gingerly, and paused to give him a grateful look. "Thanks, Luke. I don't know what I would've done if you hadn't happened by. Clay always knows what to do when my car won't start, but he's out of town until Friday."

"Say hey to him for me," Luke nodded.

"I will. Thanks again."

Luke waited until his friend got to her own door, unlocked it, and got inside the house before he backed the bike out of the drive. Lucy was married to one of his high school friends. Lucky thing he'd been in the neighborhood when her car blew a tire.

He pulled the bike out into the street. He'd come into town to pick up a few odds and ends they'd need for the riding lessons. Setting those lessons up was more complicated than he'd thought. Buck had even arranged a conference call to talk to their lawyer Eugene about it, just in case somebody fell off their horse and wanted to sue the ranch.

As for him, he didn't see how anybody could do that, it being a charity thing and all; but when he'd said so, Eugene had snorted like a horse.

So he guessed that it happened sometimes, after all.

He turned back toward town to pick up the connection to the interstate; but the road he was on took him past Trina's neighborhood, and he couldn't resist dropping in to check on her. She wouldn't answer her phone, after all. If he wanted to talk to her, it looked like he was going to have to go to her house.

Luke pulled his mouth to one side as he drove. He was willing to try one last time. If Trina still wouldn't have any part of him, he was going to have to accept that it was really over between them.

As he turned into Trina's street and neared her neat white bungalow, he noticed that her car wasn't there; but he still turned the bike into the driveway. He might leave a note on the doorstep, just to let her know he'd dropped by.

Luke parked the bike, threw a long leg over the seat, and walked up the little walkway to the front door. He rapped on the door nice and loud and waited for Trina to come open it, but there was no answer.

He coughed, looked back over his shoulder, and rapped again; but there was nothing but silence, inside and out.

He frowned and stuck his face up to the little pane of glass in the door, and was shocked to see that the foyer of Trina's house was empty.

No coat rack, no pictures on the wall, no rug. Just a bare floor and bare walls.

It looked like the whole house was...empty. But that couldn't be right. That would mean that Trina had moved.

Luke turned and hurried down the walkway and around the side of the house to the back. He skipped up onto the porch and stuck his face up to the pane in the door.

The little hallway was empty, and the dining room beyond was bare, too. Nothing but floor.

His hands drifted back down to his sides, and he stared through the window in shock. He'd still kinda hoped that Trina was just upset over their anniversary. That she hadn't really meant what she'd said.

But there was no doubting this. She'd moved right out of her house, and it had been her family's home.

Luke slowly backed away from the door. He couldn't get in touch with Trina now. He didn't even know where she was.

Luke swallowed hard, rubbed his mouth, and walked back around the house with his head down and his hands jammed into his pockets. There was a burning lump in his throat, and another in his chest as he took the handlebars of the bike, mounted it, and turned it around.

He walked it to the edge of the street, kicked it to life, and cast one last, sad glance at the empty house before riding away.

All during the ride back home, Luke was seeing his relationship with Trina, from the first time they'd met in Dallas, to their first kiss, to all the other milestones they'd shared.

I guess it was my fault that we broke up, he thought. *I can't seem to finish anything.*

Maybe I never will.

By the time he got back to the ranch house, he was starting to question more than his failure with Trina. He was looking back over his whole life; and what he saw made him start to wonder if he was even a good person.

It made him feel so low that he mostly dragged himself into the house and up the stairs to his own door; and once he got inside his own place, he closed it tight behind him.

Chapter Nine

Morgan and Heather bent over a bassinet in their dimly-lit nursery and smiled down at the baby sleeping inside it.

"Look at those long lashes," Heather breathed, and Morgan bent down to brush the baby's cheek with one brown finger.

"Casey's eyes are going to look just like yours," Heather whispered, and his arm went around her shoulders as they beamed at their newborn son. Casey looked up at them with sleepy, sapphire-blue eyes. As they watched, those eyes fluttered closed, and the baby's rosebud mouth opened in a yawn.

They both laughed softly, and Heather put a finger to her lips and nodded toward the two other bassinets in their nursery. "Let's go before the other two wake up," she whispered;

and Morgan followed her to the nursery door, checked the baby monitor, and switched off the lights.

They walked out into the living room, and Morgan looked down at his wife's heavy-lidded eyes. "You're tired," he murmured, and pressed a kiss to her cheek. "Go on to bed. I'll be along in a minute."

She shot him a grateful glance. "I am pretty beat," she sighed and rubbed her brow. "Those two o'clock feedings are catching up with me."

"Go on," he urged, and watched as Heather shuffled out of the room with her robe trailing behind her. Once she had gone, the room was empty except for him. Kit was already in bed.

He drifted over to the huge window that was the southern wall of the room. The front entrance of the house was directly beneath him, and as he watched, he saw Luke ride up on his motorcycle and park the bike.

Morgan frowned. There was something about Luke's sagging shoulders and downcast expression that went to his heart. *Lord*, he prayed, *I know I've been pestering You a lot lately about this boy. But just look at him.*

He watched as Luke paused and just stood there for a moment with his head down and his hands on his hips. He saw Luke shake his head once, then walk inside the house.

Lord, Luke's hurting. He needs You bad right now.

Maybe I can help him see that.

Show me how.

He sighed, then turned to switch off the living room lights and join his wife. He padded across the living room, down the hall, and into their bedroom at the end.

He opened the door softly. Heather was already a motionless lump curled up under the big Navajo blanket. She was out like a light, and Morgan undressed as quietly as he could, lifted the blanket, and slipped into the bed beside her.

He turned toward her and stretched an arm across her, but every time he tried to settle down to sleep, he saw Luke's stricken expression in his mind.

Lord, please.

Dawn of the next day found Morgan out in the barn, saddling Cochise. He was usually the first one in the barn of a morning, except maybe for Hank; and when the big door creaked open, and he saw Luke come walking in, he straightened up in surprise.

"You're up early," he rumbled, and threw a blanket over his horse's back. "There's coffee in Hank's office, if you want something to warm you up."

Luke ambled in slowly and leaned against a post. "I went into town yesterday to buy the blankets and tack we need for the riding classes," he mumbled. "They'll be delivered sometime today."

Morgan nodded and said nothing.

Luke hunched a shoulder and added, "If you need any help today, I'd be glad to lend a hand. I need something to do."

Morgan glanced at him and shrugged. "Sure. I can always use an extra man. We're gonna be out riding line today. There are lots of sections of fence got damaged over the winter."

"I'll saddle up one of these old girls," Luke murmured and nodded toward the mares stabled in the barn. He pushed off the post and walked away to choose a mount, and Morgan watched him go. His younger brother seemed subdued. Maybe even a bit depressed.

Morgan glanced at him again. Luke was usually the one to crack a joke or play a prank. He wasn't a man who liked to mope around, but he was moping now.

That breakup must've hit him harder than I thought, he mused.

Well, it'll be good for him to get back out in the open. Let that cold morning air blow the cobwebs away.

Hank emerged from his office with two cups of steaming coffee. He offered one, and Morgan took it gratefully. Hank's eyes moved past him to Luke, down on the other end of the barn.

"Well, look who's here," he murmured in a tone of mild curiosity. "I ain't seen Luke in awhile."

Morgan took a sip of coffee and rumbled, "He's coming out with us today."

Hank nodded. "Well, the other hands are waiting down in the pasture behind the bunkhouses."

Morgan considered, then replied, "Send 'em down to the west side of the ranch, down by the river along the border with the Lazy H. Luke and me'll hit the southern end of the ranch, down by the road."

Hank nodded. "I'll go tell 'em."

Morgan set his coffee cup down and finished saddling up his horse. He reached for the bridle and walked Cochise out of the stall, down the barn, and out the back door.

The sky in the west was pink with a new day, and the air was cool and fresh. The miles of pasture behind the barn sloped down gently and gradually to the oak-lined banks of the Big Sandy far in the distance. Morning mist lay on the river and in every hollow of the land, and the moisture was so thick that Morgan tasted it in the air, like the scent of rain-washed grass.

He climbed up onto Cochise, settled in, and sent him ambling out of the barn yard and into the green pastures beyond. He heard, rather than saw Luke following him as he nudged the black stallion southwards over the dew-spangled grass.

The southern fence line was miles away, and Morgan urged Cochise into an easy trot as they rode down into the river valley. Off to the west, he could see the other hands moving off to the western fence line, a dark knot of riders bobbing over the hills. Morgan skirted them and followed the banks of the Big Sandy down to the bridge where the road crossed the river.

The southern edge of the Seven Spades Ranch bordered the road for miles, and that was where their fences took the most damage from deer and other animals crossing the blacktop, and trespassers and petty thieves trying to grab livestock and make a quick getaway.

That fence got cut all the time.

He sent Cochise down to the point where the road began to rise up to meet the bridge, a couple hundred yards down the line. That was where the southern fence line angled sharply north to follow the banks of the Big Sandy, and ran dead east along the road to the front gates of the ranch.

It didn't take him long to start his day. There was a broken stretch of line near the bridge, and to judge by the tufts of hair on the wire, it was probably where some animal had tried to jump the fence and hadn't quite cleared it. The wire was broken and sagging to the ground.

He climbed down off his horse, reached into his saddle bag for a pair of leather gloves and a pair of wire cutters. He wriggled his long fingers into the gloves and walked through the grass to the corner post.

He jiggled it with his hand, found it sturdy, and ran his gloved hands along the damaged wire until he found the broken ends.

The soft, muddy clop of hooves through wet grass announced Luke's arrival. Morgan glanced back over his shoulder and saw his blonde brother huddled up in a denim jacket with his gloved hands crossed over the pommel of his saddle.

Morgan nodded eastward. "You go on down to the front gate, and work back towards me. With luck, we may be able to get this done in time for lunch."

Luke threw up a hand and sent the horse trotting down the line toward the front gates, miles away. Morgan watched him go and shook his head.

Lord, I don't know what to say to him, he frowned. *Maybe he'll be better off if I don't put my two cents in.*

He looked up again at Luke's tall, straight back as it slowly disappeared over a rise.

Maybe the best sermons get preached when a man's all by himself.

Chapter Ten

Luke sat cross-legged on the ground, wrestling with the lowest string of barbed wire on a section of fence. Somebody had cut the wire and made a hole in the fence about a foot across.

Probably a trespasser. They got all kinds: tourists who wanted a close up shot of a Longhorn, stupid kids cutting the fence on a dare, the occasional hobo, and every now and then, professional rustlers.

They'd even had a bunch of kids from the local college stage a protest on their land because they were raising and selling beef for people to eat. Buck had called the sheriff on 'em, and Wilmer had dragged them away; but not before they tore up a six-foot stretch of fence and littered the ground with a lot of neon-colored signs and trash.

Luke snipped the barbs off a couple feet of wire, untwined the strands, and began to splice the two ends together. It was the tenth repair he'd had to make, and he was only a mile west of the main gate. Morg was right: the fence facing the road always got the heaviest damage.

Luke tightened the twisted wire, then glanced up at the sky. It was mid-morning and beginning to get warm; but he wasn't even halfway done.

Still, it was better to be out working on something than to be back at the house.

Luke frowned at the mended wire, stood up slowly, and walked over to take his horse's bridle and walk it down the line to the next fence break.

The feeling of failure was still heavy on him. Working helped distract him, but it couldn't make that feeling go away. He squinted up at the sky again.

The sight of a fence post lying tilted over up ahead made him swallow a sigh. Barbed wire was bunched up all around it.

He dropped the reins and let his horse graze, then walked over to the mangled fence and plopped down on the grass again. He yanked the fence post upright and cut the tangled barbed wire from around it. That messed-up fence post reminded him of his life. He felt like he'd been knocked sky west and crooked, and he was all tangled up.

Didn't know what to do next.

The slow clop of horse's hooves made him wipe his brow with his forearm and look up. Morgan's big black horse was staring down at him, and when he raised his eyes further up, Morgan was too.

"How's it coming?"

Luke gestured toward the wire. "Slow. I've mended a dozen breaks this morning. The fence down here is as bad as I've ever seen it."

"Well, come and take a break. It's getting toward noon. We can rest under the shade of those trees over there." He pointed to a stand of oaks a few dozen yards away.

"That sounds good to me," Luke muttered and followed as Morgan nudged Cochise up to the trees.

Luke flopped down at the foot of a big tree and leaned against it with his hands behind his head. Morgan fumbled with his saddle bag, then walked over to join him carrying two bottles of water. He tossed one, and Luke caught it one-handed and twisted off the top.

He took a deep pull and sighed, "That sure tastes good. I was getting thirsty."

Morgan lowered his long body and sat down beside him under the shade of the big oak. He opened the bottle, drank deeply, and folded his brown hands across his belt.

They sat there in the peaceful silence, staring out across the green meadow, and time seemed to slow down. There was no sound except for the distant lowing of a cow, or the occasional swoosh of a passing car on the road.

Luke frowned and picked at a tuft of grass. "You know, Morg, I've been turning things over in my mind. This thing with Trina has got me thinking about my life."

His brother grunted but made no other reply, and Luke went on, "I think maybe God is mad at me."

At that, Morgan turned to give him a long, level stare. "How d'you figure?" he rumbled.

Luke looked down at the ground and shrugged. "I walked the aisle at church when I was eight," he mumbled. "I gave my heart to the Lord, and I meant it, Morg. But I ain't been a very good Christian since. It stands to reason that God might be jerking me sideways for it."

"Huh."

Luke scratched his cheek and went on, "When I was in the rodeo there was a lot of girls who were fans," he mumbled. "Buckle bunnies. They made a big fuss over me, and they were always around, and I—well I kinda got carried away."

Morgan stared out into the distance and said nothing, and Luke went on, "And I started going out to bars after my rides, and it was fun I guess, but I kinda got tired of it after awhile.

It started to feel fake to me. Weren't any of those bunnies really interested in me. They just wanted to be seen with a rodeo star and to have a good time.

"Then I met Trina, and she was different. She was sweet and shy. Kinda like the girl next door. And I could see that she meant every word she said. So we got together, and it was way better than what I was doing before, but"— he scratched his ear—"Trina and me weren't exactly doing like we were supposed to, either."

He looked up at Morgan. "I think God's kinda kicking me in the shins, Morg."

Morgan sighed and rubbed his eyes with one hand. "Well, Luke, I can't tell you if it's God or not," he muttered. "But if you haven't done right, then you should have a talk with Him. I know that much."

Luke frowned. "I want to do better, Morg, I really do. But it seems like I always wander off when I should be going straight ahead."

"Hum," Morgan grunted. "Well, if you know what you did wrong, then you know what to do to fix it."

"Yeah," Luke mumbled despondently, and ran a hand through his hair.

"Why don't we pray about it," Morg suggested, and he nodded. There was a long moment of silence; then his brother bowed his head, closed his eyes and sighed:

"Lord, we're here to humbly ask You for Your help. Ain't one of us always does what he's supposed to do; and Luke knows he's gone off the straight and narrow. Please help him get back where he's supposed to be with You. I know You've got a plan for his life, Lord. Please show him what it is, and give him the power to do it with all his strength.

"Amen."

"Amen," Luke echoed, with his eyes closed. He sat there in frowning concentration until he heard Morgan stir beside him. When he opened his eyes, Morgan was on his feet and towering over him.

"I'll get back to the fence line," he rumbled. "But if you want to take a few more minutes, you go ahead and take 'em."

Luke watched as his brother walked over to his horse, climbed up into the saddle, and sent Cochise down the pasture at a brisk trot.

When Morgan had disappeared, Luke looked down at his hands. It was sure true that he hadn't done what he was supposed to. He bowed his head again and prayed:

Lord, I'm sorry that I let you down. I'm sorry for all those years I put you on a shelf and went out and lived wrong. I'm sorry that I hurt Trina.

Maybe I can't figure out what I'm supposed to do in life, because I've been trying to figure it out without You.

I guess the first thing is to start doing the things I already know You want me to do.

I'm going to just trust that You'll tell me the rest later.

Amen.

Chapter Eleven

Julie sat in front of her bedroom vanity facing a starkly-lighted magnification mirror. It bathed her face in white light and blew every pore up to the size of a dime; but she was willing to face her every tiny flaw to make herself irresistible.

Julie stared at her reflection grimly as she picked up a bottle of foundation and shook it. She was going to give herself the best makeup job she'd ever had in her life.

Or maybe it was closer to the truth to say that she was applying camouflage, because she was going hunting.

She was gunning for a wild jackass.

She glanced at the bright yellow flyer lying on the vanity. The headline shouted:

RIDING LESSONS AT THE SEVEN SPADES
RANCH!

Lessons for all ages taught by Luke Spade, former rodeo star and winner of nine champion buckles.

Julie's mouth curled slightly as she dabbed foundation over her brow and cheeks. *Thanks for the invite,* she thought angrily. *I think I'll take you up on that offer, Mr. Nine Buckles.*

Since the universe hasn't taught you the lesson you so desperately need, I'll be glad to do it.

I'm going to teach you what it feels like to fall head over heels in love with someone, and then have them use you like a tool.

I'm going to do the same thing to you, that you did to Trina.

Since you think it's so much fun to dish it out, let's see if you can take it—you selfish, entitled jerk!

Julie set the bottle down with a snap and picked up a tin of powder. She shook out a dusting into her hand, swirled a fluffy makeup brush into her palm, and began furiously powdering her face. The more she'd learned about Luke Spade, she angrier she'd gotten at him; but seeing him on that motorcycle with a new girl not one day after Trina had fled in despair was the last straw.

She'd decided to stop getting mad, and start getting even.

Julie glared at her own reflection. Trina would never dream of standing up for herself, she was too shy and nice. But there was nothing holding *her* back from getting revenge for her best friend.

Julie tossed the tin of powder across the vanity counter with a clatter and picked up another tin of blush. She feathered it over the apples of her cheeks, out toward her temples, and up around her hairline.

I don't care if your family has got all the money in the world. By the time I get finished with you, Luke Spade, she fumed, *you're going to be crying like a whipped puppy.*

And it's good enough for you. Maybe next time you'll think twice before you break a woman's heart!

She dropped the powder brush, gave herself a critical look in the mirror, and picked up a shiny tube of mascara. She pulled out the wand and feathered it over her lashes with short, deft strokes.

She knew how to ride a horse as well as any woman in Texas. Her parents had started her on a pony when she was eight years old.

But she was going to those riding classes to make every stupid rookie mistake in the world. She was going to be the dumbest, most helpless rider Luke Spade had ever suffered in his life, because that would force him to spend all his time with her.

The faster she could get alone with him, the better.

Julie turned this way and that in front of the mirror, then flipped it over to the normal reflection to assess her lashes. To her grim satisfaction, they were dark and lush. They curled out slightly at the ends and made her eyes look slightly tapered.

Just the effect she wanted.

She put her hands up to her hair. Her head was covered in hot rollers, and she reached up to pull them free one by one. Her dark, luxuriant hair fell over her shoulders in curling skeins, and she fluffed it out lightly with her fingers. Then she stood up, bent over, and reached for a can of hair spray.

She sprayed her hair with a cloud of light, pleasant-smelling mist, then stood upright suddenly and flipped her hair over her shoulders. When she looked in the mirror, it was a thick, dark mane swirling around her head in glorious confusion. She sprayed it again to set it, then reached for her shirt and a pair of pants draped over the back of a chair.

She was going to wear a white cotton shirt and a pair of jeans. Simple.

Or at least, that was the effect she was going for. As if she was just another student in the class, come to ride horses.

But that tailored white shirt hugged her like a lover, and she knew that it flattered her curves. Her jeans weren't tight or revealing; but they were tapered and fit her perfectly, and her figure was such that she knew it was enough.

Julie's hand paused as she reached for the clothes. Her conscience pricked her briefly, asked her if she really wanted to do this.

To hunt a man down and do her best to break his heart.

You don't even know him, her conscience whispered; and for an instant she wavered. It was a mean thing to do; but she only had to remember the despair in Trina's eyes, and Penny's heartbreaking death, for her fury to come roaring back.

Nothing enraged her like cruelty; and at least once in the history of the world, a man who deliberately hurt a woman was going to find out what that felt like.

Yes, she was going to get payback for Trina; and maybe, in a wider and more cosmic sense, even a little justice for women like Penny.

Julie reached for a vial of cologne and spritzed it lightly over her bare shoulders; then she picked up the shirt and shrugged into it.

Watch out, Luke Spade, she thought grimly, as she buttoned it up.

You may think you're teaching a lesson. But you're about to learn one!

Chapter Twelve

Luke sat patiently on his horse and surveyed the first crowd of hopefuls who'd shown up for his riding lessons. It was a pretty mixed bag: young parents with their kids, a few senior citizens, a few teenagers, and—his brows went up—one *knockout* beautiful woman.

He blinked at her in amazement. She looked like what he imagined an angel would be. She was perched on the corral fence with her legs crossed, as if she'd just lighted there and folded her wings behind her. She had long, black, luxurious hair that curled over her shoulders, a pale, oval face, and a pair of unearthly blue eyes.

And her *figure*.

Have mercy, Luke thought in awe, then snapped back to himself. He glanced away, because it was rude to stare; but the woman almost didn't look real.

He turned back to the group, gathered his wits, and pasted on a bright smile. "Welcome to the Seven Spades," he announced. "We're glad you all came out today. My name is Luke Spade, and I'm going to be teaching these classes. Just for kicks, raise your hand if you never rode a horse before."

He saw half the hands in the group go up, and he couldn't help noticing that the dark beauty sitting on the fence raised hers, too. When their eyes met she smiled at him, big and bright and pretty.

His eyes lingered on her lips. They were fine and delicately drawn, but they were the color of ripe raspberries, and they looked just as soft and plump and tasty.

He cleared his throat and tried to focus. "Well, ah—we're going to be starting out from scratch. The first thing we're going to do is go over some safety rules." He threw a leg over the saddle, dismounted Buddy, and put a hand on the saddle.

"The first thing to remember is that horses don't like you coming up from behind. It spooks 'em, and when they're spooked, they can kick. Trust me when I tell you, you don't want to be kicked by a horse."

A ripple of laughter moved over the small crowd, and Luke's eyes moved to the dark-haired woman. She dimpled as if his joke was hilarious.

He straightened up a bit, and continued in a stronger voice, "You never want to sneak up on a horse, because it scares 'em. Always let a horse know you're coming. You can talk to it soft and gentle, and walk over nice and slow. See how I'm doing?"

He backed up a few paces and crooned to Buddy as he walked over. The palomino turned its head to watch, and nuzzled his chest as he reached up to pat its neck.

"Your horse is pretty," a little girl called out, and the crowed laughed. Luke joined in, then held out his hand to her. "Wanna come over and say hello?"

The little girl brightened and looked up at her mother; then walked up to where he was standing.

"What's your name, honey?"

The little girl turned back and forth shyly. "Ginny."

"Well, that's a pretty name." Luke bent down and took her hand and nodded toward the horse.

"Now Ginny, you just say something sweet to him, and we'll walk over nice and slow."

The little girl looked up into his face, then at the horse; but she let him lead her up to Buddy's side.

"Hello, horsey," she quavered; and Buddy turned to look down at her.

"See?" Luke smiled. "He saw you coming. Now he'll let you pet his nose."

The little girl smiled, and Luke lifted her up to allow her to stroke Buddy's nose. She shrieked with laughter, and he set her back down on the ground. The girl scampered back to her mother, crying, "I petted a horse!"

Luke watched as the little girl's mother reached for her and smiled. It made him feel good to think he was introducing a little kid to her first horse; and not only her.

His eyes moved to the gorgeous brunette, and was rewarded by the beatific expression on her face. She reached up and wiped one eye, as if she had been moved to tears by the touching moment.

Luke put his hands up and added, "Now here's something most folks don't know. It's just as bad an idea to stand in front of a horse, as to stand behind it. That's because horses have a blind spot that keeps them from seeing what's right in front of 'em. So if they get spooked, they can run right over you without even meaning to, if you're standing there.

"The safest place to stand is right beside the horse, after you walk up from the side, slow and polite.

"Now that Ginny here's showed us how, let's have everybody come up and say hello to Buddy. Who wants to be next?"

To his surprise, the beautiful woman lifted her hand. "I'll go next." She slid down from the fence in one fluid movement and smiled big and friendly as she moved toward him. Luke's eyes drifted down from her face. She moved as smooth and as dainty as could be.

Luke rubbed his chin. "Ah—why don't you tell us your name, Miss…"

"Julie," the young woman replied in a velvet tone, and smiled at the others as she moved past them. She raised her eyes to his, and when she smiled at him up close, she was so beautiful that for a second there he was struck stupid.

"Ah…well Julie, come over here and say hello to Buddy."

"Is Buddy your horse?" she asked softly.

Luke nodded. "That's right. Him and me have been together for a long time."

She shot him a warm look. "Lucky Buddy," she breathed, in a voice too low to be heard by anybody but him; and before he could do more than be surprised, she'd reached out to Buddy and murmured, "Hello, beautiful boy. What a sweetheart, yes."

Her tone was so low and caressing that Luke felt the sound crawl right up his spine like a million tiny caterpillars. He frowned and cleared his throat.

"That's right, that's the way you do it," he announced, with a nod of affirmation toward the group of onlookers. He turned to Julie and smiled, "You're off to a good start."

She arched an eyebrow. "I hope so," she murmured, but in a tone so innocent that he couldn't call it flirting.

"T-That's good," he stammered, and Julie seemed to take his words as a sign her turn was over. She whirled around, as if she was going to walk past him; but instead she stumbled over a rock, pitched forward disastrously, and plowed right into his chest.

Somehow her elbow smashed him in the gut, and it knocked the wind right out of him.

"*Oof!*"

He gasped and coughed and caught her by the shoulders; but when he rolled startled eyes to hers, she brushed her hair out of her eyes and whispered:

"Sorry."

He released her, but his smile went a bit crooked, and he looked down as she returned to the group for fear his face might be going red. "Thank you Julie, you did good," he coughed, and put a hand to his throbbing chest.

"All right, who's next?"

An elderly man raised his hand, and Luke waved him up; but he couldn't keep his eyes from following Julie as she sashayed back to the fence, hopped back up on it, and crossed her ankles primly.

Luke let each student come up to the front and pet Buddy, then continued with the first lesson: an introduction to horses and their anatomy and temperament, basic safety tips, an overview of a saddle and tack.

At the end of the hour-long session, Luke was satisfied he'd laid a good foundation for the new riders to build on. "That's all for this time," he announced. "We'll get more into tack next lesson," he promised. "I'll explain what the parts of a saddle are, and how to saddle and bridle a horse the right way. Next session is same day and time, next week. I'll see you then, and thanks for coming."

There was scattered clapping, then the group slowly broke up. A few people came up to ask questions or to chat, and Luke noticed that Julie was among them. She hung back, as if she was waiting for the others to go, and when she walked up at last, she was smiling.

She reached out to touch his arm lightly. "I really enjoyed the lesson today," she murmured. "I've always wanted to ride a horse, but I never had the time to learn."

Luke gave her a polite smile. "Well, we're glad you came."

He kept his eyes on his boots. He figured he'd better keep things nice and professional. He was starting to do right again, he was just getting his head on straight. That gorgeous brunette might look like an angel, but everything about her was a big, blinking neon sign flashing:

TEMPTATION.

If he didn't watch himself, he could go sliding right back down that old slippery slope.

Julie swayed back and forth and smiled. "I heard you were a rodeo rider."

Luke cleared his throat and tried not to be pleased. "Yep, I was there for awhile."

"What did you do?"

Luke planted his hands on his hips. "I was a bronc buster," he mumbled and felt his face going warm.

Her eyes widened. "Ooh, that sounds dangerous," she smiled.

Luke shrugged one shoulder. "Yeah, I got a little busted up sometimes," he admitted, and rubbed the back of his neck. "Got my arm broken a few times."

"Well," she murmured, and moved a step closer, "I'm glad you're all right now." To his surprise, she kissed the tip of her finger and pressed it to his arm.

"For luck," she smiled, and turned on the words. She glanced at him over her shoulder and added, "I'm looking forward to the next class."

Luke nodded. "Yes ma'am. You'll be riding a horse in no time."

She smiled and walked off, and Luke couldn't help but watch her go. She was tall and willowy and her beautiful coal-black hair was the biggest part of her. It fell down her back almost to her waist, and it was sleek and shiny as a river at midnight.

She swayed back and forth as graceful as branches in a breeze, and she filled out her clothes better than any woman he'd ever seen.

She might be a little clumsy, but she was out of this world; and she set off the warning bells in his head. He had a pretty wide experience of women, but he'd never seen any woman who had everything come together so perfect.

Who had skin so white, and hair so dark, and eyes so blue. Who had a sure-enough heavenly body.

If she'd unfurled her wings and taken off into the sky, he'd hardly be surprised.

She was just the kind of woman to cloud a man's mind, and it worried him.

Luke sighed, ran a hand through his hair, then took Buddy's bridle and led him back toward the barn. It was better to be safe than sorry. He'd just begun to pick himself up from a painful crash and burn with Trina. He didn't need to get his eyes on another woman before he'd even recovered from the last bust-up.

I better keep my mind on business, he thought ruefully. *Stick to what I know.*

I understand horses.

But I ain't never figured out women.

Chapter Thirteen

Julie pulled her car door shut. She sat there in the plush driver's seat of her VW, curled her fingers around the wheel, and smiled a smug little smile.

She'd barely met Luke Spade, and already she had his number.

He was a delicious dish up close: he was six feet tall, broad-shouldered, and blonde as summer wheat. His face was brown and his teeth were white. He was ripped, not an ounce of fat on him, but he was also relaxed and friendly and loose in the joints.

Now that she'd met him, she could confirm that he was even better looking in person than the picture she'd seen on Trina's coffee table.

He radiated an unselfconscious magnetism.

In short, Luke Spade was a classic 'howdy-ma'am' cowboy, the kind she'd often known growing up. That kind of cowboy was brave, athletic and loyal to his ideals. He was often good looking, and charming in a laid-back way.

But his disastrous blind spot was that he didn't take his personal life seriously. He sometimes never learned to value his woman until his first, second, or even third wife divorced him in despair.

Yes, Luke was brave, athletic, good looking, and charming, all right. And he'd destroyed his relationship with Trina, so he definitely qualified as the 'howdy-ma'am' type.

Julie's eyes narrowed in fierce joy. She knew his type, all right, and she was going to peel him like an orange, chew him up, and spit out the seeds.

Maybe when he learned how bad that hurt, he'd stop doing it to the women in his life.

Julie pulled her car out of the gravel lot and onto the long driveway that led to the big front gate. The lush green pasture lands rolling past were beautiful, but they only cemented her resolve. The Seven Spades Ranch was massive because its owners were wallowing in money; and Luke thought that because he was rich he didn't have to care how he treated other people.

Julie pinched her mouth into a straight line. It was going to be a pleasure to introduce him to the real world.

I was a bronc buster, she scoffed. No doubt he used that line all the time. Women loved a rodeo cowboy. And it sure didn't hurt that he was a bronzed, golden blonde with wide shoulders and narrow hips. All muscle.

Julie sighed in pity. She could see how romantic little Trina had fallen head over heels in love with him. Probably at first sight, poor thing. Luke Spade had everything he needed to break a woman's heart, and he'd used his looks and his charm to do just that.

The edges of Julie's mouth curved up. He was probably telling himself that he had a new woman on his string now. She'd gone out of her way to butter him up, and she could tell that he'd gotten the message.

Just you wait, she thought grimly. *Just you wait, cowboy.*

She pulled to a stop at the huge ranch gates and waited to exit. A big truck rumbled past, and she pulled out behind it.

She wondered, just for an instant, if she should let Trina in on what she was doing. Only after it was over, of course.

But she knew the answer, and it was no. Trina was so hypnotized by Luke Spade, even now, that she'd be against it. That was the sort of person Trina was.

Julie's conscience whispered to her again, urged her that if Trina could forgive Luke, she should too; but she dismissed it. Trina was so sweet and shy that she'd never dream of standing up for herself.

But some things were so wrong and cruel that they demanded an answer. In her book, this was one of them.

She turned off the two-lane and onto the interstate. As she drove she was plotting out her next move. She'd flirted a bit much for a first meeting, and she didn't want to overplay her hand. Cowboys liked to be the ones doing the chasing, and so next time she'd fade back a bit to see how Luke would respond.

That was going to be her game plan. Two steps forward, one step back, until she had Luke Spade tight on her hook.

She switched on the radio, and a country music singer was wailing:

You think you're tough

You think you're bad

You think you're the best thing I ever had.

You think I'm dumb

You think you're smart.

You think you're gonna break my heart.

Well I'm not dumb and I won't cry

I'm gonna get another guy

And one day you'll wake up to find

That you're the one's been left behind.

Julie hummed along as she drove, and rolled the windows down to let the breeze flow through her hair. Revenge was supposed to be sweet, and she was already getting a little taste of its sugar.

Maybe that was why it was called *just deserts.*

She giggled a little as she drove, and sang along as the radio jangled on about getting even with a bad man.

Chapter Fourteen

"Well, ain't seen you in town in a while, Luke. You been keeping busy out at the ranch?"

Luke climbed off his bike and stepped up onto the sidewalk outside the tack store in Sandy Creek. The grizzled proprietor was standing in the doorway grinning at him.

"Yeah, I've been kind of busy," Luke nodded. "I'm teaching a riding class."

The man gaped in disbelief, then burst out laughing. "What, you teaching kids and little old ladies how to ride ponies?" he scoffed. "That's babysitting. I thought you was supposed to be some kind of fire-eating rodeo star. You getting soft in your old age, Luke?"

Luke smiled and rubbed the back of his neck. "Maybe. I enjoyed teaching that class, though. It was kind of fun."

His friend shook his head and laughed. "Well, the rodeo season's cranking up again," he replied, and gestured toward a flyer posted on a light post. "Some of your old friends are coming back to Houston."

Luke glanced over, and a big red poster announced:

FIRE AND FURY RODEO!

COWBOY REUNION

THE STADIUM IN HOUSTON

JUNE 6-10

EXTRME SADDLE BRONC BUSTING!

BULL RIDING!

MUTTON BUSTING!

CHILI COOKOFF!

BOOT SCOOTIN' PARTY!

YOUR FAVORITE RODEO STARS!

JUSTICE OWENS

RED THOMPSON

BILLY 'TWO BOOTS' JENKINS

RICK SANTIAGO

Luke shook his head fondly. He knew most of the guys listed on the poster. They'd been some of his toughest competition, and he was a little surprised that they were still on the rodeo circuit. Most were about his age, in their mid thirties, and he'd figured he was almost too old to bust broncs any more.

Maybe he was wrong.

His friend shot him a twinkling glance. "Your name used to be up on those posters," he teased. "You were a real hometown hero, Luke. We even used to get your fans in here sometimes. Folks hoping to catch sight of you around here."

Luke smiled and rubbed his neck again. "No kidding? What do you know."

"Lots of folks around here'd be tickled to see you back at the rodeo," the other man replied. "In fact, you still have time to register for this one," he added, jerking a thumb toward the poster.

"Oh, I'm not planning to get back on the circuit again," Luke told him. "I might do an event now and then, just to keep my hand in," he muttered, with a glance at the poster.

His friend's face brightened. "That's right. You're not an old man, don't act like one!"

He put up a hand and disappeared inside his shop, and Luke stared after him in mild surprise.

I didn't know I was acting like an old man, he thought ruefully. His eyes returned to the bright red poster.

But maybe I did bow out too quick, after all. If those other guys still got it, why then I do, too.

Justice Owens.

Luke stared at the name, and his memory served up his old nemesis, life size and mean as original sin: a six-foot-plus cowboy with hair as red as fire and a jaw and fists made out of solid granite.

Justice had fought him tooth and nail up and down the rodeo circuit: Calgary, Cheyenne, Pendleton, Prescott, Greeley. If he'd won a buckle anywhere, he'd done it over Justice's broken body, and vice versa.

Justice had always taken losing real personal, what was more. Luke shook his head. To him, a rodeo was just a competition, and if he lost, he didn't hold a grudge toward the man who won; but Justice had begrudged every single buckle he had on his wall at home.

They'd almost had a fistfight at Prescott one year.

Luke rubbed his jaw, remembering it. Him and Justice had been tied for the round, and the first one to break it was going to win a gold buckle and thirty thousand dollars.

He'd gone eight seconds on a bronc named Catawampus, and had given the ride his best and got a high score. But when Justice rode his horse, he made just a little bobble, a technical error that had shaved a point off his score. It had been a great ride overall, but Justice lost anyway because they'd been tied.

Luke frowned and stared into space. Justice never took losing too good, and especially not to him, for some reason. When he'd won and taken his bow and went off to meet his friends, Justice had come up and grabbed him by the arm and told him he hadn't won fair and square.

He'd known at the time that Justice was blowing off steam, and he shouldn't have let it fly away with him, but it did. He wouldn't stand for anybody calling him a cheat, and him and Justice started throwing punches at each other. If his friends and the rodeo security hadn't torn them apart, the two of them might've done each other some serious damage.

Luke rubbed his jaw. Still, that had been almost five years ago. He'd long since moved on, and he was willing to bet Justice had, too.

Nobody could hold a grudge that long.

Luke's smile returned, and he glanced at the rodeo poster. The rodeo was billing itself as a 'cowboy reunion.' Maybe he should throw his hat in, after all. He had to admit that he missed the rush of pitting himself against a snorting, bucking hellion of a bronc.

Luke pulled his cell phone from the back pocket of his jeans, glanced at the poster, and murmured into the tiny mic.

"Fire and Fury Rodeo, Houston, Texas.

"Registration form."

Chapter Fifteen

"Well, would you look at that."

A sly smile curved the lips of a dark, moustachioed cowboy as he leaned against a metal fence. He elbowed his companion in the ribs and pointed toward the screen of his cell phone.

"Look who's coming back for old home week."

The other man, a towering, broad-shouldered redhead, turned his head just enough to drawl, "Why don't you just tell me. I don't like guessing games."

The two of them were lounging on the edge of a rodeo ring. The sound of sawing, hammering, and men's voices all around them announced that preparations for an upcoming event were in full swing.

The first man pointed toward the screen and chuckled, "Luke Spade's signed up for the bronc busting event the first night of the Fire and Fury. Looks like he's making a comeback."

The redhead swiped the phone out of his hands. "Let me see that." He frowned at the little blue screen, and his mouth curled down.

The other man nodded smugly. "See? I told you."

The redhead slapped the phone back into his companion's hand. "Well, I don't see what difference it makes," he shrugged. "Let him come. Luke Spade was never all that good, and now he's out of practice. He'll die on the first ride."

"I don't know," the other man parried, and raised his brows. "Nine buckles. Hundred of thousands in prize winnings. I'd say he did all right."

"Past tense," the redhead retorted. "I ain't seen him in four years. If he thinks he can come back cold and beat us out, who's been riding all this time, he's crazy." He turned to smile down into the other man's face. "It'll be fun to watch him hit the dirt."

"Yeah, you never did like him, did you?" the other man jibed.

The redhead shrugged and looked away. "I never made any secret of that."

"No, you didn't," the other man agreed, and when he caught the look the redhead gave him, he cleared his throat and added, "See you around, Justice."

"Yeah."

Justice Owens watched as the other cowboy scuttled away, then he turned his attention back to the workers setting up the stands.

Luke Spade.

He'd always hated old Luke. Luke was a golden-haired rich kid pretending to be a cowboy. His family was loaded, one of the fattest in Texas, maybe even in the country, and Luke didn't need to hit a lick at a snake.

But instead of kicking back and being happy about that, like any normal guy would, old Luke had thought it'd be more fun to show up at the rodeo. To do his best to deny as much prize money as he could to the men who worked hard for that money and needed it bad.

Luke had been real good at that. At gobbling up money that should've gone to other guys.

Yeah, it was gonna be fun to watch old Luke come strutting back to the rodeo like he owned it, get up on his first bronc in four years, and get launched across the ring in front of three thousand people. Golden boys like Luke Spade needed to eat a little dirt now and then to remind them they weren't God's gift to the world.

Justice leaned over and spat into the sawdust. Luke had been a burr in his saddle for over a decade. When they'd been coming up in the sport, Luke had always been just a hair ahead of him—a bit tougher to throw, a bit smoother on his rides, a bit more in sync with a bronc.

And when Luke picked up his hat, threw his hand up to the crowd, and walked out of the arena, the women had always been there at the gate, waiting to swarm him.Yeah, those little buckle bunnies had loved old Luke.

Women loved a brown-skinned, blonde-haired man.

As for him, with his hair as red as fire and his freckled skin that refused to tan, not so much.

Yeah, Luke was what book-smart men called 'beloved of the gods.' Young, handsome, rich, and able to get any woman he wanted.

It's a wonder more guys don't hate him, Justice thought dourly, and spat again.

Yeah, let him come.

Chapter Sixteen

Luke ambled out of the downstairs kitchen holding a plate full of warm burritos in one hand and a cold beer bottle in the other. He was making for the stairs when the big front door opened, and a gusty spring breeze blew his sister-in-law and his little niece into the house.

Luke paused to greet her. "Hey Kate," he murmured. "Molly. You two been out shopping?"

Kate juggled six striped and polka-dotted bags in pastel blues, greens and yellows. She glanced up at him breathlessly, and a shining skein of red hair fell over one eye. "Yes, I've been out getting an Easter dress for Molly and a little suit for Russ," she gasped.

Luke put his food down on a table and walked over to take the bags out of her hands. Kate shot him a grateful look and put a hand on Molly's shoulder.

"Thanks," she sighed. "I might've gone a little overboard, but the Easter clothes in that little kid's shop in town were so adorable." She glanced up at him again.

"Are you coming with us to church this Sunday, Luke? It's Easter, after all."

Luke opened his mouth to say no, but paused. He hadn't gone to church in years, and maybe that was part of his trouble.

He'd told the Lord he wanted to turn over a new leaf.

He glanced away uncomfortably. "Well...."

"Oh, come on," Kate laughed. "It's only once a year, and it's always such a beautiful service."

Luke gave her a crooked smile. "All right then," he answered weakly, and Kate's face brightened.

"Good! Donna said she'd like to come with us this year, so we'll all go together."

Luke raised his brows in surprise as he followed them up the stairs. "Is Carson coming to church, too?" His mind kind of boggled at that mental image.

Kate sigh sounded disappointed. "No, just Donna. She says she's never been in a Christian church, and she's curious."

Luke processed that. "Huh."

He followed Kate and Molly upstairs to their own door and carried in the bulging bags. The floor of the elegant great room was littered with brightly-colored baby toys and blankets. They were scattered in a wide radius around a huge playpen.

Buck was bending over it, and he turned to beam at them over his shoulder. "Kate, quick," he yelped, "come and look at this!"

Luke set the bags down and followed her over curiously. Buck was holding his little son's arms, and the baby was standing upright on his wobbly legs.

"Oh, Buck!" Kate gasped and rushed over to bend over the playpen. "It's the first time he's stood up!"

They both laughed indulgently. Luke smiled to see his little curly-haired nephew look up at his parents with shining blue eyes, then stomp his foot triumphantly.

He glanced behind them. It wasn't as happy a story on the back end. Molly was standing behind her mother with her eyes on the floor and a dejected slump to her shoulders.

Luke smiled a bit. It looked like little Molly was feeling replaced by the newcomer, and he knew how that went. It had happened to him three times when he was a kid.

He walked up beside her and ruffled her hair with a big hand. She looked up at him glumly, and he reached into his pocket and pulled out a shiny nickel. He took Molly's hand and pressed the nickel into her palm.

She looked up at him. "What's this, Uncle Luke?"

He stared down into her face as grim as a judge. "I need you to keep that safe for me," he told her, as Buck picked up the baby and Kate laughed and stroked her fingers over its fuzzy cheek.

Molly frowned faintly. "Why? It's just a nickel."

Luke squatted down on the floor beside her. "Well, now, that's where you're wrong," he told her in a confidential whisper. "That's a magic nickel that I got from an old Indian man in

New Mexico. He said it'd make me feel ten feet tall as long as I had it in my pocket, but that it'd only work for five years. He said if I didn't pass it on to somebody else after the time was up, the magic would go away."

Molly looked up at him in wonder. "You're giving it to me?"

Luke reached out and pinched her button nose. "That's right. My five years are up. I got to pass it on.

"But you keep that magic nickel on you, and you'll feel ten feet tall. You'll go strutting down the street like a peacock. Not a care in the world."

He watched in silent amusement as Molly looked down at the nickel in her hand, then slowly slipped it into the pocket of her pink dress. Luke nodded and winked.

"Don't you spend that on candy, now!"

Molly pulled her shoulders back and nodded regally. "I won't."

Luke ruffled her hair again. "That's a smart girl."

She flounced around and walked out of the room with her head held high, and Luke smiled and shook his head.

Kate turned around an instant later and asked, "Where's Molly?"

Luke nodded toward the side hall. "She went off yonder."

Kate sighed and crossed her arms. "She's feeling a bit left out. We have been paying a lot of attention to the baby. I should go and talk to her."

She turned back to him. "We'll be having lunch in a few minutes. Why don't you have some with us?"

"Oh, thanks, but I already have my lunch downstairs," Luke smiled. His eyes moved to little Russ, who was now sitting down in the playpen with his chubby legs stuck out. "Congratulations, though. Russ is a fine little boy."

Kate's face brightened. "Thank you. We are proud of him." She glanced toward the hall and added, "Of both our children."

Luke waved and moved off toward the door. Kate waved back, but Buck was so engrossed with his little son that he didn't turn his head or give any sign that he'd noticed a guest had entered his home; and Luke chuckled to himself as he walked out of the apartment.

There had never been a prouder father in the world, than Buck.

Luke skipped down the stairs, ready for his beer and burritos, but when he reached the foot, his plate and bottle were gone.

It wasn't hard to find out where they'd gone, though. Jesse was in the atrium, sitting on the couch next to the big fireplace, and he had one end of the beer bottle to his lips, and the other tilted up to the ceiling.

Luke stuck his hands on his hips and sauntered over. He pointed to the empty plate sitting beside his brother and drawled, "That was my lunch."

His dour brother turned to look at him, then turned back around. "I thought Conchita left it out for whoever wanted it," he grumbled.

"Uh huh," Luke retorted, but decided not to argue. Jesse was so grumpy that you had to be really mad to stir him up; and he wasn't mad.

Just hungry. It wasn't worth getting pounded over.

Still, his stomach rumbled all the way up the stairs; and he made a mental note not to leave a meal lying around undefended in that house.

Chapter Seventeen

Luke breezed into his apartment, whistling as he went. He probably had something edible in his own kitchen, though he'd probably have to dig to find it.

His refrigerator was covered with souvenir magnets from rodeos or horse shows, and when he opened it, an empty can of beer fell out.

He bent down and peered in. The news wasn't good: the inside of his fridge looked like a mushroom farm.

He closed the door and straightened up to open his kitchen cabinets. He found one box of mac and cheese, some coffee filters, a salt shaker, and some Christmas cookies that had expired four years ago.

He tossed the container into the trash, sighed, and dug his phone out of his jeans. He pressed the screen and stuck it to his ear.

"Hello, is this Smoky Sam's? Yeah, I'd like to order the grilled Mexicali pizza with a big green salad on the side. Spicy salsa dressing. Yeah.

"Luke. The Seven Spades Ranch." He paused, then laughed, "Yeah, it's me.—We're all right, how are you? Your Mamma doing all right? Yeah, I'm glad to hear she's out of the hospital.

"That's great. Tell her hey for me.

"Okay. Thanks, Sam. You, too."

Luke hung up and sighed. It was going to be thirty minutes to his lunch, and in the meanwhile, he needed to go find out if he had something proper to wear to an Easter Sunday service, since he'd promised to go.

He drifted out of the kitchen and down a long hall to his bedroom door. He wasn't sure that he even owned a Sunday suit. If he did, it was probably buried in the deepest, darkest corner of his closet.

He flicked on the light as he entered. His bedroom, like the rest of his apartment, was a scrambling mess. His clothes were on the floor, the bed was unmade, and every table and dresser was covered in a jumble of small appliances, unopened mail, loose change, and other odds and ends.

Discouragement slapped over him as he looked around the messy bedroom. *I need to clean up,* he told himself, but instead walked over to the closet and pulled the doors open.

A mountain of clothes came tumbling out onto the floor, and Luke grumbled under his breath as he picked up the mound, wadded it together, and threw it onto the bed.

He turned back to the closet with a frown and went rummaging through it. He threw out a fringed leather jacket that had once been part of a rodeo costume; a half-dozen plaid shirts; jeans, jeans, and more jeans; and a pair of black leather pants.

Luke frowned as he pulled them out. *What in the world,* he thought in confusion, then tossed it onto the bed.

He reached back into the further reaches of the big closet, hoping to at least find a jacket. *I may have to borrow a suit from somebody,* he thought in regret. *Doesn't look like I have one.*

He reached into the closet as far as his arm could reach, and his expression lightened. He pulled out a heavy hanger, and when he pulled it out, a nice navy suit dangled from his hand.

But his expression slowly clouded, because he remembered it. It was the suit he'd bought for Trina's grandmother's funeral, two years ago.

Luke tossed it onto the bed, sank down into a chair, and ran a hand through his hair. He'd gathered up all the photos he had of him and Trina and dumped them in a cardboard box. But seemed like every time he started feeling better, something popped up to remind him that him and Trina hadn't worked out.

Seems like I'm my own worst enemy, he thought in exasperation. His memory projected Buck's happy face as he took his baby son in his arms, and Kate's eyes gazing up at him adoringly.

That could be me, Luke thought wistfully. *Trina wanted that to be us, and I bucked sideways and took off running.*

What's wrong with me?

He sighed and pulled a hand over his face. *I guess if I could figure that out, I wouldn't be where I am right now.*

But maybe going back to church is a start.

Luke stood up slowly, walked over to the bed, and picked up the suit. He hated suits, he'd never worn one in his life that he hadn't been desperate to get out of; but he was going to put one on and go to church for Easter Sunday.

Guess that's what it means to cowboy up, he thought grimly. *A kid does what it wants to do.*

A man does what he needs to do; and this is what I need.

Chapter Eighteen

This is what I need.

Julie pulled a plaid cotton shirt out of her closet. She walked to her mirror and held it up to herself.

It gave her a cute, cowgirl kind of look, and that was what she was going for. Something girly and earnest to wear to her next riding class at the Seven ranch. Like she was so eager to learn to ride that she was dressing the part.

Julie smirked at her reflection and turned back and forth. She was going to stop short of a country-star bouffant hairstyle, but she was going to the trouble to give off that general vibe.

She tossed the shirt down on a chair and rummaged around in her wardrobe until she found what she was looking for: a denim riding skirt and a pair of cowgirl boots that she'd bought before she left for L.A.

She might even have a cowgirl hat back in there somewhere; but on second thought, she didn't want to lay it on too thick.

Julie wriggled out of her pajamas and pulled on the skirt and top to judge the effect. She was going to leave nothing to chance. No detail of her appearance, no matter how small, would be overlooked.

It seemed she had at least one competitor, the blonde that she'd seen on the back of Luke's motorcycle; and she was willing to go the extra mile to push that girl right out of Luke's mind.

Julie planted her hands on her hips and stared at her reflection. The red plaid shirt was a nice foil to her pale skin and dark hair, the riding skirt showed off her flat stomach and slim hips, and the red panels in her black boots matched the shirt and tied the outfit together.

She pursed her lips as she gave the ensemble one long, last appraisal. For her purposes, it was perfect. It made her look like the sweet, slightly goofy cowgirl next door. Shy and naive.

Just like Trina.

With any luck, at their next lesson Luke was going to let them start climbing up onto a horse to learn stirrups and saddles. That would give her the opportunity she needed to slip and fall so he'd have to catch her.

She was going to throw her arms around his neck and do her best to look helpless and terrified. Her lips curled up as she assessed herself in the mirror; and she practiced a "help me" face, followed by a "my hero" face.

This is going to be fun, she told her reflection, then turned away from the mirror to choose an appropriate fragrance. Something light and sweet, she'd say.

She had a whole library of designer fragrances that she'd picked up during her time as a model, and she sank down in front of her dresser and scrabbled through the ornate glass bottles. She finally chose a pale green bottle labeled *Ingenue*. When she spritzed it, a delicate floral scent curled through the air: a base note of fresh grass, overlaid with honeysuckle and a faint top note of jasmine.

Julie hummed to herself and set the bottle off to one side. It was Easter weekend coming up, a long weekend and extra day off for her; so she had all the time in the world to refine her plan for revenge.

The riding class lasted only two months— that came down to only a few classes, so she had to plan carefully. She ticked off her goals on her fingers. First class, get noticed, make Luke notice her. Second class, get into his arms, kiss him if possible. Third class. fade back to see if he'd pursue her. Fourth class, arrange to see him outside of the class, kiss him again. Fifth class, invite him to her home, and then move in for the kill.

She studied her reflection in the mirror. It was like a play. She had to hit her marks.

She peeled off the cowgirl outfit, shrugged into a fuzzy housecoat, and padded off to her office. She sank down into the desk chair and fired up her computer.

Now that she had her costume picked out, and had the bare bones of her overall plan, it was time to flesh it out with all the little details that would make it come alive. That would convince Luke Spade that this little cowgirl had it for him, bad.

Most men loved to be buttered up; and so she was going to get all the information she needed to butter that blonde donkey up one side and down the other.

She tapped the keyboard. *Luke Spade.*

A preliminary search pulled up a smorgasbord of rodeo photos, stats, and biographical information. Julie leaned over the keyboard to study them.

There were dozens of splashy color shots of Luke in mid-air: Luke riding a bucking horse with its hooves kicking higher than his waist; Luke riding sideways on the back of a twisting bronc; even Luke mostly airborne, with a good four inches of air between him and the saddle.

Julie narrowed her eyes and thought sourly: *It's a shame they didn't get one of him on the ground.*

She scrolled down to the bio. It read:

Luke Spade burst onto the American rodeo circuit when he was only sixteen, and quickly established himself as a rising star in the saddle bronc busting category. In his first year of competition he became the PRCA Saddle Bronc Riding Rookie of the Year and went on to compete in national finals sixteen times in his twenty-year career. He became known for his smooth technique, technical skill and ability to stay with even the most violent broncs.

His first big championship win was...

Julie snorted and scrolled on to the next article. She had all she needed there. All she needed to do was bat her lashes and *ooh* and *ahh* over Luke's rodeo pictures when he showed them to her.

She had no doubt he was going to.

She returned to her search results. Her eyes flicked down to a general article on bronc busting. It was pretty generic, but it might help her to know something about the sport.

The goal of every bronc buster is to stay atop a bucking horse for eight seconds. Saddle bronc busters hold onto a thick rein with one hand, but must keep the other in the air throughout the ride.

If the rider's hand touches the horse or himself at any time, the rider is disqualified.

Julie raised her brows. *That* sounded like a neat trick. As much as she hated to admit it, any man who could ride a bucking horse one-handed had mad skills.

Quite the athlete, old Luke.

Well, buddy boy, she thought dryly, *let's see how you do with this little filly. You think you're big and bad, but you're about to eat dirt.*

Julie smirked at a picture of Luke flying through the air on her computer screen.

Yee haw, baby!

Chapter Nineteen

Luke walked out of his apartment door, closed it behind him, and paused in front of the hall mirror. It was Easter Sunday morning, and he didn't recognize the man staring back at him. The other fellow was shaved clean and all slicked up in a dark linen suit.

He was even wearing a tie.

There was a sound of motion on the stairs, and as he stuck his hands in his pockets and walked out to the landing, Kate and Molly descended in front of him.

Buck's voice greeted him from above. "Well, I can't remember the last time I saw you in a suit! You clean up pretty good."

Luke glanced up to see Buck saunter down the stairs in a nice brown suit. His older brother clapped him on the shoulder.

"Come on, let's go. Morgan and Heather and Donna are downstairs waiting on us."

"Where we going?" Luke muttered.

Buck half-turned to answer as he descended. "You know that little church we used to go to when we were kids!"

"Oh, you mean the brick church in town?" Luke replied in surprise.

"That's the one."

Luke raised his brows in surprise. He hadn't been there since he was fifteen. He'd walked the aisle in that church.

It'd be kinda nice to see the place again; but it was gonna be kinda embarrassing to explain why he'd been gone so long. He half expected that one of his old Sunday school teachers was gonna pull him aside and demand an explanation.

They all filed outside, and the breeze met them with open arms. It was a clear spring morning, and the sky was a deep, porcelain blue. A cloud of pink petals swirled by from the crepe myrtles lining the courtyard, and the breeze ruffled Kate and Donna's Easter hats.

Luke stood there and surveyed the family. Everybody was all slicked up pretty as chocolates in a box. Kate was wearing a pale blue suit dress, a corsage of pink roses, and a floppy-brimmed hat of pale blue that was mostly transparent and big as a platter. She was holding the baby, and to Luke's amusement, they'd dressed him up in a little blue suit with a pale blue bow tie. Molly was dressed up cute, too, with a little white dress with pink polka dots and a big pink sash, and little pink sandals.

Donna had on a little cream-colored dress that hugged her without being tight, cinched with a skinny little gold belt. A little cream-colored hat tilted slightly askew on her head, and there was a shiny gold bow on top, like the cherry on a sundae.

Morgan was wearing a black suit—Luke couldn't remember ever seeing him in any other color—and Heather was wearing a white cotton blouse with long puff sleeves and a dozen little buttons up the front, and a long lavender skirt with a ruffled hem. She'd dressed Kit up in what looked like his first fancy church suit, a pale beige linen suit, blue bow tie, suspenders, and dress shoes.

Luke smiled. His sisters in law and his little niece and nephews were always cute, but he couldn't remember seeing Buck and Morgan look so good.

Of course, everybody there was uncomfortable, but they looked great.

Buck walked out into the center of the circle. "Are we all here?"

"I think so," Kate replied.

"All right then! Let's go." Buck walked over to a big SUV, slid the door open, and beckoned to Donna. "Come on and ride with us," he invited, and Donna smiled and climbed into the van. Buck glanced over his shoulder. "Luke, you too. Unless you're going to ride to church on that motorcycle."

Luke sighed and pulled his mouth to one side. "I'm coming."

He walked over, climbed into the van, and settled down beside Donna. But he fidgeted in the seat like a dog on the way to the vet, and the smile he gave his sister in law was a little weak.

He was dreading having to face the people he used to know at church as a kid. Some of 'em were bound to still be there; and he wondered what they thought of the man he'd turned out to be.

He hadn't exactly walked the straight and narrow since he last walked through those church doors; and now he was going back.

He was beginning to wonder why he'd agreed to go; but then he remembered that stranger he'd seen in the mirror. The man in the suit.

He was going to church because he needed to straighten up and fly right; and so he set his mouth and steeled himself to endure. No matter what those church people might say to him, he was gonna have to suck it up.

His sister in law's amused voice brought him back to reality. There was a smile in it.

"You look like you're going to a funeral," she observed.

Luke gave her a startled look and adjusted one shoulder. He wanted to tell her that she wasn't far off; but he just shrugged.

"I haven't been to church in awhile," he muttered, and glanced out the window.

She cocked her head to one side, like a bird.

"Do they beat you for that?"

Chapter Twenty

Twenty minutes later they all arrived at the little Friendship Church of Sandy Creek. It was a red brick church with a tall steeple and ornate stained glass windows. It was in the heart of town, facing the courthouse, and had stood there for as long as Luke could remember. It had been built in 1919 and still looked pretty much the same as when it was first dedicated.

Buck parked the van on the street, and Luke slid the van door open, unbuckled his seatbelt, and climbed out. He stood there and extended a hand to help his sister in law out.

Luke saw Donna light down safe from the van, then offered her his arm on the way to the front doors. There was a big flower cross in the front yard of the church, and all the worshippers streaming in were dressed in their Easter best: little girls in frilly pastel dresses, women in fancy hats and matching dresses, and men in their best Sunday suits and hats.

The inside of the old church was just as Luke remembered it. It was more than a hundred years old, and whole families in that area had lived and died as members of it. The wooden planks in the floor squeaked underfoot, and the pews were still the original 1919 vintage, as were the stained glass windows.

Luke glanced up at them as he passed. As a kid, he'd memorized every detail in those windows; the carefully painted scrolls and flourishes, the delicate colors, the painstaking detail on the faces.

The first window on the right was the miracle of the loaves and fishes, with Jesus surrounded by his disciples. The second was the healing of the blind man, with Jesus reaching down to touch the man's upturned face. The third, was Jesus being baptized in the Jordan, with a dove descending to him on a beam of light.

Yeah, he knew every last detail of those windows, and of the little four-row choir loft, and the little altar.

The pastor was standing at the lectern. He was a smiling young man, Luke guessed about the same age as him. He had dark hair with streaks of premature gray at the temples, but his face was brown and smooth.

"Well! I'm always glad to see so many smiling faces," he beamed. "This is Easter Sunday, a very special time for us. This is the day we celebrate the resurrection of Jesus Christ.

"We celebrate that we no longer have to struggle to earn our way to heaven. We accept that we can never measure up; but the good news of Easter is that we don't have to. Jesus' death on the cross paid for all our sins.

"All we have to do is believe in Him. To accept the free gift of salvation."

He picked up a hymnal. "Let's open the service with an old favorite. Turn to page 340 as we sing 'Christ the Lord is Risen Today.'

Luke reached for a hymnal and flipped to the hymn. He offered one side of it to Donna, but she smiled and shook her head.

Luke held the hymnal, but he didn't really need it. He'd sung that hymn a million times as a kid, and he still knew the words.

When the song ended and they all sat down again, Luke noticed that Donna was listening intently, but his own mind drifted from the sermon right away.

Well, I'm here, he thought to himself. *I guess it ain't right to expect God to change me like a lightning bolt from the sky.*

I'm gonna have to get used to doing things different one day at a time, like the people trying to go dry.

The thought made him want to scratch his neck something fierce; but he sat there quiet and ramrod-straight. He was determined to go through with his plan.

He lasted through the whole sermon without so much as a twitch, and when it was closing, the pastor stood at the lectern and said solemnly:

"If the Lord is calling you right now, come on, while the congregation sings. Come to the foot of the cross."

The choir began to sing the old hymn, and the congregation joined in:

"Just as I am, without one plea

But that Thy blood was shed for me

And that Thou bid'st me come to Thee

Oh, Lamb of God, I come, I come

Just as I am, though tossed about

With many a conflict, many a doubt

Fighting and fears within without

Oh, Lamb of God, I come, I come."

Luke took a deep breath, stood up, and shuffled down the pew past his astonished family. He stepped out into the center aisle and marched down to the front, just like he had as a kid.

The preacher was standing in front of the altar, and he smiled and extended his hand in welcome as Luke approached him. Luke clasped it, and the pastor shook his hand heartily and pulled him in close.

"God bless you, son," he murmured. "Come and stand here beside me."

Luke inhaled, turned around, and clasped his hands together in front of him. Every eye in the sanctuary was on him. The congregation went on singing the invitation hymn, but Luke noticed that nobody in his family was singing. He saw Buck's eyes glistening, saw Kate put a hand to her mouth. Molly and Kit were staring at him round-eyed, Heather's mouth crumpled up.

Morgan had his arms crossed, and he was looking down at the floor.

"Just as I am, Thou wilt receive

Wilt welcome, pardon, cleanse, relieve

Because Thy promise I believe

Oh, Lamb of God, I come, I come."

The last notes of the organ faded into silence, and the pastor raised a hand.

"You may be seated. Well, I'm glad to report that Luke Spade has come forward during the invitation this Easter Sunday to rededicate his life to the Lord," he announced. "Please come up after the benediction and welcome Luke to our church family, and pray for him."

Amen, the congregation replied, and Luke felt his face going red.

"Let us pray."

Luke bowed his head and tried to pray as the pastor murmured his own prayer.

Lord, I came up here today because I want You to know that I mean business. I'm gonna do my best to be a better man, with Your help. Amen.

"Amen," the pastor echoed, and raised his hand again. "May the Lord bless you and keep you; may the Lord make His face shine on you and be gracious to you; the Lord lift His countenance on you, and give you peace."

The congregation murmured its assent, then moved to greet their neighbors and gather their things.

Buck rushed up to the front and closed Luke in a big bear hug. He turned his head to murmur, "You made me real happy today." Buck squeezed his arm, and the next thing he knew, Kate was smiling up at him. She reached up to hug him and pressed a kiss to his cheek.

"I'm so glad for you, Luke."

Heather crowded in after. She stood up on tiptoe and Luke bent down to let his tiny sister in law give him a peck on the cheek.

But Morgan's eyes were dark. He extended his hand and leaned in to offer an embrace, but he looked troubled.

Luke returned his handshake, then answered his unspoken question. "I'm doing what I need to do, Morg."

There was no time to say more, and other church members crowded in to offer their congratulations. Luke searched his heart. He felt none of the emotions that Buck and

Morgan had described when they came to the Lord: joy, peace, happiness.

He didn't feel anything. Not one solitary thing, not even relief; but he'd done what he needed to do, and that was what mattered.

Sometimes you just had to power through a tough job and get it done.

Chapter Twenty One

"All right, I've shown you all the parts of the saddle, and the bridle, and the cinch. Now who's ready for some hands-on experience?"

It was the second lesson of his riding class, and Luke scanned the group of students standing in the pony ring. A half-dozen hands went up, but his eyes moved to the pretty brunette, Julie. She was perched on the fence, all prim and proper, and dolled up like a cowgirl in a plaid shirt and a denim skirt.

It was cute.

She smiled big, stuck her hand up high in the air and wiggled her fingers, and he wanted to pick her first. But he didn't want the rest of the folks to think he was unfair. That he chose her just because she was a beautiful woman.

Then too, he was walking the straight and narrow road now; and that gorgeous brunette didn't look like she was gonna help him do it.

He pointed to an older man in the middle of the group. "Come on up, Mr. Schwartz," he smiled, and the other hands descended. Luke couldn't help glancing at Julie, and he was oddly pleased to see a disappointed pout on her pretty face as she lowered her hand.

The gray-haired man walked up, and Luke grabbed a mounting block up and set it on the ground beside Buddy. The patient palomino turned his head to watch as Luke took the man's hand and helped him slowly climb up the steps.

"That's great, Mr. Schwartz," he murmured. "Now I want you to grab the pommel right there, and throw your right leg over the saddle. I'll help you."

Luke stood there, ready to catch the man, as he grasped the pommel, pulled himself up, leaned into the horse's flank, and lifted his right leg.

He floundered there, reaching with his right leg, and Luke zoomed up to give him a boost. He pushed the man's leg all the way over the saddle and helped him sit upright.

"That's the way," he nodded, and was gratified when the other folks clapped for their fellow rookie. "That's real good for a first try. Let's give him another hand, folks."

When the clapping faded, Luke stuck his hands on his hips. "Let's do man, woman, man woman," he suggested. "Come on up, Miss Julie."

She hopped down instantly and sashayed up to his side, all smiles. Luke watched her in amusement. It was cute how excited she was to learn.

It didn't hurt that she was pretty as a hat full of kittens, either.

She smiled at the crowd, then up at him. "I'm a little nervous," she confessed. "This'll be my first time." She glanced up at him appealingly, and Luke felt his mouth drop open slightly. Up close, those big, pretty eyes were as blue as turquoise.

He cleared his throat and put a hand lightly on her arm. "Don't be nervous," he assured her. "I'll be here to help you. Just take my hand and climb up on those steps." He nodded toward the mounting block.

She dithered a little, and glanced up at him again, as if she still didn't know what to do; but she took his hand and held it tight as he walked her up to the steps.

Buddy turned his head to look at her as she grabbed the saddle pommel and pulled herself up with a tiny gasp. Luke rubbed his nose and glanced to the side, because Julie was turned away from him and he was getting a way nicer view than he needed to see. But to his relief, when he looked up again, she was safely in the saddle.

She smiled down at him. "I didn't think I could do it!" she exclaimed.

Luke nodded and turned to the crowd. "See how easy that was?" he told them. "There's nothing to it."

He looked up and motioned to Julie. "Come on down now. Stand up in the left stirrup and throw your right leg over the saddle."

A look of confusion flitted over her pretty face, but she smiled uncertainly and prepared to comply. Luke saw her stand up in the left stirrup and throw her right leg over the saddle; but somehow, the next thing he knew she'd crashed onto his chest and was scrabbling for something to hold onto. There was a gasp from the onlookers, and Julie gave a little shriek.

"*Oh!*"

She rolled wild eyes to his, clutched his collar, and half-fell. He grabbed her to keep her from hitting the ground, and they stood there for an instant looking into each other's eyes.

Terror flicked through those beautiful blue depths; then Luke felt her go limp in his arms. He tightened his grip on her, thinking, *She's going to fall.*

Julie licked her lips, put a hand on his chest, and glanced down, as if she was embarrassed. He bent his head to murmur, "You okay?"

She nodded and said nothing more, and Luke glanced at the startled onlookers.

"It's okay, she just missed her step," he announced, and took hold of her shoulders. He pressed her away from his chest gently but firmly, and was relieved to see her smile weakly at the others.

She shot him a grateful look, smoothed her mussed hair back from her brow, and went a pretty, delicate pink.

Just before she staggered sideways and accidentally stomped his foot. *Hard.* Luke bit back an expletive and half-swiped at his throbbing toe.

"Sorry," Julie yelped, and scampered off; but when she hurried away, Luke noticed the whisper of honeysuckle that eddied in the air after her, more than his mashed toe.

His worried eyes followed her; then he cleared his throat, straightened up, and announced, "All right, who's next? How about you there, Billy?"

He didn't wait for a reply, and motioned a freckle-faced, startled-looking teen to come up. "That's right! Come right on up."

But he couldn't keep his eyes from wandering to Julie. To his dismay, she was sitting up on the corral fence, dabbing her eyes with a hanky.

Why, she's really upset, he thought with a frown. *I hope she didn't get hurt.*

"Um...come on over to the mounting block, Billy," he mumbled; but his eyes moved back to the fence.

Chapter Twenty Two

"You sure you're okay?"

Luke stuck his hands in his jeans pockets and stared at Julie's face. She closed her eyes and nodded briefly, but she still looked upset to him.

The lesson had ended, and the meeting had mostly broken up. There were only a few other people in the parking area beyond the corral, and they were all out of earshot.

"I'm sorry," Luke mumbled and rubbed the back of his neck. "I should've caught you. I would have, if I'd watched you closer."

She raised her eyes to his, and the look in them made his skin tingle. "Oh no, it's not your fault," she breathed. "I'm just clumsy." She shrugged one shoulder, and the hopelessness in that gesture went to his heart.

"No, now, you got to get that idea right out of your head," he told her earnestly. "You ain't ever been on horse before, remember. You're not clumsy, you just need practice, is all."

She pulled her mouth down like a child and slumped back against the fence. "Oh, you're sweet, but—I really am clumsy. Real accident prone. I've always been that way. Probably always will be." She shook her head.

Luke frowned and leaned against the fence beside her. He crossed his arms and looked down at the ground. "Well, you're never going to make a rider if you let yourself think that." He looked over at her.

She glanced up at him, and there were tears in her eyes. "I knew it," she murmured. "I'm hopeless!"

She pushed off the fence, but Luke reached out and caught her arm. She stopped to look at him pitifully.

Luke dropped his hand. "You're not hopeless," he told her firmly. "You just got to keep at it. Keep coming back to class, and before long, you'll be riding around and wondering why you didn't do it sooner."

"I don't know," she murmured, and Luke took her by the shoulders and turned her around to face him.

"You can do it," he told her firmly. "You just had a little bad luck, is all." He gave her a tiny shake, and let her go.

She shrugged again, then shot him a look brimful of gratitude. "You're sweet to say so, Luke." She tucked a tendril of dark, curling hair behind one ear, then raised her eyes to his again.

She leaned over and gave him a quick kiss on the cheek, then turned and half-ran away. Luke raised his brows in surprise and followed her with his eyes as she hurried to her little VW and slipped inside.

His cheek was tingling with the soft, fleeting touch of her kiss, but he frowned as he watched Julie's car disappear down the long drive.

He was trying to turn over a new leaf, but it looked like he wasn't off to a very good start. He shook his head. He *always* got tangled up with women.

Well, this time was going to be different.

Luke set his jaw. He couldn't afford to get involved with a new female. He'd promised the Lord. Then, too, he was toying with the idea of doing more than just competing in a rodeo now and then. He was thinking about going back on the circuit, and that meant travel.

He had to concentrate on his goals.

Luke drifted back to the corral and climbed up onto Buddy's back. He nudged his horse out of the pen and across the parking lot on the way to the barn.

It was a lovely, warm spring day, and he glanced up at the banks of fluffy white clouds as he swayed in the saddle. Yeah, he was gonna have to be more deliberate about his choices if he wanted his life to change direction.

He couldn't let himself just drift along any more. He wasn't gonna fall into a new romance as thoughtlessly as he'd fallen into all the others.

Even if the woman in question was a gorgeous brunette with coal-black hair and eyes as blue as the sky.

Luke closed his eyes as he rode and pictured Julie again in his mind. She was so cute in her little cowgirl getup, and she'd looked so helpless and scared when she fell on him. Kinda like she was begging him to help her.

And he did want to help her, all right. The trick was gonna be, wanting to help her just like he wanted to help all his other students.

Because he was already imagining himself giving her special attention. It was true that she seemed to need extra help, but that was no excuse to play favorites.

He was gonna have to be strict and fair. He owed that to his other students, he owed it to the Lord, and he owed it to himself.

But as he rode along, he kept seeing the desperate look in Julie's pretty eyes, and his memory kept on replaying the depressed note in her voice as she sighed:

I'm clumsy...I'm hopeless...I've always been that way.

Luke gave his head a shake, as if that could dispel the memory, but it couldn't. There was

something about that little girl that had
touched his heart.

She just looked *so* sweet and helpless.

Chapter Twenty Three

"So, you're thinking about going back on the circuit, huh?"

Luke looked up from the dinner table in the act of shoveling a spoonful of refried beans into his mouth. He closed his mouth, blotted it with a napkin, and nodded.

"Mmm-hmm."

Buck tilted his head in approval. "That's what I'm talking about. I still don't understand why you quit the rodeo the first time. You were crushing it."

Kate shot her husband a worried look, then glanced at Luke. "I'm sure Luke had his reasons," she amended, with a smile. "Rodeo competition is dangerous."

Conchita leaned in to lay a massive platter of *huevos rancheros* on the big table and drifted out of the dining room. Luke reached over and ladled a big mound of food onto his plate.

Carson smirked at him from across the table. "Oh, no worries Kate," he laughed. "Luke won't be hurt even if he falls on his head. It's as hard as a rock."

Luke pulled his foot back and kicked Carson smartly in the shins under the table, and watched in satisfaction as his brother jumped, but didn't yell out.

He had to give Carson that. He might look like a pretty boy, but he rolled with the punches.

"Yeah, I signed up for the rodeo down in Houston next month," he told the table at large. "It'll be fun to start up again. I've been away a long time."

Morgan gave him a worried look from the end of the table. "Luke, you ain't ridden a bronc in four years. If you go in cold, those monsters'll kick you to the moon!"

Luke shot him a confident smile. "Oh, don't worry Morg. It's like riding a bicycle. You never forget."

"Still and all," Heather put in quietly from beside Morgan. "You might want to try your hand in one of the smaller rodeos around town to warm up for the big one."

"Hey, that's a great idea," Buck yelped, and pointed at Luke with his spoon. "Give you a good sense of how ready you are. I know one thing, you don't want your first ride in years to be one of those killers down at the Fire and Fury!"

Luke addressed his dinner. "I might try my hand at one of the smaller ones," he shrugged. "Kinda warm up. But I'm not worried about it."

"Huh," Jesse grunted, and lifted a cup of coffee to his lips. Luke felt himself going red, but he didn't dare kick Jesse under the table. Jesse wasn't like Carson. He got mad quick and didn't hold back.

"We'll all have to come down and see you at the Coliseum," Buck announced through a mouthful of beans. "Nothing like a good rodeo."

Luke glanced up in pleasure. "Yeah, why don't you?" he nodded. "We could all go out to eat after." He shot Jesse a short, straight look.

"Help me celebrate my win."

Jesse chewed his dinner and looked at him. "I heard Justice Owens is still on the circuit," he mumbled, and took another bite. "Didn't he used to bust your chops?"

Luke frowned at him. "Sometimes," he grumbled. "Sometimes I used to bust his. You saying I can't win against him?"

Jesse hunched a shoulder and kept his eyes on his plate. "I'm saying it's one thing to talk, and another to back it up." He raised piercing eyes to Luke's and added, "If I was betting on it, right now, I'd put money on Justice. You're going in cold, and he's been in the saddle ever since you left the rodeo."

Luke sat up ramrod straight with indignation, and the table broke out into shouting. Luke pointed a fork at Jesse's face and retorted, "You go ahead and bet on him. You'll lose your money!"

Buck scowled at Jesse and called out, "You telling me you'd bet against your own brother? What's wrong with you, boy?"

Jesse picked up a roll and threw it at Luke, and Morgan frowned, "No call to start a ruckus at the dinner table!"

Luke ducked the roll and threw another back, and it hit Jesse in the mouth and bounced across the table. Jesse rose up from his chair and yanked his napkin out of his collar.

Carson picked up his plate and sidled out, and Donna quickly trailed out of the room after him, followed by Kate and Heather.

Buck pointed at Jesse and yelled, "You better not make me come down there!" But Jesse's answer was to scoop up a mound of refried beans into a spoon and lob it across the table right into Buck's chest. Buck flicked it off his shirt and looked up in outrage.

Morgan gestured at Jesse in disgust as Buck surged up from the table and dived for his brother.

"Now see what you've done!"

Luke kicked free of his chair and lunged for Jesse but got there a second after Buck. Luke piled on as Buck grabbed Jesse in a bear hug and they all fell onto the floor in a tangle of elbows and knees.

Conchita appeared in the doorway and threw her hands up in dismay. "*Ay!*" she shrieked, and the platter of churros she'd been carrying fell on the floor with a clang. She turned and fled, wailing in outraged Spanish.

Luke held Jesse's hands down, and Buck wrapped him in a head lock with one arm and rubbed his brother's salt-and-pepper hair with the other hand.

"Say it!" he demanded, as Jesse sputtered and squeezed his face into a knot of outrage.

"Let go of me!"

"Not until you say it!"

Morgan stood up from the table and stalked out in disgust. "You all should be ashamed of yourselves. You're acting like little kids," he rumbled in passing.

Jesse struggled to be free, and Luke held him down fast. One of Jesse's eyes opened up, and his mouth twisted. "All right, I'll say it, let me go!"

"Say what?" Buck demanded, and rubbed his bristly head again.

"Uncle!" Jesse growled, and Buck let him go. Luke sat up and leaned back on his heels, and their grumpy brother clambered up from the floor in a huff. He stalked to the door and rounded on them to deliver a parting shot.

"I'm still betting against you!" he declared, and Buck waved him off.

"Aw go on!" he laughed, and sat back on the floor with his hands draped over his knees. He looked over at Luke, and they stared at one another for a pregnant instant—then they both sputtered and burst out laughing.

Chapter Twenty Four

The next afternoon Julie twirled a long, dark tendril of inky hair around her finger and rolled her eyes up to Luke's in rueful appeal. "I—I can't do it," she stammered. "I know I'm going to fall again!"

They were standing in the middle of the corral Luke was using to teach his riding lessons. He'd given Julie a pretty lazy horse, and it turned its head to look at Julie as she stared up at him pleadingly.

Luke put his hands on his hips and shook his head. "No, you won't fall, I won't let you. Go ahead on." He turned to appeal to the other students. "Go ahead and clap, folks. Let's give Julie the boost she needs to get up on that horse and take her first ride!"

There was scattered clapping, and Luke smiled up at Julie's frightened face. She gulped, scratched up her courage, and slowly climbed to the top of the mounting block. She reached out, grabbed the saddle pommel with both hands, and glanced at him over her shoulder.

Luke nodded at her. "Go on."

He stood there and watched as she gave him one last pitiful look, then pulled herself up, threw her leg over, and straightened in the saddle.

He brightened in relief. "See now, you did it perfect," he told her, and was gratified to see the look of pleasure on her face. "Now pull the right hand rein to turn her head, and give her a little nudge to go join the others." He nodded toward a small group of mounted students. "Now that everybody's on a horse, we'll start our trail ride."

He watched as Julie nudged the horse around to join the group other riders; but she turned her horse just close enough for its swishing tail to hit him in the face and knock his hat right off his head.

It stung.

Luke clapped a hand to his face, and there were gasps and muffled laughter from his students. He looked up in chagrin to see Julie staring at him in dismay. Her open mouth made a perfect O.

"Oh, did I do that? I'm so sorry," she murmured.

Luke bent down to swipe his hat off the ground. "That's all right, it happens now and then," he smiled, and walked over to Buddy. He climbed up easily, turned his horse's head around, and sent it trotting to the head of the line.

"We'll just be going on a short ride today," he told the group. "Out into the big meadow over yonder." He pointed to a gently-swelling line of hills out to the west.

"Let's go."

He led the line of riders out into the parking lot, behind the riding ring, past the stables, and on through a line of slowly-rising meadows up to a low ridge. He kept an easy pace, always making for the top of the rocky ridge and the little oak grove just on the other side. There was a little spring there, with fresh water that came bubbling out of the rocks, and he planned to stop there and let everyone have a cool drink.

He maintained a slow, easy pace, and glanced back over his shoulder now and then to make sure everybody was following along okay. Everybody seemed to be doing all right.

He noticed that Julie was riding along in the very last place, kinda lagging behind. He raised his arm to wave her along, and he noticed that she saw him, brightened, and nudged her horse into a faster walk.

He smiled and tipped his hat to her, then settled back in. Slowly they crossed the gently rolling meadow lands and began to climb up to the little ridge. The trail he was following wound around the foot of the rocky hill, and rose at an easy, gentle grade.

They'd just begun to wind around the foot of the hill, when a piercing scream made the hairs on his neck stand up. He pulled Buddy up and turned around to see Julie's horse running away with her. He watched in disbelief as it roared up the steep side of the hill, went flying over the crest, and disappeared down the other side.

Luke turned and shouted to the dumbfounded riders behind him. "Stay here," he yelled, and clapped Buddy's ribs hard. The palomino bounded up the grassy hill like a rocket, and when they reached the top, Luke's eyes darted down the steep grade.

To his horror, the riderless horse was sliding down the hill, and there was no sign of Julie.

He sent Buddy down the incline as fast as he dared. "Julie!" he shouted. "Julie, where are you?"

He swung a leg over Buddy's neck, slid to the ground, and clambered down the slope as fast as he could go.

"Julie!"

He glimpsed movement off to the right, and to his horror, he saw Julie's booted leg just beyond the roots of the big oak tree. He scrabbled down the hill and landed beside her with a gasp.

"Julie, can you hear me?"

He crouched down and climbed over the tree root. To his alarm, Julie was lying face up on the ground with her hair splayed out around her head like a dark halo. Her fingers were curling into her palms on either side of her head, and she pulled one leg up to her chest and moaned as if she was in pain.

"Julie, are you hurt?"

He bent down over her in dismay, and her jeweled eyes fluttered open. She moaned out something he couldn't quite understand, and he bent lower to hear it. And then, to his astonishment, she raised her hands to cup the back of his neck, and a languid look spread across her pretty face.

"Oh, Luke," she whispered and pulled him down to her lips.

He closed his eyes, and the first touch of those plump, soft rose petals set him on fire.

He grabbed her shoulders, and before he knew it, he'd lifted her up into his arms and was devouring her mouth like a starving man.

Oh man. Oh no, he thought as his fingers curled around her shoulders; but he couldn't make himself stop. Julie's lips were pure velvet, and they melted away beneath his, reformed, and kissed him back so soft and sweet that he couldn't think about anything but *more.*

Her hand moved from his neck to his cheek, and her fingers caressed his face as sweet and delicate as a feather. She looked up at him with those bottomless blue eyes. They were as pure and innocent as a baby's, and he kissed her again.

The sound of a voice calling from the other side of the hill slowly pulled Luke back to reality. He cleared his throat and slowly and reluctantly disentangled himself from Julie's lips. He gave her an apologetic look.

"Julie, I—I'm sorry," he stammered. "I don't know what came over me." He licked his lips. "Are you hurt anywhere?"

Julie's big blue eyes were shining. They were full of a look he knew all too well—that hero worship look he always got from fans when he won in the rodeo ring.

Only he wasn't a hero.

"My ankle hurts," Julie whispered, and cast her eyes down demurely. "I don't think I can walk."

The distant voice called out again. "Luke," it was yelling faintly. "What happened?"

Luke glanced back over his shoulder. He couldn't see anybody, but any minute somebody could come riding over the rise and catch him bending over Julie. He didn't want anybody to get the wrong idea.

"Julie, I'm going to pick you up," he murmured. "Do you think you can ride on Buddy?"

"I might," she murmured, and reached up to twine her arms around his neck. Luke glanced down into her face and felt a flush of— something warm his heart. Something soft and gentle.

It was sweet how Julie trusted him.

"All right, here goes," he murmured. "Try to stay loose, and I'll help you up into the saddle."

He leaned down and scooped her up as gentle as he could. She was light as down on the breeze, she didn't weigh anything at all, and it was no trouble to stand up and carry her over to his horse.

He reached up and practically sat her in the saddle, and she took the reins and smiled down at him a bit crooked.

"I'm sorry I'm so much trouble," she whimpered, and her face crumpled up; but he rushed to reassure her.

"Oh, you ain't no trouble," he told her earnestly. "Nobody can stay on a bolting horse for long. You don't worry about it one bit."

He took Buddy's bridle, turned him around, and started to walk him back up the hill.

Julie's trembling voice quavered: "You're not going to walk me *all the way back to the corral,* are you?"

Luke shrugged and replied, "That's what I'm going to do. It won't be the first time I've had to hoof it on this ranch."

He glanced back at her, and for an instant he caught what looked like a smirk on her face. But that couldn't be right.

He'd probably imagined it; and when he looked again, it was gone.

Chapter Twenty Five

Julie watched in grim satisfaction as Luke Spade climbed up the steep, rocky hill in front of her, paused on the crest to catch his breath, then led her mount back down again, step by gruelling step. It was a long, hot slog back to the corral for a man on foot, and she was enjoying every minute of it.

She glanced back over her shoulder. That tired old horse she'd kicked to a gallop was probably at the bottom of the hill, grazing and switching its tail.

Her eyes glowed with secret amusement. She'd spurred that lazy old plug hard enough to send it up the hill at a run, and had screamed and pretended to yank the reins to make it look like she'd lost control.

As soon as she'd topped the rise and got out of sight, she'd pulled the horse up short and sharp, jumped off, and sent it down the hill alone. She'd hurried down to a nice grassy spot under a tree, crumpled herself up under it, and closed her eyes.

She shook with silent laughter as she remembered it, and as she watched Luke stumble and huff over the rocky terrain in front of her. She didn't feel one bit sorry for him. On the outside, he looked as kind and warm as a summer day—but on the inside? On the inside, that golden boy had the head of a goat. He was an ice-cold, manipulative monster.

He was a really good actor, though—the snake. If she didn't know all about him already, she'd be tempted to believe he was really worried about her.

All that 'Julie, where are you?' stuff, all that rushing up to see how she was—it might almost be convincing if she didn't know what he'd done to Trina.

She adjusted a shoulder uncomfortably. Luke was a—really, a shockingly good kisser, too; but then, playboys usually were. She frowned at his broad back. He seemed to know by some kind of dark instinct just how she liked to to be kissed; and he'd used his mouth to tell her all kinds of things without saying a word.

He was fluent in that language, she had to admit. That series of kisses had felt like getting surprised by a live wire a couple of times, and she tossed her hair back over her shoulder to shake off the last of the tingles.

She watched Luke as he led her horse down the rocky hill. There was no denying that he was a healthy specimen, broad in the shoulders and narrow in the hips. When he stopped for a minute to roll up his sleeves, she was treated to the sight of brown forearms, smooth and firm and muscular and plainly well-used.

The reptile was good looking, all right. Julie crossed her hands on the pommel, pressed her lips together and flicked a speculative glance from his head to his boots.

None of that was going to save him, of course. She was going to teach him a lesson he'd never forget; but in her heart of hearts, she was beginning to admit that it wouldn't be an *entirely* revolting task.

As she watched, Luke took off his hat and fanned himself with it. The sun glimmered in his flaxen hair, and Trina's words replayed vividly in her mind.

Something about how she'd been spellbound by Luke's beautiful blonde hair. How the light shining down on it had made it glow like gold.

Like it was doing now. Julie tilted her head and stared at Luke's thick, glorious head of hair. It was shaggy and rough, lapping the back of his neck in layered waves, like ripe wheat. It needed to be cut, it looked as if it had only been finger-combed, but there was something seductively wild about it. It reminded Julie of the coat of a golden bear, or a puma.

"Isn't it?"

Julie snapped back to herself and stared at Luke's upturned face. She switched back into character and plastered a goofy, demure look on her face.

"Oh...oh, yes it is," she chirped, and flashed him a big, bright smile.

Luke glanced down at the knot of riders at the foot of the hill as he fanned his face. "It's not usually this hot so early. It's gonna be a warm summer."

One edge of Julie's lips curled up as she sat atop the horse and enjoyed the sight of sweat beads popping out in Luke's glorious hairline. She glanced at his squinting face, then down at his saddlebag. She leaned down suddenly to open it. She pulled out a canteen, unscrewed the top, and took a long, deep pull of water.

"*Ahhh,*" she sighed, and closed her eyes in deep satisfaction. "Cool water really hits the spot on a hot day."

Luke's face brightened, and he reached out for it. "Hand it to me," he begged, and Julie smiled and gave it to him. Her smile deepened as it lifted it over his mouth, only to frown and shake it.

Nothing came out.

"Ohh..." she murmured, and rubbed her nose. "I'm sorry, I must've drunk it all."

"Oh." Luke squinted up at her and handed her the canteen, and Julie took it with downcast eyes.

She didn't want him to see the laughter in them.

She rubbed her nose and purred, "You're real sweet to let me ride your horse, Luke. I know it can't be easy to walk *so far* on such a hot day. Without any water, too! Your throat must be as dry as chalk."

Luke licked his lips and took the horse's halter. "Yeah, it is," he confessed, and started trudging down the hill again. "But I'm glad I can help you back to the corral."

Julie's smile faded, and she glared at his back in frowning consternation. *Do you expect me to fall for that?* she wondered irritably. *What kind of fool do you take me for?*

She frowned at him in deepening confusion. Luke Spade was burning up, he was sweaty and thirsty. His feet were probably killing him in those big leather boots.

He should be cursing under his breath; but instead he started to hum, and then to whistle a cheerful tune as he walked. He began to sing softly, and to Julie's surprise, she discovered that Luke Spade had a deep, resonant singing voice.

To her dismay, that low, beautiful murmur zapped up and down her spine like the kiss of electricity.

He went on humming as he walked, but Julie's mouth dropped open in dismay. The song was a lullaby, and she had no idea why he was singing it; but for a song meant to lull a baby to sleep, it sure had an electric effect. Julie could feel her lids going heavy in hypnotized fascination, could feel her chin tilting up. She stared down at Luke as she swayed in the saddle, and for an instant, she could've slipped down off that horse to plaster her lips against his.

She frowned and shook her head slightly. *I'm the one who's supposed to be doing this to him,* she told herself angrily. *He's good, I admit it. But not good enough.*

I'm not going to let him do to me, what he did to Trina!

He glanced up at her as he walked and chuckled. "Don't know what put that into my head," he grinned. "It's a little ditty I heard somebody singing once at a rodeo."

He went on humming, and Julie closed her eyes and frowned: "It doesn't sound very much like a rodeo song."

Luke glanced up at her and smiled, "No, it doesn't. I think a lady brought her little baby to the rodeo and was trying to stop him crying. I heard her singing that, walking by." He shook his head. "Funny the things that stick with you."

Julie opened her eyes and shot him a resentful glance. *Funny the things that don't*, she thought tartly.

"Maybe it came to me because I'm going back to the rodeo."

Julie pursed her lips and gave his back a narrow glance, but kept her tone light and happy as she replied, "Oh, you're going back to the rodeo? How exciting!"

He shrugged and smiled at her. "Oh, not for keeps," he replied easily. "Just for fun. Just to keep my hand in."

Julie inhaled and straightened up in the saddle. "I heard that you won nine buckles," she replied dutifully, though she was tempted to roll her eyes. "You must be very good!"

He lapsed into a thoughtful silence. She was beginning to think he wouldn't answer, but he finally replied, "Lucky would be more like it. Blessed."

Julie put on her adoring fan face and cooed: "Oh, I'd love to see you ride a bronc! Are you competing anywhere near here?"

A look of undisguised pleasure flitted over Luke's face as he glanced up at her. He smiled and nodded. "Yeah. I'm going to ride in the Sandy Creek rodeo this weekend. It's just a local event, nothing fancy, but I've been gone four years. I need to get back in the saddle."

Julie trained her baby blues on Luke's face and poured all the innocence she could muster into her expression as she breathed: "Oh, would you mind if I came to see you ride? Just as a fan," she added with a shamefaced smile. "You wouldn't have to talk to me if you didn't want to."

Luke's brows drifted up. "I'd be proud to talk to you," he replied in a tone of faint puzzlement. "You're more than welcome to come over after my ride, if you like."

Julie frowned faintly, swallowed the lump of gall in her throat, then forced herself to smile with all her teeth.

"Oh, *could* I?"

Luke smiled and nodded. "Sure you can." He licked his lips. "I'd like that."

Julie cast her eyes down and tried to blush. "Well, then. I'll be there with bells on."

His reply was soft as a sigh. "Good."

She sat there in an attitude of maiden bashfulness, waiting for him to kiss her again; but when she looked up, Luke had taken the bridle and was leading the horse down the hill.

The steep, rocky path made it a bumpy ride, and Julie saw, with a stifled sigh of impatience, that the moment had definitely passed.

Still, she'd made progress toward her goal. Her little trick had made Luke grab her up and kiss her. Enthusiastically, too.

It was a start.

She gave his back a smug little glance. *I'll bet that little rodeo fairground has plenty of dark nooks and crannies,* she thought. *And we're going to find at least one of them, buddy boy.*

Luke glanced over his shoulder and grinned at her, and she gave him a sour little smile.

Chapter Twenty Six

Julie set a pot of her famous homemade spaghetti sauce on her stovetop and flicked the front burner on. She hummed a bit to herself as she worked.

Her plan was right on track and going smooth as silk. She was confident that she had that worm on her hook now. The only thing left for her to decide was whether she wanted to finish him off quick, or toy with him a little before she told him off and dumped him.

Yes, indeed, the old saying was true: revenge was going to be sweet.

She was therefore in a bit of a triumphant mood. She'd decided to celebrate her imminent victory by pulling out all the stops and cooking herself a luscious, homemade, high-calorie feast.

She opened a packet of spaghetti noodles and poured them into a pot of water on the back burner. She dumped in a handful of salt, reached for a wooden spoon, and began to stir the bubbling pots.

Her cell phone trilled from the kitchen table, and Julie picked it up and stuck it against her cheek as she stirred the steaming pot. "Hello."

To her surprise, Trina's quivering voice answered. "Jules? I'm so glad I caught you! It's Trina."

Julie frowned and set her wooden spoon on the stove. "Trina, are you crying? What's wrong?"

There was a sob on the other end. "Oh, Julie, I don't know what to do," Trina wept. "I've been feeling a little sick lately, and I thought I might have the flu. I went to the doctor. She gave me an exam, and...and she says I'm not sick.

"I'm pregnant!"

Shock wiped Julie's mind blank for an instant. "What?" She closed her eyes, frowned, and tried to gather her scattered wits. "Oh, Trina. What can I do to help?"

"Nothing," Trina wept. "I just needed to talk to you." She sniffed and added, "I'm going to have my baby, there's no question of that. I just don't know how I'm going to afford it. I'm barely making it on my salary!"

Julie pulled herself together. "Well, you need to call Luke and tell him the baby is his," she replied tartly. "It's his responsibility to help you! Have you told him?"

Trina's voice gathered strength. "No," she replied. "No, and I'm not going to tell him."

Julie's frowning eyes flew open. "Why on earth *not?* He's rolling in money, and it's his duty to support his child!"

Trina's voice was clear and strong. "I won't have Luke thinking that I'm trying to use the baby to force him to marry me," she replied proudly.

Julie sputtered impatiently. "He's been with you for five years, Trina," she retorted. "If he doesn't know you any better than that by now—"

"No, I mean it Julie," her friend replied. "I don't want you to breathe a word of this to anyone. Promise me!"

"Oh for crying out loud, Trina!"

Trina's voice turned soft and pleading. "Promise me, Jules."

Julie shook her head. "Oh, all right," she replied in exasperation. "But I think you're making a huge mistake. Luke is responsible for that baby no matter what he thinks of your reasons for telling him. And as much as I hate to admit it, he has a right to know that he has a child on the way."

"Maybe I'll tell him later," Trina hiccuped. "I just don't want to do it right now, Jules. It's too soon. He might misunderstand."

Julie closed her eyes and bit back the shout that was building up in her. *Why do you care what he thinks*, she wanted to yell. *He used you heartlessly—for years! He doesn't love you. He doesn't love anybody but himself!*

But she forced her temper down and replied, slowly and evenly: "Do whatever you need to do then, Trina. I've got your back."

Trina's voice overflowed with gratitude. "I know it, Jules. It makes me feel better just to talk to you."

"You know, I'm off this weekend," Julie told her. "What say I come up and help you get your apartment ready for the baby? You're going to need some maternity clothes and shoes, of course. And I think I'll ask around at work and see if I can get the names of some top obstetricians in Oklahoma City."

The relief in Trina's voice was palpable. "You're an angel, Jules," her friend sighed. "I've been so scared. I always wanted a baby, of course, but—I always saw it happening after I was married."

"You're going to be just fine," Julie replied instantly. "Don't worry about anything. You just concentrate on getting your rest and eating right."

Trina's voice was wistful as she replied, "You know, I used to dream about having Luke's baby. Of the two of us being married and snug in our little house, and finding out one day that I was pregnant. I used to imagine how I'd break it to him, and imagined him looking so surprised and happy.

"I never, ever thought it would happen...like this."

Anger flared in Julie as she imagined Trina huddled up on the other end of the line, all alone and miserable in a little apartment in a strange town.

Luke Spade's just the gift that keeps on giving, she thought resentfully. *Blast him! Poor Trina's never going to be free of him. Well, don't worry you rattlesnake*, she thought grimly. *I'm going to make you pay for this and everything else you've done to my poor friend. You'll curse the day you met me, I promise you that!*

"Jules?"

Julie snapped back to the present. "Right here, sweetie."

"Thank you for being such a good friend. I always know I can count on you."

Julie's anger melted before the wave of affection she felt for her best friend. "Yes, you can," she replied softly. "I've got your back, girl. Everything is going to turn out just like it should, I promise you."

There was a brief pause on the other end of the line, and Julie could almost feel the question in Trina's mind; and so she changed the subject before her friend could ask it.

"Is Friday afternoon a good time for me to arrive?" she asked brightly.

"Oh, you can come here any time you like, you know that," Trina replied quickly. "I work from nine to five, but I usually get home around six. I'll leave the key under the mat, so you can let yourself in."

"I'll be there Friday then," Julie promised. "And...in spite of everything, Trina, I can't wait," she confessed. "This is going to be your first child, and I'm over the moon for you.

We're going to have such a good time preparing for your baby."

Trina's laugh sounded a little weak, but it was a laugh, and Julie was glad of the change. At least Trina wasn't crying and scared any more.

"Yeah," she replied. "I can't wait for you to get up here either, Jules. It's been kind of lonely up here."

Julie's heart twisted in pity, but she put on her brightest and most confident tone as she replied, "Well, not for long. Hold down the fort until Friday, and then we'll turn that apartment upside down."

Trina's laugh sounded more natural as she giggled, "It's upside down now. But I can't wait." She paused and added, "Thank you, Jules. Really. You're a life saver."

Julie went warm, but murmured: "What are friends for? You go and eat a healthy dinner now, and get a good's night sleep. I'll see you soon.

"Everything's going to be all right."

Trina thanked her again, sighed, and said good night; and as she hung up the phone, Julie exhaled in deep relief.

She'd been genuinely scared there for a minute. Trina had sounded desperate.

Julie turned back to the stove to find her spaghetti sauce burned and her noodles swollen and mushy, and she spat out an exclamation as she hurriedly switched the heat off.

Her dinner was ruined; but at least her friend was okay.

Barely.

Julie sighed, picked up the potholders, and threw out her ruined meal. She tossed the dirty dishes in the sink and stuck her hands on her hips.

But she couldn't be irritated for long. *I'm going to be an aunt*, she thought to herself in dawning pleasure.

Kind of.

I hope it's a little girl.

Julie decided right then and there that she was going to be an important part of the baby's life; and now that she considered it, her involvement in its upbringing would be a lot easier and happier without Luke Spade. If Luke never found out about his baby, well, it was his own fault. She'd lodged the proper objection, and if Trina decided not to tell him, it was totally her call.

Trina had given Luke his chance, and he'd blown it. In fact, considering what a snake Luke was, the baby would be better off without him.

Julie hurried out of the kitchen, down the hall, and into her little office. She sat down at her desk, fired up her computer, and pulled up the search tab.

Maternity shops+Green Oak.

Baby clothes+Green Oak.

Baby furniture+Green Oak.

Rental vans+Green Oak.

A smile spread over Julie's face as she surveyed the results. *This is going to be fun,* she thought in pleasure. *Just wait until Trina sees a van parked outside her apartment!*

By the time I'm finished with her, she won't be able to wait until her baby is born.

I know I can't!

Chapter Twenty Seven

Julie pulled the rental van up into the parking space outside Apartment 350. She'd arrived in Oklahoma City, and it was Friday afternoon around two o' clock. Trina wouldn't be back home for hours. She had plenty of time to get unpacked, and that was a good thing, because she wanted to turn the inside of that apartment into Christmas morning.

But she had her work cut out for her. Julie's heart sank as her eyes flicked over Trina's drab gray door. The Sunset Apartment complex was a drab, seedy collection of one-story buildings that looked as if they'd been built in the fifties. They were red brick, ranch-style buildings with air conditioning units in the windows, overgrown weeds in the tiny lawns and cracked, ancient concrete walks leading up to each door.

Still, she'd arrived safely. Julie set the brake, curled her fingers over the steering wheel, and allowed herself a moment of relief that she'd made it all the way up to Oklahoma City without incident.

Julie glanced at the weedy patch of grass and the cracked walkways to each door. This time she noticed what looked like spent joints and beer can tabs on the neighboring walk.

It might be a good idea to get the van unpacked while the sky was still light.

Julie climbed out of the van and walked up to Trina's door. When she lifted the mat, the key was there, just like Trina had promised.

Julie unlocked the door and walked into the apartment. To her dismay, the whole apartment smelled faintly of stale cigarette smoke and dog, even though Trina didn't smoke and didn't have a pet.

She flicked the lights on. The front room was mostly bare, except for an ancient shag carpet, a sofa, a coffee table, and a television.

Julie frowned and moved into the little kitchen tucked behind the front room. There was a little kitchenette table and chairs, a coffeemaker on the counter, a stove, a small fridge, and a microwave.

There was no decor, no curtains on the kitchen window over the sink. Julie walked over and glanced through the window. It looked out over a parking lot and another red brick apartment building.

Julie blinked back tears. Trina hadn't been kidding. She was barely scraping by.

No wonder she was scared.

Julie set her mouth, turned around, and marched back outside. She opened the back door of the van and climbed up into it.

She'd gone a little crazy at the furniture store, but now that she'd seen Trina's place, she was glad she did. She'd bought a little crib, a rocking chair for Trina, some pretty butterfly decals for the wall, a little rag rug for the nursery, some pretty curtains.

Nothing she couldn't carry herself, if she took it easy.

She picked up a box and began unloading the van, and within thirty minutes the apartment floor was covered in cardboard boxes and plastic bags. Julie opened the rocker box first. She sank to the floor, sat down cross-legged, and pulled it down beside her. She found the instructions and unfolded them.

Some assembly required.

Julie sighed, but dove in. She discovered the screws, screwdriver, and other tools and began to attach Part A to Part B. Slowly the white rocker took shape in Trina's living room, followed by a white crib.

When they were finished at last Julie exhaled and wiped her brow. She was a bit tired, but a glance at the clock told her that she only had another hour to get ready. She pulled the rocker and the crib around to face the door, so Trina would see them when she first walked in.

Then she slowly began to fill the chair, the crib, and the floor around them with pretty pastel-wrapped presents filled with little fuzzy white onesies for the newborn baby, soft stuffed lambs for the crib, little baby socks and caps, embroidered white nursery drapes, and a whole wardrobe of maternity clothes for Trina.

Julie pulled an armload of tops out of a big bag with a smile. She'd chosen them all to flatter Trina's pale face, brown hair, and gray eyes. There was a white cotton peasant top with a scoop neck and big blousy sleeves; she'd paired it with a pair of jeans that had a stretchy panel to accommodate a pregnant woman. There was a darling pastel yellow top with a duck and little ducklings embroidered across the neck and hem, and a pair of white maternity slacks. There were three adorable maxi dresses in pale pink and blue and green.

Julie surveyed the floor happily; then she reached for the bag with the wrapping paper and bows.

By the time another hour had passed, the last box and gift bag had been packed, lined with tissue, and wrapped. Julie glanced at the clock. She had just enough time to order delivery for dinner, and she reached for her phone.

By good fortune, the delivery driver arrived before Trina did. Julie answered the door, tipped the driver, and carried the bags back to the little kitchen and unpacked them on the table. She'd barely finished setting out a jug of tea, some plates, and an aluminum container of Mongolian Beef, when she heard the sound of a car outside.

Julie smiled and hurried out to the living room. She was just in time to see the door open, and Trina's astonished face as she glanced up.

"Surprise," she smiled, and Trina put a hand to her mouth, squealed in joy, then rushed over to hug her tight.

"Thank you Jules," she whispered, and Julie frowned and pulled out of her hug.

"It's nothing to cry over," she smiled. "Half the fun of getting these is going to be watching you open them!" She took her friend by the hand. "Come on, I ordered Chinese. Dinner's ready, and you can open your presents after."

Trina tossed her bag down on the soft and followed her wearily. "I can't believe you did all this. You can't know how amazing this feels right now," she confessed, with a hungry glance at the Mongolian Beef. "You're an angel, Jules."

Julie poured tea into a cup and passed it to her friend. Trina raised the cup to her lips with a sigh of relief, then smiled.

"It's so good to have you here," she sighed. "I've missed you, Jules." She took the plate Julie offered her and walked out into the dining room. She glanced at the Christmas-like profusion of gifts on the floor, and her mouth crumpled up as she sank down onto the couch.

Julie followed and plopped down on the sofa beside her. As they ate, she stole little glances at her friend's face, and the relief she saw there made all her exertions worthwhile.

Nothing made her happier than to see that look of sweet relief dawn over a patient's face; and the fact that her newest patient was also her best friend only deepened her pleasure.

Julie set her plate down on the table beside her. "Come on now, Trina," she smiled. "I want to see you open these presents.

"The pink package first!"

Chapter Twenty Eight

Luke scanned the little group of students gathered in the corral for his riding class. To his surprise, Julie wasn't perched on her usual spot on the fence.

He scanned again, but he came up with the same result. Maybe she's late, he thought with a frown; but worry sparked in his heart.

I sure hope she didn't get scared off riding horses because that mare ran away with her, he thought; and his frown deepened.

I sure hope she wasn't worse hurt than she made out.

But he couldn't postpone the lesson to fret about Julie, as much as he might want to; and so he cleared his throat and smiled, "Welcome back, folks! Well, now that we've got the basics down, and we've had a nice trail ride, so now we can practice what we've learned."

A couple of hands went up in the group, and Luke pointed to a lady in a baseball hat.

"Julie."

The lady frowned in confusion. "Um...my name is Joan."

Luke felt himself going beet red, and he coughed, "Sorry, Joan. What was your question?"

"Can you tell us what to do in case a horse runs away with us, like what happened to that girl last time?"

Luke coughed into his hand and nodded. "Um...sure." He felt himself going red as he explained.

"So...the first thing to understand is that horses don't usually bolt," he assured her. "If a horse bolts, there's something wrong. They usually bolt when they're scared or in pain. Maybe they're girthed too tight, maybe they saw a booger, maybe they've picked up a burr. Sometimes a horse'll give you a warning that it's about to bolt, and if you're quick, you can head it off."

He glanced up at Joan, but his eyes skimmed past her to scan the corral and the parking lot beyond. Julie still wasn't there, and it looked like she wasn't gonna show.

It wasn't a good sign.

Wonder if she decided not to come back, he thought. *Guess I wouldn't blame her.*

A voice called from the back of the group. "What signs?"

Luke's mind returned to the question. He rubbed his chin and scanned the parking lot a last time. "Ah...the horse acts skittish, or feels tense, or starts fighting you." He shook off his worry with an effort and continued:

"So today we're gonna be pairing off into groups of two. We'll be practicing mounting a horse, turning its head, and pulling it to a stop. One person will hold the horse still as the other one mounts. Everybody choose a partner. If you don't have a partner, come up front and I'll help you."

The group broke up into murmuring groups, and motion from the drive jerked Luke's attention to the parking lot. A car came scooting in and parked.

Luke's heartbeat sped up and he craned his neck to see if it might be Julie. It wasn't her usual car, but maybe she had more than one.

Luke dropped his gaze. He was surprised by how deflated he was when a teenaged boy climbed out and came skipping across the lot to the corral.

I'm in trouble, he thought, and rubbed his jaw. *I'm thinking about Julie way too much. Daydreaming about her, really.*

But I don't know thing one about her, except that she's pretty and she likes to flirt. That her eyes are bluer than blue.

That her lips are the softest thing I've ever touched.

Luke frowned and shook his head, as if he could shake the thoughts out of it. *I thought I was doing better, but maybe I'm not doing so good after all. I hate to think of Julie quitting the class and being scared of horses, but maybe it's a good thing for me that she skipped out.*

Maybe it's for the best.

He looked up again in time to see the students staring at him expectantly. He mustered a smile and clapped his hands together. "All right, everybody have a partner?"

"Everybody except you," somebody quipped, and the class laughed. Luke laughed with them, but when a car passed by on the road, he turned to see who it was, again.

Chapter Twenty Nine

"A warm Sandy Creek howdy to all our rodeo guests," a deep male voice announced over the loudspeakers. "We're glad you came out to support our local contestants tonight. You folks ready to see some rodeo action?"

There were yips and yells of affirmation from the stands and scattered clapping, and the announcer replied, "Let's get the show on the road then!"

Julie settled down onto the metal bleacher seat between a pair of young blonde women in tank tops and faded jeans and an elderly couple in red cowboy hats. She'd indulged in a bag of buttered popcorn, and she nibbled on it absently as she scanned the rodeo ring. She searched the stands and the roped-off area behind the ring fences, but she saw no sign of Luke.

She'd just returned from Oklahoma, and her sense of outrage against Trina's baby-daddy was still fresh. There was no sign of him, and that irritated her, too.

Hmm, she thought darkly. *It'd be just like that lizard to flake after inviting me to join him here.*

The spotlights zoomed to the main gate, and it swung open for a pair of riders who galloped out carrying billowing American flags. The crowd roared its approval as the riders circled the ring, then rode out again.

Julie glanced down at her own bare knee. She was big game hunting that night, and she was dressed for it. She was sporting a black cowgirl hat, a tied-off cotton shirt in a tiny red check, a pair of jean shorts that showed off her long, sleek legs, and a pair of black cowgirl boots.

It was time for her to up her game, and that night, she'd decided to show Luke Spade why she'd made the cover of a dozen magazines and even refused an offer from *Playboy*. She had a killer figure, and she was going to use it like a loaded pistol.

Julie's lips curved up. Some hopeful cowboys had already hit on her, but she'd told them she was waiting for her husband, the marine, and that got rid of them.

A pair of rodeo workers entered the ring, set out big barrels at different points in the arena, and hurried out again.

"Ladies first this evening," the announcer declared. "Let's put our hands together for the contestants in our barrel racing competition!"

There was enthusiastic clapping and yelling from the stands, and Julie glanced at the gate in boredom, then scanned the people standing just behind the nearby fence. Her eyes focused in on one man in a white hat and a white shirt. He was taller than the men around him, and his shoulders looked familiar; but he was talking to someone and facing away from her.

"Let's welcome our first contestant, Mary McKenna," the announcer intoned, and someone close by screamed out, "Let's go Mary!"

Julie rubbed her right ear. The first contestant burst out of the gate and sent her horse flying low around the first barrel, but Julie's eyes moved to the man in the white hat. He turned his head to laugh at something, and she got a glimpse of his profile. Her hand drooped down from the popcorn bag and her eyes narrowed.

"Twenty seconds!" the deep voice announced, and the crowd burst into applause. "Well, the bar's been set high this evening."

Julie stared as the man in the white hat laughed again, then glanced out at the ring. Her eyes narrowed in a flash of predatory joy, and she rose smoothly, tossed away the popcorn bag, and sidled across the aisle and down to the gate. It was Luke, all right.

Let the games begin, she thought grimly, and fluffed up her hair as she sashayed through the crowd. She slipped smoothly past groups of cowboys and smirked to herself as their words trailed off into silence. The men she passed turned their heads and smiled at her in open admiration, and other women gave her short, unfriendly once-overs and crossed their arms.

But she kept her eyes on that white hat. It was visible just over the heads of the crowd.

She knew her makeup was nearly perfect, but she still pinched her cheeks and bit her lip as she closed in. There wasn't a blush or a lipstick in the world to match her own natural coloring.

Julie reached up to gently push the last shoulder out of the way. She stepped up a couple of feet away from Luke and waited for him to notice her.

Her eyes flicked over him. She was quick to notice that he'd taken trouble over his appearance. His vivid blue eyes reflected the overhead lights and his face and neck were glowing and squeaky clean.

He was wearing a black string tie, and his white hat and shirt were spotless, starched and pressed. His jeans were slightly worn, but clean and pressed and held up by a belt with a glorious silver concho buckle.

She even thought she caught a whiff of...yes, of Old Spice. He was clearly expecting a little female attention.

It was a good sign.

The announcer's voice blared out overhead. "Let's welcome our next racer, Sue Lynn Tompkins!"

The crowd erupted in applause and the mounted racer burst out of the nearby gate. Luke glanced up to watch, and as he turned back his glance grazed over her as she stood there.

Julie smiled knowingly as visible shock washed over his face. He turned to look at her with his mouth still slightly open.

Her smile deepened, and she sauntered up to him. "Hi Luke. Are you surprised to see me?"

He recovered instantly and returned her smile. "I'm glad to see you made it, Julie," he amended. "I hope you'll enjoy the rodeo."

Julie lowered her eyes and curved her lips. "I'm sure I will."

Luke took off his hat and ran his hand through his hair. "My event's last, so I been hanging around to chew the fat. I know most everybody here."

He nodded toward the stands on the opposite side of the arena. "If you stay until after my ride, I'll introduce you to my family. Some of 'em came out tonight to see me."

Julie followed the line of his pointing hand and noticed a large group of people all sitting together. Her brows twitched together in frustration. The last thing she wanted was to get tangled up with Luke's family. She was there to get Luke off in a dark corner alone; but she smiled and murmured, "I'd love to meet your family, Luke. Is that them—the ones with the white hats?"

"Yeah, the ones with the white hats. They all decided to match my hat," he added with a shamefaced laugh. "They're a little goofy that way."

Julie glanced up at him and took his arm. "Oh, I don't blame them," she smiled. "I wish I'd known you were wearing white. I would've worn a white hat, too. I'm rooting for you."

Luke's face split into a beautiful white smile. "Well, I guess I can't lose now," he joked. "Look, we've got a few minutes. You want to get a snack while we wait?"

"That sounds wonderful," she murmured. "What's good?"

Luke put his hand lightly over hers and led the way toward the concession stand. "Oh, I wouldn't know," he teased, and shot her a mischievous look. "I never eat or drink before a ride."

"Well, of course not," Julie sputtered. "I suppose I shouldn't tempt you, then."

"Oh you go ahead," Luke told her. "I don't mind."

Julie pinched her lips together and cast an amused glance at the little food truck in the parking lot. The scent of roasted hot dogs and funnel cakes greeted them from twenty feet away, and she was willing to bet that Luke had arrived with an empty stomach.

The two of them strolled up to the counter. Julie raised an eyebrow. The little truck was selling beer and wine. She could take beer or leave it, but she was willing to bet that Luke loved it.

The concession clerk leaned across the little counter. "What would you like, little lady?"

"Hmm," she murmured. "I....I think I'll have a big, frothy beer, a hot dog with lots of chili and cheese, and a big cup of onion rings."

She turned to Like with an innocent look and murmured, "Are you sure you don't want anything, Luke?"

To her delight, his smile looked pained; but he shook his head. "No, thank you. Nothing for me."

"Oh, that's too bad," she sighed, and took the beer that the clerk handed her. She took a sip, then smiled with all her teeth.

"*Mmmm,*" she sighed, as if it had been delicious, and enjoyed the sight of Luke licking his lips.

"Here's your order, miss."

Julie reached for her bag to pay, but Luke reached out and took her hand. "I'll get it."

She rolled amused eyes to his, but murmured: "Are you sure?"

He nodded and slapped his card on the counter. "Sure. I invited you. I want you to have a good time."

Julie's smile faded, and a flick of conscience stabbed her. She shot him a stricken look. "Well...thanks. That's nice of you." She grabbed an onion ring and took a small, guilty bite.

Luke took the plastic basket and led her back toward the ring. "Let's go back and see the action," he smiled. "Lots of new talent here tonight. It'll show you how good a rider you can be if you stick with it."

Julie sputtered and shook her head. "I'll be happy if I can stay on board," she demurred, and noticed a cloud pass over his face.

"Julie, I...I hope you aren't gonna let that horse bolting put you off riding," he replied earnestly. "I noticed that you didn't show at the last class."

Good, was Julie's first thought; followed instantly by a flush of guilt over her mean intentions.

What's wrong with me, she thought impatiently. *I've got this guy where I want him. I can't let him get to me now. Make me forget what he did to Trina.*

He's a snake!

"You ain't quitting, are you?"

Julie rolled stricken eyes to Luke's. His eyes were big and blue and clear as the sky. He looked 110 percent sincere.

To her own dismay, Julie felt her resolve crumbling. *What if I'm wrong about him,* she thought in sudden panic.

She looked up at Luke in a moment of disastrous doubt, and he took her arm and pulled her behind a stack of hay bales. She watched him set the little plastic basket down and reach for her beer as if she was hypnotized. As if it was watching it happen to someone else.

He turned back and stared down into her eyes in concern. A lock of his wheat-blonde hair fell down over his brow, and those clear, sky-blue eyes clouded with worry. He looked genuinely troubled for her, and when he licked his firm, chiseled lips, Julie swallowed hard. Luke was gorgeous, a golden statue backlit by the halo of stadium lights, almost irresistible in that moment, and she was in deep trouble.

Julie felt herself slipping away. She made a desperate grab for her wits—and missed.

Luke looked down at the ground, licked his lips. "Julie, I—I didn't ask you here as my student," he stammered, as if he was a schoolboy asking a girl out for the first time.

Julie reached for his chin, gently lifted it, and stared up into his beautiful eyes.

"I didn't come here as one," she whispered.

They stared at one another for a pregnant moment, then Luke's arms clamped around her waist, and her arms twined around his neck, and they kissed one another like two starving people.

Julie closed her eyes and abandoned herself to a wild swirl of reckless pleasure. The first thing she discovered was that Luke Spade knew how to kiss a girl. His mouth on hers was delicate and deliberate and delicious, and her brows shot up in surprise. He had moves she'd never felt before, and it didn't take him any time to make her nerve endings start throbbing like a big bass drum.

Julie felt herself start to go limp in his arms, heard soft laughter from passersby as they clinched, but Luke was blowing her mind.

A voice in the back of her mind was screaming at her to remember why she was there, and she paused long enough to catch her breath and regain control. She was breathing heavily, she was staring at Luke's chest, and he stood there patiently and waited for her.

All right, Julie thought grimly, and pressed her brow against Luke's shirt. *I've seen what he's got. Now I'm going to show him what I can do.*

I'm going to do what I came here to...

Her nails dug into his shoulders and she stood up on tiptoe to kiss him. She threw everything she had into that kiss, because this was her chance. She had to make a big impression if she wanted to tear Luke's heart out and stomp on it.

She was going to tear it out and...

Luke's hands wandered from her waist and tangled into her hair, and Julie lost her train of thought. Her eyes rolled up in her head and she lost track of everything except Luke's lips on hers. She was floating on a pink cloud.

Then suddenly, she wasn't.

Luke raised his head and frowned toward the ring. Somewhere in the background the announcer's voice was saying, "Next up, the bronc buster category! Put your hands together for a rodeo champion and hometown boy Luke Spade!"

Luke gasped and gave her an anguished glance. "I'm sorry Julie," he gasped. "I got to go!"

He dashed off at a run, leaving her holding air, and she stared after him in outrage. His blonde head bobbed through the crowd, leaving her flustered and alone.

She exhaled, clapped her hands clean, and sashayed through the onlookers to the ring fence. She was just in time to see Luke jump up into the chute, settle in on top of the bronc, and grab the thick rein that was all he had to hold onto.

Julie leaned against the fence and watched him through angry eyes. Her pulse was still pounding.

Well, I guess I know where women rank with him, she thought resentfully. *Way below a horse.*

I can't claim to be surprised.

But still!

I'm glad he wasn't carrying me in his arms, she thought tartly. *He would've dropped me on my head!*

The gate suddenly flew open, and she watched as the bronc burst from the chute and launched into the air. Julie bit her lip, watching with an uncomfortable mixture of resentment and admiration as Luke jerked and wheeled with the horse. She saw him hold one hand high in the air and grip the rein with the other.

Time seemed to slow down, and Julie watched as Luke's hair bounced and floated in the air over his head. She traced the taut set of his jaw. Her eyes followed as his hips rose and fell with the screaming bronc, how they flowed with its every twist and turn.

Julie stared at Luke in unwilling fascination. She didn't know anything about bronc busting, but she had to admit that it was a pleasure to watch Luke ride. He moved so smoothly with the horse that he made it look almost easy.

That was always the mark of a pro.

She blinked, and it was suddenly over. The horse was now halfway across the ring, bucking and snorting, and Luke was holding his white hat high over his head as the crowd burst into thunderous applause.

To her own surprise, she found herself clapping with them. The announced crowed, "Well, we can all see that Luke's still in top form, can't we folks? Let's hope this is the start of a comeback!"

The applause jumped to a roar, and Luke raised his hand again, smiled into the light, and walked back to the gate. He was swallowed up by a mob of admirers waiting there, and Julie watched in disapproval as two scantily-clad blonde women rushed up and kissed him.

She was still glaring at them when an ironic drawl made her turn her head.

"Yeah, you wouldn't be the first girl ol' Luke made mad."

She turned indignantly. A giant of a redheaded man was grinning down at her. He was lounging against the fence with a straw in his teeth, and he took it out to gesture toward her.

She scoffed and turned on her heel, but his voice stopped her. "Oh, I don't mean no harm, miss," he called out. "It's just that I hate to see him hurt somebody else. Ol' Luke likes to love 'em and leave 'em, that's a fact."

Julie turned to face him. "How do you know?" she demanded. "Who are you to him?"

"Oh, just a bronc buster, miss," the big man chuckled, and tipped his hat to her. "Come down from Houston to keep an eye on the competition.My name's Justice. Justice Owens."

Julie's eyes flicked over him, and she sauntered over, hands on hips. "Well," she replied softly, "I like your name anyway, Justice." She cocked her head to one side. "What kind of justice do you think 'ol' Luke' deserves for skipping out on me?"

She nodded toward Luke, who was now so mobbed by fans that only his white hat was visible.

The redheaded cowboy lowered his eyes and pulled a face. "Well, miss, that depends on you," he replied softly, and raised keen eyes to hers. "But if you ask me, I'd say ol' Luke deserves to see you walk out of here on the arm of a tall, handsome cowboy. A guy who knows how to treat a lady right."

Julie's lips curled up. She was in the mood to do just that: and so she took the arm the redheaded man offered her.

"I think you're right," she murmured, and smiled up into his eyes. "Let's serve a little justice, shall we? Be sure to take me right past him."

"Yes, ma'am," the big man smiled, and squired her through the crowd right past the knot of giggling women surrounding Luke. Julie turned her head just enough to enjoy the moment when Luke raised his head and caught sight of her, just before she passed by with a smile.

The look of open-mouthed dismay on his face was the best thing about the whole night; and she savored it as she smiled up into Justice Owens' beaming face.

Chapter Thirty

"Well, you can forget about seeing Luke again tonight," Carson sighed as he handed Donna a glass of beer and settled down on the metal bleacher seat.

Buck leaned out from behind Morgan and shot him a troubled look. "Why?"

Carson took a sip of beer, grimaced, and set the cup down on the seat beside him. "He's found a new friend. I caught a glimpse of them behind a hay bale on the way back from the concession stand." He glanced toward the gate, where a throng of mostly female admirers were still clustered around Luke's white hat.

"I don't see her now, though."

Morgan and Buck both frowned at him and subsided into a troubled silence; but Donna smiled and raised an eyebrow. "I'm not surprised," she murmured in amusement. "Luke is a very handsome man. Why shouldn't he have—new friends, as you put it?"

Buck waved toward the gate dismissively. "Aw, Luke can't help it if he gets swarmed at the gate," he retorted. "He wouldn't have gone with that little girl he did so long, if he was just playing around. He ain't interested in them hooch—"

"Buck!" Kate hissed in an urgent undertone, and her husband shrugged and took a drink of beer. She turned back to cradling their son, who had fallen asleep in her arms with one chubby fist in his mouth.

"It's the truth," Buck grumbled in an unrepentant murmur.

"Well, Luke seems to have gotten over his blue funk, anyway," Carson observed. "And since we've seen him ride, I think Donna and I are going home now."

"Oh, you aren't going to stay to watch the other riders?" Kate objected, and Carson smiled, but shook his head. "No, I'm afraid not. We can rest assured that Luke's as wild and woolly as ever, so I'm done for the evening. I'm here for family solidarity, not because I'm a big rodeo fan."

Heather glanced up at Morgan. "I think we better go, too," she murmured. "We told the sitter we'd be back at ten, and it's almost nine-thirty now."

"Well, we're staying," Buck replied. "I like to keep up with the new riders coming along. And," he added, with a defiant glance at Carson, "I think Luke'll be back to say hey in a little while. It'd be bad if nobody was here to meet him."

Morgan and Heather looked stricken, but Carson smiled and tilted his head. "Bye, all." He put a hand around Donna's waist and followed her as she descended the bleacher aisle.

"Bye, Carson. Donna," Kate called out. She watched as they slowly disappeared into the crowd, and looked up as Heather and Morgan stood and collected their things.

"We'll see you back at the house," Heather murmured, and leaned down to give her a peck on the cheek.

"Y'all be careful," Buck told Morgan.

"Tell Luke he did good," Morgan rumbled, and he and Heather walked down the aisle and into the crowd.

Kate watched them ruefully and turned to Buck. "Are you sure you want to stay, Buck?" she asked softly. "Look at little Russ—he's all in." She leaned down to give his chubby cheek a kiss.

Buck gazed down fondly at his son. "No, he's having the time of his life," he smiled. "Look at those cotton candy stains on his mouth. He's still dreaming of 'em, I bet."

Kate smiled in spite of herself, but added, "Well, if Luke isn't back in awhile, we need to take this baby home."

Buck leaned back and stared wistfully at her, and then at little Russ. He sighed.

"All right, then Kate. I'll give him thirty minutes, then we'll go." He returned his attention to the ring, where a rider was unceremoniously hurled off the back of a twisting bronc. Kate screamed softly and clapped a hand to her mouth, and Buck shook his head. He took a sip of beer.

"I know that stung," he mumbled, as the rider pulled himself up off the dirt and dusted off his pants. His roving eye caught the sight of a tall, approaching figure, and he let out a whoop that startled his wife.

"There he is! I told 'em you'd be back! You just missed everybody. Carson and Donna and Morgan and Heather left just a few minutes ago!"

Luke walked up, took his hat off, and sank down on the bleacher beside Buck as every fan within ten feet lifted their phones to snap a picture.

Buck clapped him on the back. "That was a great ride, boy," he approved. "You showed 'em you still got it!"

Luke bent over on the seat and rubbed the back of his neck. "Yeah, my muscles are cussing me right now," he laughed. "They're telling me I ain't sixteen anymore."

"Well, you went the whole eight seconds, that's what counts," Buck beamed. "We're proud of you."

Luke glanced across him, nodded and smiled at Kate, and glanced beyond.

"Um...has anybody come over here tonight?"

Buck took a gulp of beer and looked a question. "Who do you mean?"

Luke looked embarrassed, but mumbled, "Ah..a woman. Long, dark hair, red checkered top, shorts. I was kinda hopin' she'd come by to...say hello. I told her my family was here."

Buck shot him a short, straight look. "Didn't see her," he replied, and crossed his arms. "Saw a lot of others with you over there by the gate, though."

Luke leaned forward and clasped his hands over his knees. "Yeah, that tends to happen," he admitted. "I don't think she liked it."

"Well, why don't you go find her, if you're worried about it?" Buck demanded. "She's probably still here somewhere."

"I don't think so," Luke mumbled, and looked the other way. "I saw her leave with another guy."

Buck raised his brows, then handed his beer over. Luke took a gulp, and subsided into a depressed silence that he finally broke with:

"Not just any guy, either. Justice Owens."

Buck turned toward him in surprise. "What's Justice doing up here at Sandy Creek's little podunk rodeo? He's not riding tonight, is he?"

Luke shook his head. "He's not on the list."

"No, because that don't make no sense," Buck retorted. "There's hardly even a purse here." He adjusted one shoulder and muttered, "I'll tell you what he's doing here. He heard you're going down to that rodeo in Houston and he came here to see how you'd do tonight. He wants to know if you're still a threat!"

Buck grumbled under his breath. "I never did like that guy. He rides good, but I've never seen him but what he looked like he was sucking on a lemon."

Luke shook his head. "He's a sore loser, that's for sure," he grinned. "I've never met a man in my life who hates to lose so bad. Guess it makes you look mean."

Luke's smile slowly faded. "Maybe I should go look for Julie after all," he mumbled half to himself, and handed back the beer. "If she happens to come by, tell her that I want to talk to her."

Buck nodded and watched Luke get up and descend the bleachers; then he turned to Kate.

"He's off to find some woman named Julie. What d'you make of that?" he demanded; and Kate smiled a bit.

"It looks like Luke's found a new girl. And that she sent him a message tonight," she giggled.

"What message?" Buck frowned, and Kate shrugged and smiled up at him.

"Why, the oldest one in the world—'*Two can play at that game.*'"

Chapter Thirty One

"So you're a bronc buster."

Julie lifted a glass of wine to her lips, and the candle at their restaurant table glimmered in its ruby red depths.

Justice shot her a quick glance from his brown eyes. His eyes were dark, almost black, and the candle flame shimmered in them.

"That I am," he sighed, and downed a draught of beer. "For almost fifteen years now. I've paid my dues busting broncs on the circuit, that's for sure."

Julie shot him a sympathetic glance. As a physical therapist, she could guess what fifteen years of that life had done to his body. The redheaded man sitting across from her at the table was six feet tall and built like a brick wall, but she knew that cracked bones, torn muscles, and injured joints were likely the price of his rodeo glory.

Her tone was soft as she replied, "I can imagine."

He took a deep breath and went on more strongly, "But I can't lie, the rodeo life suits me. Never did like to stay in one place for long. I love to go, and the rodeo takes you from the Mexican border, all the way up into Canada."

Julie shook her head and smiled. "It sounds very romantic."

His eyes flicked to her face again. The look in them was direct, almost intense; but she smiled and looked a question, and he finally shrugged and smiled.

"Some people think it is. I guess it is, if you're watching it. But if you're competing, it's a lot of hard work. Lot of hard knocks, too." He took another drink of beer. "Lots of time in airports and hotels." His eyes returned to hers.

"It gets lonely."

Julie's glance flicked over him, and she smiled. "No woman in your life, Justice?"

He shrugged and took another drink. "I was married there for awhile, but my wife died three years ago."

His words wiped the smile from Julie's face, and she leaned back into her chair. "I'm sorry."

Justice tilted his head. "We would've busted up if she hadn't took sick," he confessed. "We'd been on the rocks a long time before that happened. It's tough to stay married when you got to travel all the time."

Julie shot him an awed glance. *He must really be serious about his career,* she thought. *It sounds like he's sacrificed everything for it.*

Justice set down his beer glass and took a deep breath. "What do you do?"

Julie glanced up at him and smiled. "I'm a physical therapist at the hospital in Green Oak," she told him.

"Huh. Maybe I should come by and get my shoulder seen to," he replied in a low, gravelly voice.

The waiter's arrival made a reply impossible, and Julie stifled a sigh of relief as he leaned across the table to set a bowl of salad and a platter of tamales down between them.

"Enjoy."

Julie shot her companion another glance as she reached for the salad bowl and began filling two plates. Now that she'd had a chance to talk to him, Justice didn't seem nearly as magnetic and appealing as Luke Spade, but then, Luke was like a unicorn, and Justice looked like an ordinary, down to earth man.

She handed him a heaping bowl of salad and reached for the tamale platter. "I guess you're in Houston for the rodeo, then, Justice?" she queried, as she spooned out a generous portion onto his plate and handed it to him.

He took it from her and nodded. "That's right. The Fire and Fury Rodeo in June. You should come down and see it. It's a lot of fun. You don't have to be into the rodeo to have a good time."

"Maybe I will," Julie smiled, and thought: *I think Luke's competing in that rodeo, too. Wouldn't it be fun to pull his nose by showing up there with Justice?*

She shot him a mischievous look, but was a little taken aback when Justice seemed to read that thought right off her face. The look in his eyes hardened, and his next question was like a fork pointed at her face.

"You and Luke been seeing each other a long time?" he demanded, and Julie hunched a shoulder and looked away.

"I'd hardly say that," she replied, but shot him a hard look of her own and thought:

Not that I owe you an explanation.

Justice seemed to read that thought, too, and to her relief, he leaned back in his chair and smiled. "Didn't mean to be nosy," he told her. "I just like to understand, that's all."

"Well, you saw pretty much all there was to see," she told him briskly, and shook out her table napkin. "Because I think your opinion of Luke Spade is the right one." She raised her eyes to challenge Justice with a short, sharp look.

That's the Gospel truth, anyway, Julie thought to herself, and lifted the glass of wine to her lips.

She glanced at her big companion over the rim of her glass. It was easy to see that she and Justice had something in common. He was trying hard to play it cool, but she could tell that Justice hated Luke's guts, and it wasn't hard to guess why.

Justice had to work for what he had, and she knew he was carrying the scars of a hard and lonely life. Luke, on the other hand, was a careless playboy who didn't have to worry if he won any money or not. His looks and fortune ensured that he'd never be lonely or desperate.

It wasn't fair, and it would be hard for a man like Justice to not resent it. Naturally he'd dislike Luke. And she certainly couldn't blame him for noticing that Luke used women. She glanced at him again.

She discovered that his eyes were on her, and that he was giving her an odd, speculative look. Probably he was wondering if she was using him to get back at Luke, and that was fair, too. She kind of was.

But she sympathized with Justice, and when she searched her own heart, she could honestly say that she was willing to give him a chance for his own sake. Their dinner was a bit awkward, and Justice Owens was definitely rough around the edges; but he seemed like an honest, hard-working man.

And his blunt candor, even though a bit uncomfortable, compared very favorably to Luke's fake charm and selfishness.

Justice shook his head and addressed his salad. "Yeah, I always felt kinda sorry for the women in Luke's life," he muttered. "There used to be a little brown-haired gal who came to the rodeo with him," he reminisced, and gazed past her, as if he was seeing someone else. "Looked kinda shy. Followed Luke around like a little puppy. You could tell she thought the sun rose and set in him."

Julie's eyes snapped up to his in dismay as he went on, "Yeah, you could tell she was just dying for him for him to pop the question, but he wasn't never gonna do it. It was sad to watch." He munched a salad and reached for his beer. "I guess she finally figured it out."

Julie stared at him in shock, both at his unnerving insight and his painful timing. She lowered her eyes to her plate and took an apathetic bite of food.

Even the other rodeo riders saw it, she thought numbly. *Everybody saw it but poor Trina.*

If only I'd come back home sooner! Maybe Trina would've listened to me. Maybe she wouldn't be alone and pregnant and broke right now.

The bitter anger that had bloomed in her heart slowly melted into a terrible regret.

Maybe this is partly my fault, too.

Justice's voice broke into her thoughts. "Did I say something wrong?" he asked with a raised brow. "You look downright sad."

"Oh...no," Julie murmured, and took a bite of salad. "No, you didn't say anything wrong."

A sympathetic look flitted across his dark eyes, and she could tell that he was interpreting her sadness as being about Luke dumping her that evening. She had no intention of telling him the real reason, and so she let him think it.

But the painful reminder of Trina cast a pall over the rest of their dinner. Julie lapsed into a stricken silence and said little more, and to her relief, Justice didn't push her to make conversation. She experienced that as a kindness, and she blessed him for it.

Chapter Thirty Two

"Thanks for the nice dinner, Justice," Julie smiled.

They were standing in the parking lot of the little restaurant in downtown Sandy Creek. The parking lot lights cast the silent rows of cars in ghostly white light.

"And for the pleasant company," she added. "It sure is nice to be with a gentleman who doesn't make me feel like I have to *compete* for his attention."

"Why, it was my pleasure, miss," the big man smiled. "It's not hard at all to concentrate on such a pretty girl." He took her hand, kissed it lightly, and released it with a smile.

He opened her car door for her, let her slide in, and closed it after her. Julie rolled down the window, and he leaned against the car to smile at her.

"I have to go back to Houston, but I'll be back before long," he told her softly. "Can I call on you?"

Julie dimpled at him. "Sure can."

"Well, if you'll give me your number, I'll call you before I come up. Maybe we can go out dancing or something."

"I'd like that." Julie found a piece of paper and scribbled down her number, and Justice took it and tucked it into his shirt pocket. He tipped his hat to her gallantly and sauntered away, and Julie shot him a satisfied glance before she rolled up the car window and cranked the engine.

She wasn't at all displeased with the evening. That blonde donkey had insulted her at the rodeo, but she had her answer ready. If

Justice Owens wanted to squire her around, that was all right with her.

I'll flash him around like a diamond necklace, all over this little town, she thought grimly.

Mr. 'Love 'Em and Leave 'Em' can put that in his pipe and smoke it.

Julie smiled grimly, remembering the look of staring amazement on Luke's face when she blew past on Justice Owens' arm. His eyes had been as big and round as two blue marbles, and his mouth had fallen slightly open.

She pulled out of the parking lot and into the street, but she was still seeing Luke's shocked expression. *You thought I'd just stand there behind that hay bale and wait for you to get good and ready to come back to me, like Trina would've.*

I suppose, after you'd got bored of being kissed by that pack of painted cats at the gate!

She gunned the motor and sent her car down the street a bit too fast, came to herself, and slowed to a more reasonable speed. She had to remind herself that she didn't need to get angry.

She wasn't really interested in Luke Spade, and so it didn't matter what he did. Her goal was to get him on her hook, and them torture him for as long as she could before she dumped him flat.

Poetic justice for Trina.

But it wasn't long before she was fuming about Luke again: and she hissed in exasperation and turned on the radio to take her mind off him.

She arrived home at midnight, and by the time she'd parked the VW, locked up behind her, and shuffled up to her bedroom at the condo, her long night was beginning to catch up with her. She yawned at her own reflection in the bathroom mirror, brushed her teeth quickly, and slipped into a pair of white silk pajamas.

She stretched, yawned, and drifted into her bedroom. She had a huge antique sleigh bed placed squarely between two French doors leading out onto her third-floor balcony. Moonlight was streaming across the hardwood floor as she walked to the bed, threw back the puffy, pink chintz comforter, and climbed into bed.

Julie sank deep into her pillow, sighed deeply, and closed her eyes. Weariness pushed her deep into the soft darkness, gently but irresistibly; and she felt herself drifting away into a comfortable sleep. She settled deeper into her pillow as her mind released conscious thought and floated down into restful nothingness.

She drifted there in contented unconsciousness for an indeterminate time; but the silent nothingness was gradually replaced by sound. Slowly, a distant but beautiful male voice rose and fell in melodious song. At first it hummed incoherently, but slowly it resolved into soothing words, sung as soft and low as a sigh.

Get along home

Get along home.

Julie murmured in her sleep and turned on her pillow. The voice was indescribably comforting, like a loving hand on her brow. It echoed in her mind like a benediction.

Hush now my baby,

Don't you moan.

Julie's lips silently mouthed the words as she slept, and slowly the darkness melted away before glittering green light, like sunlight through summer leaves.

She looked up into the branches of a huge oak tree. She was sitting at the base of its gnarled trunk on a pillow of new grass. Somehow she was wearing a white cotton nightgown that covered her almost to her feet. Only her bare toes peeped out from underneath the hem, and she wiggled them like a child.

She was perfectly comfortable, and as she closed her eyes and leaned back against the tree trunk, the male voice murmured again, closer and stronger, as if its owner was walking up the green hill.

Get along home

It's time to go home.

She opened her eyes in her dream, and as she watched, a blonde man appeared over the rim of the hill. It was Luke Spade, and he was somehow different, younger. He looked as innocent as if he was some new Adam on the first day of the world, and singing out his wonder and joy.

He smiled and extended his hand to her as he walked up and sank down onto the grass by her side. He was wearing a white cotton shirt open to the middle of his chest, and a pair of loose white cotton pants.

He was holding a single white daisy, and he gave it to her with a sweet smile.

Julie frowned in her dream, but she saw her dream self take the daisy with delight and twirl it in her fingers. Luke's face split into a beautiful white smile, and he leaned over to give her a kiss on the cheek.

Hush now my darlin',

Soon we'll be home.

She put a hand to her cheek in surprise, because the touch of his lips was warm on her skin and made it tingle. She looked up at him, and he took her in his arms and kissed her again, and it was right and natural and their lips blended into one another as easily as breathing, like two clear streams converging into a single one.

And a voice, not his and not hers, murmured through the fluttering leaves:

This is how it can be.

Like the first day of the world.

Julie frowned in her sleep and turned her head on her pillow, because even in her sleep, the suggestion made her angry.

It isn't this way, she objected in her dream. *Life isn't this way. Luke isn't this way and I'm not this way.*

Luke is a selfish snake and I'm...

Julie woke suddenly with a gasp and sat bolt upright in bed. She rolled wild eyes from one end of her moonlight bedroom to the other, then closed them in relief and fell back onto her pillow.

It was only a dream.

But her relief faded, because the lovely peace of the dream lingered with her, left a shimmer of green leaves and a whisper of sweet kisses in her memory.

She put a hand to her head and closed her eyes in frowning impatience. Somehow her subconscious had scrambled her real-life clinch with Luke at the rodeo, served it back up to her in a weird mishmash of images.

Julie licked her lips and stared up at the ceiling as her mind spun back to that little hidden nook behind the hay bales. She got a little shudder up her back in spite of herself. There in the solitude of her own bedroom at 3 in the morning, she could admit to herself that no man had ever kissed her like Luke Spade did that night.

That was why she was having strange dreams.

She hadn't exactly been short of admirers in L.A., and she'd dated some gorgeous men; but that grinning cowboy had taken her in his arms and flown her right to the moon.

Julie closed her eyes and frowned, but she couldn't banish the memory. She and Luke had just melted into one another *perfectly*. That had never happened to her before, and she'd begun to think it never would.

But somehow, Luke knew that she wanted to be kissed like it was the end of the world; that she loved that first rush of passion to taper off into slow, deliberate, thorough kisses, and then to have his lips wander down her neck and over behind her ear.

He's known it without asking and he'd done it all flawlessly, and she'd responded without thinking, in perfect rhythm with his mouth. It had been so amazing, so delightful, that her pulse jumped just remembering it.

Julie opened frowning eyes and picked at the coverlet. When she was in Luke's arms, she had to fight herself to keep on course, to remember why she was there.

Her frown deepened. Even knowing what she knew about him, he'd *still* swept her away. Julie stuck her thumb in her mouth and nibbled her fingernail nervously. Of course, capturing Luke was the plan, and so it hadn't really been a mistake, except in her head.

But still—there for a few minutes, he'd come between her and her goal.

He'd made her lose control of herself; and she frowned and tightened her fingers on the steering wheel. Next time she was going to be more deliberate and careful.

Now that she knew what to expect from him, she could be ready for it.

He'd surprised her, that was all.

But as she pulled the covers up around her chin, her memory replayed the day Luke let her ride his horse and walked in front of her for a long, hot hour to spare her discomfort.

It reminded her that he'd invited her to come meet his family at the rodeo.

It replayed Trina's voice admitting that Luke would do anything for her, if he knew she needed his help.

It whispered: *Are you sure you're right about this man?*

She frowned, turned over with a sigh and closed her eyes; but she didn't fall asleep right away. She was little bit afraid that if she fell asleep, she'd dream of Luke again; and she held out at long as she could.

Chapter Thirty Three

Justice Owens pulled his battered truck away from the last stoplight in Sandy Creek and past the old gas stations and older shops on the outskirts of town.

He turned away from the interstate and down the old two-lane that ran parallel to it all the way down to Houston. It was past eleven, and it was a fine, warm spring night with a wide Texas sky full of stars. Justice rolled the windows down with a flick of a button and let the cool night breeze ruffle random papers in the cab as the clover-scented air flowed through it.

Justice's lips curved up a bit as he drove. It was a pleasant night on the little rural back road. He could hear crickets humming in the fields as they rolled by, mile after mile of them, punctuated only by little stands of mesquite or cottonwoods, dark blurs flashing by in the night.

He sat up suddenly as a brightly-lit archway appeared on the right side of the road. He pulled his mouth to one side in disgust. It was the massive gateway to the Seven Spades Ranch, a giant portal of natural rock barred by massive wrought-iron gates. He turned his head to glare at the entrance as his truck flashed past. There were no buildings visible beyond that gate—just a faint glow on the horizon off to the east.

A *mile* away.

Justice shot the ranch another resentful glance. There were no other lights visible, except the faintest blush, far to the northwest, that might have been another building complex; but it was too faint to be sure.

Blast him, he growled to himself, and muttered under his breath until the big, lighted ranch gate faded over the horizon behind him.

But one thing almost evened the scales, for once in his life: he'd stolen that breathtaking brunette right out from under Luke Spade's nose.

He shook with silent laughter. Yeah, ol' Luke hadn't seen that coming. His eyes had just about popped out of his fool head as they'd strutted past, and his mouth had flopped open like a fish.

Justice shook his head. He didn't know what Luke used for a brain, but any man with half of one would know you didn't go from kissing one woman, to running off to be with a dozen others. Not if you wanted to keep the first one.

Justice licked his lips. Yeah, Luke was a fool, all right. When he'd first seen that dark-haired beauty, she'd made him doubt his own eyes.

He'd never seen a more beautiful woman, at least not up close. Guys like him would give anything to have a woman like her kissing 'em; but when the bell rang, Luke had tossed her aside like an old shoe, and after his ride, he'd let himself get swarmed by a bunch of buckle bunnies.

Just like old times. Ol' Luke had gotten older, but not smarter; and it was a good sign.

Justice opened the dash, pulled out a pack of cigarettes, and lit one. He held it to his lips with one hand and blew smoke from his lips that swirled over the seat and was sucked out the window into the night.

That little girl was still thinking about Luke, of course. She'd only gone out with him to spite Luke. She thought she was hiding it, but it was plain as print.

He wasn't surprised, and in a way, he didn't mind. He didn't expect much else. He'd literally swiped her right out from Luke's arms.

His smile deepened. She'd still been mad at dinner. She'd stabbed her salad with that fork like she was stabbing Luke Spade's sorry butt. Couldn't say he blamed her: and he was hoping that she stayed mad.

He'd decided that he was going after her himself.

He narrowed his eyes in amusement. She might be willing to keep him company just to spite Luke, and he'd take it in the hope that he could build on it. Because nothing would be better than beating ol' Luke at the rodeo, than stealing his girl.

Yes sir, that would be extra *specially* good.

His shoulders shook with silent laughter. Luke was so used to getting all the girls and hogging all the glory that it hadn't occurred to him that some other guy might move in on him.

Well, he was about to find out.

Justice let his mind linger on Julie's little checkered top and shorts. She'd be a cozy armful, that was for sure; but he was going to go slow and work on her bit by bit.

Julie was a skittish filly, and he'd worked with 'em long enough to know that moving too quick scared 'em off.

Her mind was still full of Luke Spade; but he was confident that if he worked with her long enough, he could push Luke right on out.

It was a very pleasant thought; and he lingered on it as he drove through the darkness.

Chapter Thirty Four

"Julie!"

Julie glanced up, stiffened, and turned her back on the voice. She was standing in the middle of a little mom and pop grocery store in downtown Green Oak, and Luke was walking down the little bread aisle toward her. He was dressed like a cowboy in a plain white tee shirt and jeans. His blonde head was taller than the top shelves, and his boots rattled the old wooden floors.

Luke walked up and planted himself in front of her cart, and she frowned at him, crossed her arms, and looked away.

Luke's voice was soft and regretful. "Julie, I'm sure sorry I missed you at the rodeo last night. I would've called you, but I didn't have your number."

Julie dropped her arms and glared up at him. "How did you find me?" she snapped and grabbed the plastic cart handle. She tried to wheel the cart past him, but he grabbed the metal rungs with his hands.

"Julie, please don't be mad with me." His blue eyes pled with her. "I wouldn't have left you so quick unless I had to. You"—he rubbed the back of his neck and looked sheepish—"you kinda made me lose track of time."

Julie's eyes blazed with anger. "Well, I saw you got over it," she snapped, and gripped the cart handle. "Let me pass!"

"Julie, I can't let you go away mad," Luke pled. "And all kinds of people come up to say hello to me at the rodeo," he added earnestly, "I can't help it if some of 'em are girls. I didn't ask 'em to do it."

Julie hunched a shoulder. "You needn't explain to me," she retorted proudly. "Your friends are your business. Now let me pass!"

Luke raised his hands from her cart and stepped aside, but he walked alongside her as she pushed forward. "They ain't my friends," he explained. "They're fans. Haven't you ever been to a rodeo before, Julie?"

"Plenty of times."

"Well, you see it happen to other riders, don't you? I promise you, I can't help it unless I'm downright rude. I'd hate for folks to think I was stuck up, or didn't appreciate them."

"Well, I think you've proven that," she retorted. "Leave me alone!"

He stopped dead in the aisle to let her pass, and his voice went low and soft. "Please, Julie," he pled, and in spite of herself, the pained tone in his voice made her stop and glance at him over her shoulder. His big blue eyes were on her, and the look in them was as full of *I'm sorry* as a little boy's.

Julie paused in doubt, and in that split-second of indecision, Luke moved up and put his hand beside hers on the cart handle.

"Why don't we start over," he pled. "Go out to lunch or something." The look she shot him made him add, "Oh, I know it was bad, Julie, and I wish I could go back and change it, but I can't. I can only say I'm sorry and try to make it up to you."

Julie stared down at her hands and tried to get control of her anger. *Remember why you're doing this*, she told herself. *Don't get sucked into his games.*

She took a deep breath, took a fresh grip on her resolve, and forced herself to smile—just a *little* bit.

Luke brightened instantly. "Why don't you go ahead and check out, and we'll go to a little place I know outside of town. It's just a little shack, but it has the best barbecue in the world."

Julie tried to look gracious, but the best she could scrape up was a sour smile. "Well...all right, Luke." She glanced down at her cart. She'd barely started shopping, but she'd finish later. It was more important now to take advantage of Luke's reappearance. To let him think that she was seething with jealousy, but that he'd won her over.

His shock would be that much greater, when she showed up in Houston with his rival.

She comforted herself with that mental image as she waited in the checkout line.

She watched through the big front window as Luke walked outside to his car. She'd agreed to let him drive her over to the little barbecue place for lunch, and then bring her back to the grocery.

Julie frowned as she set a bottle of dish washing liquid on the little checkout belt. She was becoming impatient with her own plan. Spending time with Luke had become frustrating, because half of her wanted to punish him, and the other half...

She glanced out the window again. Luke was leaning against the wall outside with his hands in his jeans pockets and his eyes on the ground.

She slapped a bottle of mineral water down on the counter, trying to block out the memory of Luke's big, hurt eyes. From replaying the pained tone in his voice.

She used to think he was play acting, but now she wasn't so sure, and it shook her confidence. He was behaving just like a decent man. He'd explained what happened at the rodeo, he'd apologized for it, and he'd looked and sounded sincere. Unless he was the world's best actor, he'd meant at least *some* of what he'd just told her.

The elderly clerk smiled at her as she reached to scan the groceries. "Having a nice day, dear?" she murmured.

Julie shot a frowning look at Luke. "I'm not sure," she murmured, and ignored the startled look the clerk gave her.

She picked up the paper bag of groceries and walked out of the store. Luke stepped up and reached for it.

"I'll take that," he offered. "Let's put the bag in your car, and you can ride to the restaurant with me."

Fine, Julie thought dryly, and led him to her car. She waited as he slid the bag into the back seat.

Luke straightened, took her elbow, and walked her toward a gleaming motorcycle parked near the curb.

Julie looked up at him in alarm. "Wait, we're not going to the restaurant on *that*?" she objected.

Luke grinned at her. "Sure. It's safe."

Julie's eyes returned to the motorcycle. She'd have to climb onto his bike and slide her arms around him to avoid falling off, but it wasn't just the sketchy safety that irked her. She couldn't help remembering the blonde she'd seen on that seat a few weeks before.

Her anger whisked to life in a shower of sparks, but she snuffed it out again with a deliberate effort. She was going to have to play along if she wanted to teach Luke the lesson he needed to learn.

She stood in the parking lot, arms crossed, as Luke climbed onto the bike and cranked it up. He turned to flash her a big grin.

"Come on."

Julie inhaled deeply, but walked up and climbed onto the bike behind him. She looked, but she couldn't find anything to hold onto except Luke; and he half-turned to smile, "Hold onto me."

Julie pulled her mouth to one side in exasperation, but sent her arms sliding around the white tee shirt he was wearing. She could feel the smooth muscles of his back and chest through it.

She frowned and tried to clear her mind, but Luke was all muscle, and she could feel the tiniest move he made through that thin cotton.

Luke turned again. "Tighter," he smiled. "You don't want to fall off!"

Julie frowned, but laced her fingers loosely over his chest. She closed her eyes as the bike started rolling, then opened them with a gasp as the engine roared and they blasted off like a rocket down the street. She dug her nails into Luke's ribs, then scowled as he half-turned to laugh at her.

"You did that on purpose!" she cried into the wind, and he laughed and gradually slowed the bike down again.

"No I didn't," he teased.

"Yes, you did!" she fumed, and then pinched him hard to hear him yelp.

"Ow!"

Chapter Thirty Five

To Julie's relief, it didn't take them long to get to the barbecue joint. Luke pulled the bike up onto the lawn of what looked like a private home on the edge of Green Oak. The yard was filled with cars and trucks, and the ancient gray clapboard house had a rusted tin roof, a stone chimney, and a sagging porch. It looked a hundred years old at least.

The front entrance of the house was covered only by a screen door, and a neon beer sign over the counter was dimly visible through it. The sound of country music and laughter wafted through it, along with the heavenly aroma of a mesquite wood smoker somewhere in the back.

Luke nudged the bike's kick stand out and glanced at her over his shoulder. "Hate to say it, but we're here," he grinned.

Julie blew her hair out of her eyes, released him, and dismounted the bike. She smoothed her hair back self-consciously as Luke threw his long leg over the seat and reached for her hand.

Julie bit her lip, but let him take it and followed him across the lawn to the porch steps. Julie looked up as the climbed up to the porch. It was her home town, but she'd never been to this house before, didn't even know who'd lived there.

Luke opened the groaning screen door and led the way inside. The little dining room was crowded with patrons, mostly local men, and they turned to look, then looked again.

Luke led her up to the counter and glanced down. "What d'you want?" he murmured.

Julie glanced up at the menu board. It was on the wall behind the counter and it listed only six items: pork sandwich, beef brisket, pork ribs, cole slaw, beans, mac and cheese, Texas toast.

She shook her head. "You're the one who knows this place," she told him. "What's good?"

"The ribs are the best in town," he told her. "I like the cole slaw, too. It's dry and it's got a nice kick of vinegar. Not too sweet, or swimming in mayonnaise."

Julie nodded. She was a Texan. Barbecue and its attendant sides were a local art form; and nothing was worse than soggy cole slaw.

"I'll have that, then," she nodded. "And a glass of half-and-half tea."

Luke nodded at the waiting cashier. "Make it two." He glanced around the room and added,

"It's a little crowded in here. Wanna go outside and eat out there?"

Julie nodded. There was a thin white layer of smoke hanging just under the ceiling from the cigarettes, and she felt a dozen pairs of appreciative eyes on her.

Luke touched her arm lightly. "Why don't you go outside and find us a place, and I'll bring the food with me."

Julie glanced up at him in relief and replied, "Look for me behind the house. There's no room in the front yard."

She slipped out of the little room and out onto the porch. The old boards of the porch creaked as she pattered down the steps and drifted around the side of the old house, looking for a picnic spot.

It was a warm, sunny day, and she discovered that the back yard of the little house was green and pleasant. The lawn was covered in old oak trees, and their huge branches were only half-visible through clouds of bright spring leaves.

To her relief, the back yard was empty; and she meandered under the shade of the old trees, looking for a soft spot to sit down and eat. She found a big oak tree in a quiet corner at the very back of the yard and sank down onto a patch of new grass at its foot. She was wearing a pink cotton top and a pair of jeans and loafers, nothing that a little grass would hurt; and so she crossed her feet at the ankles, looped her arms around her knees, and waited for Luke to find her.

She looked up at the sky through the fluttering new leaves. The breeze was pleasantly cool and caressed her cheek.

It was a nice place to spend a little time. Restful.

Julie glanced behind her. There were no other houses nearby; the metal fence that formed the back yard had a pasture on the other side of it, and she could just make out a few tiny horses grazing in the distance on its far side.

"There you are!"

She looked up to see Luke walking toward her. He had a smile on his face and a cup caddy in one hand and a bag in the other. He walked over, handed her the bag, and flopped down on the ground beside her.

"Whew!" he sighed and handed her a sturdy plastic cup. Julie took it and sipped a bit of tea. It was just right: crisp, ice cold, not too sweet.

Luke opened the bag and tossed a roll of paper towels down on the grass. "I got us some paper towels," he began, and dug out a square styrofoam container. He handed it to her and pulled out another one.

Julie opened the lid of her container. A heavenly aroma of smoked pork and barbecue sauce came curling up to kiss her nose. She licked her thumb hungrily.

Luke set his container down on the grass and reached for her hand. Julie frowned and tilted her head.

"What?"

Luke's blue eyes stared into hers earnestly. "Grace."

Julie glanced down at the ribs, but closed up the container and reached out for Luke's hand. He closed his big brown hand over her fingers, clasped them warmly, and bowed his head.

"Lord, we thank You for this beautiful day, and for the chance to enjoy this good food." He paused, then went on, "And I thank You,

Lord, that I have the chance to be here with Julie."

Julie frowned and opened her eyes to shoot a glance at Luke's face. His eyes were closed tightly, and he was frowning in concentration.

He looked sincere.

"Amen," Luke murmured, and squeezed her hand before releasing it.

"Amen," Julie echoed weakly, and opened up her lunch container hungrily. She had no fixed religious belief, but it was easy enough to humor Luke's.

She picked up a pork rib. It was a glossy burgundy shading into a deep brown on the ends. She took a delicate bite and was immediately rewarded with a rich, smoky, tangy sauce over meat so tender that it that practically disintegrated in her mouth.

"*Mmm*," she moaned, and licked the sauce off her fingers. "This is really good."

Luke nodded. "I told you." A thoughtful look crossed his face and he raised his eyes to hers.

"Julie, you're still coming back to class, aren't you?"

Julie shrugged and didn't answer right away, and Luke's expression clouded. He put the rib down.

"I'd hate to think that you gave up on learning to ride," he said softly. "You've been doing good."

She glanced at him, and he put his meal down and scooted over the grass to sit beside her. He watched as she set the rib down, and he added: "Julie, I—I didn't have a chance to ask you before, but I'd like to get to know you better."

Julie picked up another rib and smiled a bit. "What would you like to know about me?"

Luke pulled up a blade of grass, twirled it in his hands. "Well...are you from here, or somewhere else?"

"I was born in Gween Uk," she mumbled through a mouthful of pork.

"Huh," Luke muttered. "I never saw you growing up, and it's a small world around here." He turned his head to look at her. "I'm sure I would've remembered you."

Julie dabbed her mouth with a paper towel and weighed her answer. She didn't know how much Trina might've told Luke about her; and so she chose her words.

"I moved out of state when I was eighteen," she replied carefully. "I went away to school to learn to be a physical therapist. I just moved back here a little while ago. Now I work over at the hospital part time."

Luke took a spoonful of cole slaw. "Mind if I come over to your work sometime?"

Julie smiled and looked a question, and he pointed to his leg.

"My knee's been griping me for the last few days."

Julie shrugged and tried not to feel pleased. "Of course you can," she smiled. "But I won't be allowed to help you. You'd get a male therapist."

His face fell. "Oh."

Julie lifted her cup with a little smirk. "It's office policy." She glanced at Luke sideways to enjoy his reaction. It wasn't true, but she wanted to see how he'd respond.

She couldn't say she was disappointed. He'd looked as crestfallen as she'd hoped he would. She wasn't sure if that was because she still wanted to punish him, or because she wanted him to be eager to get her personal attention.

Luke pulled up another blade of grass. "Julie, I'd like to see you again. Away from the riding class, I mean." He looked over at her with an almost pained expression on his face.

Julie tried her best to seem indifferent, but inwardly she was elated. She placed the bare rib bone daintily on the little pile she was building on the ground and said nothing.

"I like you, Julie," Luke told her softly. "I guess you've figured that out by now," he added wistfully. "Can I call you?"

She turned to look at him, paused to deliberate, and finally sighed: "I guess so."

Luke scooted so close that they almost touched. He took her chin in his hand to turn her face toward his.

"Julie, I want to kiss you," he whispered. "Can I?"

Julie lowered her eyes to hide the pleasure in them. It was exactly what she wanted, but she judged it wise to show some hesitance.

"Well, I…"

The light blotted out, and Luke's lips touched hers, then moved softly over them. Julie closed her eyes and thought jubilantly: *I've got him now.*

She turned to twine her arms around Luke's neck and murmured her own soft reply. She gave him little teasing kisses astray of his lips, on the tip of his nose, across his chin.

The object was to frustrate him, and it worked. He suddenly turned his head and crushed her lips under the same rush of kisses that had swept her away the first time, and Julie smiled and sent her hands down his back. She closed her eyes and let Luke run wild, because that was the plan.

To get him hopelessly tangled up with her. To make him fall in love.

She turned her head just enough to gasp, "Oh, Luke..." She rolled her eyes up and dug her nails into Luke's back as his lips wandered down her neck. She struggled to stay in control, to hang onto her wits, but in spite of everything they were beginning to slide away.

Julie's chin tilted up. She'd never met a man who sent her to the moon like Luke Spade; and just as her pulse was throbbing in her ears, and her breath was coming in gasps, and she was ready to throw all caution to the wind, Luke's kisses suddenly paused.

The shadow over her lifted, and Luke let her go. Julie frowned in confusion, and she had to brace herself to keep from falling backwards on the grass.

She brushed a tendril of hair out of her eyes. "What's wrong?" she murmured, then bit her lip for admitting she was upset; but Luke didn't seem to notice. He was sitting cross-legged on the grass, and he was staring down at it with a troubled look on his face.

When he turned to answer her, his blue eyes were clouded and worried. "Julie, I—I wasn't handing you a line when I said I want to get to know you," he mumbled. "I really do. But I can't do that right if we go too fast." He bowed his head. "I want to be a gentleman. But I guess I haven't done such a great job of that so far."

Julie's concern vanished. She dimpled and reached for him. "What if I tell you that I don't mind at all?" she whispered, and held out her white arms.

Luke shot her a longing look, but he shook his head. "I'm sorry, Julie," he told her, and straightened suddenly, as if he'd made up his mind. "I've got into all kinds of messes going too far, too fast. I don't want to do that with you."

He raised his eyes to hers, and the look in them now was soft and pleading. Julie stared at him in frustration, because she had no choice but to sputter: "W-why—I don't understand why you're worried, Luke, but—if it's *that* important to you, then I guess I understand." She bit her lip in irritation. Luke had been right on the edge of losing control, but he'd regained it at the last minute.

Now she was going to have to try again later.

Luke's tone was soft and genuinely grateful. "Thanks, Julie," he murmured, and he reached out for her hand, squeezed it.

Julie mustered a smile that she hoped was gracious, but a swirl of conflicting emotions were fighting each other in her chest. Her heart was still pounding, her mouth was dry, and she wasn't sure why she was frustrated— because she wanted Luke, or because she wanted revenge.

At that moment, both seemed to be true, and both had been delayed. Worse, it was the second time that going into Luke's arms had made her lose sight of everything except how good he made her feel. And that was bad. That was *dangerous*.

She wanted to get revenge for Trina, not to end up just like her.

Luke pulled a piece of paper out of his shirt pocket. "Give me your number, Julie," he murmured. "I'd like to call you later."

Julie shot him an exasperated glance and thought tartly: *Why, so you can come over and tease me a third time?*

I'm supposed to be torturing you!

Luke looked up at her, pencil poised over the paper, and she sighed and gave him her number. He smiled at her, tucked the pencil and paper back into his pocket, and reached for a barbecued rib.

He took a bite, made an *mmmm* face, and smiled at her with his cheeks stuffed, like a kid.

Julie stared at him in a mix of exasperation and dawning affection, and a troubled frown clouded her face as he mumbled:

"Tell me about your family growing up. I still think I should know you."

She licked her lips, reached for the cup of tea, and stalled for time to dream up an answer.

Chapter Thirty Six

"Well, would you look at that."

A grin spread across Buck's face, and he nudged Kate in the ribs as Luke breezed past them. They were relaxing in the lounge chairs around the pool, and Luke waved as he walked across the patio.

As he passed, they smiled to see a pair of small brown hand prints tattooed across the back of his white tee shirt, and they both hunched down with smothered laughter.

Buck sat up and called, "Hey Luke, where you been all day?"

"Buck, don't," Kate whispered in amusement as Luke paused with his hand on the sliding patio door.

"Aw...just over to Green Oak," Luke mumbled, and rubbed his hair with one hand. "Just messing around."

"Well I can see that," Buck nodded, and pointed to his shirt. "You must've had some help."

Luke frowned and pulled his tee shirt around his body. His face fell as he saw the telltale barbecue prints on the back.

He looked up and his face went red. "Ah..."

Kate rose gracefully and pulled a caftan over her swimsuit. "I think I'll leave you two alone," she murmured, and breezed past Luke with a smile.

He watched her go into the house, then turned back as Buck called, "Come on over and tell me about it."

Luke ambled over, dropped down onto the recliner Kate had vacated, and pulled the shirt over his head. He held it in his hands and looked down at the sticky prints.

Buck reached over, swiped a bit of barbecue sauce off, and put his fingers to his lips. His brows rose.

"*Mmm-mm,* that's good! Where'd you go?"

"Over to a little place I know in Green Oak," Luke murmured. "I took a girl there. She signed up for the riding class I'm teaching."

Buck nodded. "The girl you were looking for at the rodeo?"

"Yeah." Luke stretched out in the recliner and leaned back into the cushions.

Buck shook his head. "Well, I guess you talked her back around," he drawled.

Luke turned to look up at him. "No, that's just it," he murmured with a troubled expression. "I didn't do much talking at all. Not near as much as I should've." He sighed and shifted in the chair impatiently.

"I always go straight to necking," he admitted with a sigh. "I've been told I'm kinda good at it, so when I want to impress a girl, I— I kinda fall back on it. I know it'll give me a better chance with her. But I always get in a mess because of it, because then things don't have nowhere to go but—well, *on*." He threw the shirt onto the ground in frustration and glanced up at his older brother.

"I promised the Lord I was going to turn over a new leaf, and I'm trying, Buck. But I never knew till now how *hard* it is," he exclaimed. "I've never really tried before. And now I meet the prettiest girl I've ever seen in my life, and I got to hold back. I'm all worn out from it.

"She makes me awful weak."

Buck nodded and did his best to hide his smile. "Yeah, it ain't easy to do right sometimes, that's a fact," he agreed solemnly. "What's this girl's name?"

"Her name's Julie," Luke replied softly. "Prettiest girl in the world, Buck. Her hair's as black as night, and her eyes are as blue as the sky. And she's got a figure that like to popped my eyes out, the first time I saw her." Luke shot him a wistful look.

"I think I'm in love with her."

"Oh, Lord have mercy," Buck sputtered and shook his head.

"No, I mean it," Luke told him earnestly, and leaned over to poke his arm for emphasis. "I've never felt this way about any other girl."

Buck gave him an amused look. "Haven't you just met her? How long have you known her?"

Luke leaned back into his own chair. "Oh, I know it hasn't been long," he replied. "But she's hit me right between the eyes, Buck."

"That's not the same thing," he replied with a twinkle; but he decided not to chaff Luke any more about it. He could see that Luke was taken with this girl, whoever she was; and he could at least be glad that Luke wasn't moping around over the other one any more.

"Why don't you invite her up here?" he suggested. "Introduce her. I'd like to meet this girl that's roped you up so tight after just—how long has it been?"

A reluctant smile spread across Luke's face. "About a month now," he admitted. "And I want to bring her up here, but I wasn't even sure she'd go out with me today. She was pretty mad at first." He rubbed the back of his neck. "She thought I was flirting with those girls at the rodeo."

Buck raised an eyebrow and tilted his head. "Can't say I blame her," he replied. "That's how it looked to me."

Luke raised startled eyes to his face. "Now you know that's not right," he objected. "I can't help what they do. That's what I told her, too. I guess she must've seen I was telling the truth, because she let me smooth her down."

"Wait, now, I'm confused," Buck objected. "Is this the same one you told us left the rodeo with that other man, what's his name?"

"Justice Owens," Luke replied glumly, and frowned. "Yeah, she's the one."

"Maybe she's not as smoothed down as you think," Buck smiled.

"She was mad," Luke mumbled. "I wanted to ask her about that, but I was kinda on credit with her today. I didn't want to push my luck." He adjusted one shoulder. "But I am gonna ask her. I don't like to think of her with Justice. He's got a mean streak. He's ugly inside and out."

"He looks bad tempered, I'll give you that," Buck agreed. "Well, I wouldn't worry about it. It looks like you beat his time with her today, anyway," he sighed.

"I hate the thought of Justice even being around her," Luke growled. "I know why he was at that rodeo, and why he left with Julie. He was there to spy on me, and he must've seen me and Julie together, and figured out she was mad after I left her. He saw a chance to get at me, and nothing makes him happier. I don't know why."

"I do," Buck retorted. "He always looked as green as a new apple when you were around. He's jealous of you, boy. He knows you're a better rider than he is."

"Maybe," Luke shrugged. "We were pretty even matched most times. He hates to lose, I know that."

Buck clapped his shoulder. "Well, don't worry about it," he replied. "You're not going back onto the circuit, so you don't have to be devilled with him. And I'd be willing to bet that if you put your mind to it, you can make little Julie forget all about him."

Luke turned to give him a wistful glance. "I hope she went with him just because she was mad," he murmured. "I can't think of any other reason she'd do it."

Buck burst out laughing and shook his head, and Luke turned to look at him.

"What?"

Buck gripped the arms of the recliner, stood up, and wrapped a towel around his trunks. He smiled down at his younger brother, patted his shoulder, and returned to the house.

He walked slowly up the staircase, right to the top flight. He turned into the only door on that level, and as soon as he walked in, his little daughter came running up to him with her arms held out.

"Daddy!"

Buck reached down and took her in his arms. "Well, doodle bug," he smiled. "How's my best girl?" He gave her a smack on the cheek and looked down at a book she was holding.

"What you got there?"

Molly showed it to him. "It's a book of paper dolls," she replied proudly. "Princesses."

"Well now, ain't they pretty," Buck agreed, and set her down. She skipped off to her bedroom, and Kate walked up to him in a flowing cotton caftan. Buck slid an arm around her waist and led her to the couch.

He sat down with a sigh and stretched an arm across the back of the couch. Kate sank down beside him and snuggled onto his bare chest.

"How's little Russ?" he asked her.

"I just put him down for his nap," she sighed. "He should be good for a few hours now." She turned to look up at him. "What were you and Luke talking about, or is that prying?" she smiled.

Buck turned to kiss her hair. "Aw, he thinks he's in love with a little girl he just met," he sputtered and shook his head. "That's Luke all over. He's easier than any man I ever knew. He takes to folks just like a kid."

Kate giggled and looked up at him. "Well, you said you were worried about him," she murmured. "If he's found a new girl, that's a good thing, isn't it?"

"Real good," Buck agreed. "I told him to bring her by the house, so we can all meet her."

Kate ran her fingers absently through his chest hair, then looked up to ask, "That would be fun. Why don't we have her and Luke over to

a big pool party or a treasure hunt or

something? Nothing too fancy, just a fun time

together. It'd be a good way for her to meet

the family without feeling awkward or singled

out."

"That's a nice idea," Buck sighed. "I'll talk to

Luke and help you if you want to put it

together." He stretched his arms wide. "That

swim made me hungry," he yawned. "Got

anything for dinner?"

Kate patted his chest and stood up. She

glanced down at him over her shoulder. "I have

a roast in the crock pot," she told him. "It's my

own recipe. The splash of whiskey's the secret

ingredient."

"Bring it on," Buck told her, and she laughed

and walked off to the kitchen with her

diaphanous gown rippling gently behind her.

Buck watched her go, and his smile faded.

He didn't let on, but he was a little worried

about Luke's new girlfriend. Luke was a grown man, but it was still true that he fell in love way too easy, and way too soon. Usually before he had a chance to really know the girl.

He just hoped that this time, it'd work out.

But there was nothing he could do except let Luke figure it out for himself: and so he got up and went to see if he could snitch something to eat before dinner.

Chapter Thirty Seven

"Julie?"

Julie pulled her ponytail over her shoulder and looked up from the foam mat. The secretary was standing in the doorway of the physical therapy room with a knowing smile on her face.

"You have a patient."

Julie stood up, clapped her hands clean, and frowned. "I don't have an appointment for ten today," she replied in surprise. "Is it some kind of emergency?"

"I don't think so," the girl replied with a puzzling smirk. "Just a walk in."

Julie shrugged. "All right, post the questionnaire. I'll see them in five minutes."

The girl smiled and pulled the door closed behind her, and Julie readied the therapy room for a new patient. For a walk in, she'd probably just be doing an interview to determine what the problem was, and maybe a brief examination to see how extensive it was.

She sat down at a little computer console and pulled up the patient calendar. The secretary had already scanned the questionnaire.

Male, Julie mused, *early thirties, sports injury to the shoulder. Probably a sprained or torn muscle, or a rotator cuff injury; though it says the pain is persistent, not severe.*

She tapped a pencil against her mouth for a moment, then called the front desk.

"Barb, you can send him back now."

"Okay." The receptionist sounded amused, and Julie frowned in puzzlement as she hung up the phone; but the mystery was solved as soon as the door opened.

Luke Spade's six-foot frame filled the opening, and Julie rose with a flush of surprise and—she wasn't sure what else.

"Luke!"

Luke' face split into a sheepish grin. "Yeah, I was in the neighborhood and thought I'd drop by," he smiled. His bright eyes skimmed the big therapy room, and he walked over to plop down on the corner of one of the exam tables. He swung a long leg back and forth.

"This is a nice place," he approved. "Lots of windows, plenty big."

Julie's eyes narrowed in exasperation, but she pulled a chair up beside the table and sank down into it.

"Are you gonna be my doctor today?"

Julie felt her face going hot. She'd told Luke she wasn't allowed to see male patients.

"Um...it looks that way," she replied uncomfortably, and tucked a sprig of hair behind her ear. "The male therapist is out sick today.

So your shoulder's been hurting you?" she added, and tried to keep her embarrassment out of her voice.

"Yeah," he smiled down at her.

"Which one?"

Luke raised a hand to his right shoulder. "This one."

"*Mmm*. When did you injure it?"

"I think at the rodeo," he told her solemnly. "It's the shoulder that gets jerked around when I ride. From me holding my arm up."

Julie felt a flick of concern and glanced up at him. "You haven't done anything else lately that might hurt it?"

Luke scratched his ear. "I guess not."

Julie stood up beside him. "Do you feel like you've lost any strength in that arm, any range of motion?"

"No, can't say I have."

"Let me see you raise that arm, slowly and gently."

Julie watched as Luke raised a muscular arm, and crossed her own. She tilted her head to one side. "Now stretch your arm out in front of you...now out to the side."

She watched as he moved his arm, smoothly and without any apparent hesitation.

"Are you feeling any pain right now?"

Luke glanced at her out of the corner of one eye. "Well, ah...yeah, I got a little twinge there."

"Where, exactly? Show me."

Luke gave her a crooked smile and slowly pointed to a spot on his right shoulder.

Julie frowned. "Do you mind if I look at it?"

"You go ahead."

Julie shot him an exasperated glance, then reached up and gently palpated his shoulder muscle. "Does that hurt?"

Luke rolled his eyes to hers. "Maybe a little bit."

Julie tried to raise his shirt sleeve further up, but it obscured her view of his shoulder. She struggled with it for a moment or two, then murmured, "Do you mind taking your shirt off, so I can see it better?"

Luke replied, "No ma'am! Here we go." He reached back and yanked the tee shirt off his back like he was casting a line, and Julie's eyes widened for an instant. Luke's bare chest and arms were sold muscle, golden brown, and looked smooth as silk. She swallowed and closed her eyes and frowned.

"Ah...just...sit still for a minute," she stammered. She could hear her own heart thrumming in her ears, and she had to catch her breath before she could go on.

Luke sat on the edge of the exam table and stared at the far wall as she moved her fingers over his firm brown shoulder. Julie closed her eyes and tried to focus on her job, but the knowledge that Luke was faking made that harder than she expected.

He'd come in to flirt with her, and she was enjoying that as much as he was.

"I don't see any inflammation," she coughed, and released him.

Luke rolled his eyes to hers. "Well, ah— maybe it's the kind that comes and goes."

He twisted around to face her and added, "Julie, since I'm here, I thought I'd ask if you'd want to come up to the house."

She turned away from him and retreated to her little desk. "I'm working today until five," she replied, in as professional a tone as she could muster.

Luke wriggled back into his shirt, hopped off the exam table, and came over to stand beside her. "Oh, I don't mean today. The family's having a big party out at the ranch. We're gonna cook a whole cow on the spit, and have a treasure hunt and a dance and all kinds of stuff. I'd sure be glad if you came. It's next weekend, on Saturday."

Julie stared at the computer screen without seeing it. For an instant the sight of his bare chest shimmered in her imagination. She couldn't keep it out, and she could feel herself weakening.

"Well, I—"

"Aw, come on," Luke grinned. "It'll be fun."

Julie bit her lip and shot him a wavering glance. The boyish, eager look in his eyes was the *coup de grace*.

"Okay then, Luke."

He brightened instantly. "Good!" He stuck his hands in his jeans pockets, swayed back and forth, and lowered his eyes to the floor.

"What about a kiss for a hurting man?" he asked, and raised hopeful eyes to her face.

Julie reached for a purple brochure and stuck it in his face. "This is what I have for a hurting man," she replied briskly. "It's a leaflet on sports injuries. It tells what to do for a minor sprain."

Luke took it with a disappointed glance. "Aw come on, Julie."

"I'm not allowed to fraternize with my patients," she told him matter of factly, and moved past him. She walked across the room to the door and held it open for him.

He shuffled to the door with every sign of reluctance and paused to give her a puppy dog look.

"Not even one?"

Julie cast an embarrassed glance behind her. The secretary and two patients in the waiting room were staring at her. She cleared her throat.

"If you have any other problems, follow the instructions in the brochure," she announced.

Luke stuck the brochure in his shirt pocket. "Yes ma'am," he murmured sadly, and walked to the outer door. He gave her another sad look before walking out, and Julie coughed and walked back inside the therapy room.

She'd no sooner gotten inside than she leaned against the door and giggled; but the laughter suddenly died on her lips. It struck her just then, that she hadn't thought of revenge even once that day.

And what shook her even more, was that she found the reminder almost unwelcome.

Chapter Thirty Eight

Julie arrived home that afternoon, pulled her phone out of her purse, and was finally free to check her messages. She found that she had a half-dozen. She set the phone down on the kitchen table and pressed the red button on the little screen. Justice Owen's gravelly voice instantly reminded her that she'd gone out with him. A little flush of guilt heated her cheeks as his message swirled out into the air.

She opened her refrigerator door and looked for a TV dinner as he growled, "Hey Julie, this is Justice. Just wanted to tell you I'll be down your way in a few days. Thought I'd see if you'd like to go dancing. Call me."

Julie grimaced as she peered into the fridge. Justice reminded her that she was supposed to be keeping her mind on revenge, and that he could help her get it.

It also sparked a twinge of guilt, because while she was willing to go out with Justice a time or two, she couldn't honestly say she liked him even a fraction as well as Luke.

Which also was a problem. She didn't like Luke, or at least she wasn't supposed to.

Julie pulled a bottle of pomegranate juice out of the fridge, opened it, and took a swig as the next message played. It was from Trina, which caused her a rush of dismay. She hadn't thought about Trina in days.

To Julie's relief, Trina sounded much more like herself. Almost cheerful. "Hi Jules," she chirped. "Just wanted to call you. I know you've been worried about me."

The bottle in Julie's hand drifted down from her mouth as she frowned in remorse. She *was* worried about Trina. She just hadn't been as focused on her lately, that was all.

She'd been too busy making out with Trina's ex-boyfriend.

I'm getting distracted, Julie frowned. Maybe I'm even in danger of getting sucked in. It's all very well to make Luke fall in love with me, but I can't let myself feel anything for him. I can't lose sight of what he did to Trina.

And yes, it's true that Trina still thinks Luke is a great guy, but Trina's naive. I can't take her word for it, and I can't let him get to me.

Luke may seem caring, but he's an 'aw shucks ma'am,' cowboy. That means he's a train wreck when it comes to women. Bad news.

Trina's baby probably isn't the only one he's got out there.

Who knows, he could have a small army of them!

Julie came back to herself, and Trina's voice was saying, "....and she told me that I was eligible for an automatic pay increase when I'd worked there three months. I was *so* relieved, Jules!"

Trina's voice nattered on about her job and how the apartment was coming along, and Julie listened patiently; but when the message was over, she switched the phone off.

I need to call her back, she thought, *but not now. I'm too beat tonight.*

She opened the fridge, pulled out a t.v. dinner, and walked across the kitchen to pop it into the microwave. She glanced at it as she slid it in. It was some kind of quinoa veggie bowl thing that she'd bought after she found out she'd gained a pound.

As the bowl started to rotate, Julie's memory served up Luke's smiling invitation to their party.

We're gonna cook a whole cow on the spit.

Julie closed her eyes and bit her lip, because she could just see it: a glossy brown roast turning slowly over an open fire as a plume of barbecue smoke curled gently into the air.

Her stomach growled, and she frowned and leaned against the cabinets. Her memory was showing her something else, too: the way Luke had looked shirtless back on the exam table. The sight of his glorious brown chest—all muscle—was the most perfect and beautiful she'd ever seen outside of an art museum, and one thing was becoming crystal clear.

This revenge thing wasn't going to be as easy as she'd thought. She hadn't counted on Luke being so gorgeous. If and when she reeled him in, it was going to be tough to throw him away after, even if she did it in the name of justice.

The microwave beeped, and Julie opened her eyes and popped the door open. Her quinoa salad was ready: but when she grabbed a pair of pot holders and pulled it out, her salad was mostly beige, and the steam rising up from it smelled of...nothing.

Julie stood there for a moment, staring down at it: then she marched to the trash can, dumped it in, and went to the fridge to search for bacon.

Thirty minutes later, Julie had polished off a BLT sandwich with potato salad and a pickle on the side. She'd brought a little paper container of rum raisin ice cream, too, and sat watching t.v. and absently eating it.

Maybe I should just drop this revenge thing, she thought as she watched a ballerina leap across a stage. *Trina doesn't seem to even want revenge, and the more I see of Luke, the more I wonder if I'm wrong about him.*

So far at least, he doesn't seem to be a mean person.

She took a spoonful of ice cream. *Maybe he isn't a bad guy,* she mused, *or at least, not bad enough for me to hunt down. He's hardly the only man in the world who didn't want to commit to his girlfriend; and as painful as that was for Trina, it was their business, after all.*

Maybe I overreacted out of sympathy for Trina. Maybe I was too quick to make Luke out the villain.

Maybe I should just...leave him alone. Let the universe take care of him.

Julie sighed and took another bite of ice cream. She *was* involved with Luke, though; and even if they weren't deeply involved, letting Luke go might still be a little awkward. She'd agreed to go to the party at his ranch, and the odds were good that Luke would get her off someplace alone while they were there.

Julie frowned as she stared at the t.v. She hadn't dreamed, when she'd started out, that she could ever *want* Luke Spade to kiss her; but that was before she'd found out how good he was at it.

Julie suddenly dropped the spoon into the ice cream container. *What am I saying?* She thought in irritation. *I'm so confused, I don't know what I want.*

I don't even know what to do right now.

And as for Justice—I told him I'd go out with him, so I suppose I should keep my promise. But if Luke isn't the monster I thought, I have no reason to make a habit of it.

My life is getting complicated.

Chapter Thirty Nine

"Well, this is the house."

Luke killed the motorcycle and nudged the kickstand out. Julie let her eyes roll up the front wall of the huge house in awe. She hadn't seen a house so big since she came home from L.A.

"You say your whole family lives here?" Julie murmured.

"That's right," Luke nodded. "Most of 'em are here today."

Julie pulled her arms reluctantly from around Luke's chest and dismounted the bike. She untied the kerchief she'd wrapped around her head and shook her long, dark hair out.

Luke sat on the motorcycle watching her. "Law," he grinned, "do that again!"

Julie laughed with him as he hopped off the bike. "Silly," she smiled.

Luke walked up, took her elbow, and squired her toward the massive front door. "Everybody's around the pool," he told her. "I'm going to introduce you. Don't expect to remember everybody's name. There's a lot of us."

Julie raised her brows in surprise. "I don't have any trouble remembering names," she told him, as they walked inside. She gazed around her in wonder as they walked into a huge, sunlit atrium. Dozens of people were milling in it, and Luke nodded to several as they moved through the crowd toward a massive staircase.

But Luke steered her across the marble-tiled space toward the eastern wall, which was mostly glass. She could see dozens more people gathered around a pool, and Luke opened a portion of the glass wall for them to walk out into the sunshine.

The first thing Julie noticed was that there was a massive side of beef turning on a spit, and that it was flanked by two industrial grills with all kinds of meat sizzling on them. The patio was littered with plates and glasses, and there was a mouthwatering aroma of wood smoke and barbecue in the air.

Luke walked up to a big man with coal-black hair and clapped him on his broad back. "Buck, I want you to meet Julie," he smiled, and took her hand. "Julie, this is my oldest brother Buck."

The big man turned to smile at her. "It's great to meet you, Julie," he nodded. "I'm glad you came to our party."

"I'm glad to meet you," Julie smiled back; and as she watched, a beautiful redheaded woman walked up and put her arm around

Buck. He looked down at her and murmured, "Julie, this is my sweetheart, Kate. Kate, this is Luke's guest, Julie."

"We're so glad you could come, Julie," Kate smiled. "Would you like a drink, or maybe some barbecue?"

"I'd love that," Julie murmured, and shot a sideways glance toward the grill. There were ribs, chicken, and steaks on it.

"Would you like tea, or wine, or maybe a margarita?"

"Tea would be lovely, thank you."

"I'll bring you one." Kate walked away to fetch the tea, and Luke nodded toward another tall, dark man sitting on the edge of the pool in his swim trunks.

"That's my other brother Morgan," he told her, "and the blonde woman sitting beside him is his wife Heather. The couple lying on the lounge chairs over there are my brother Carson and his wife Donna.”

“Morgan-Heather, Carson-Donna,” Julie murmured, to commit the names to memory.

“And the two guys on the other end of the pool arguing, that’s my brother Jesse and my other brother Chance.”

“Jesse, Chance,” Julie frowned.

Luke pointed to a little boy and girl splashing in the shallow end of the pool. “And those kids are my nephew Kit and my niece Molly. Kit is Morgan and Heather’s son, and Molly belongs to Buck and Kate.”

Julie’s frown deepened. “Kit and Molly.”

Luke turned to her and smiled. “I got another brother named Will, but he’s active duty Air Force and can’t be here.—Got it now?”

Julie smiled crookedly and nodded, because all the names had just jumped up and flown out of her head.

The smiling redheaded woman reappeared with a glass of iced tea, and Julie received it gratefully and took a sip.

"Would you like a plate?" Kate asked, but Luke shook his head and put a hand lightly on her arm.

"Don't worry, Kate, I'll get it for us," he smiled. "Thanks."

Kate smiled at him, and then at Julie. "We're glad you came, Julie. If you need anything, just ask."

"I will, thank you."

Luke took her hand and pulled her behind him to a big table set up beside the grill. "You tell me what looks good, and I'll get it for you," he offered.

Julie cast an awed glance at the groaning table and answered, "I'll have the potato salad, and the grilled corn, and some barbecue chicken," she added, with a sidelong glance at the grill.

"Coming up," Luke sang out, and grabbed a couple of plates.

Julie glanced over her shoulder at the all the people in Luke's family. *I'll say one thing,* she thought to herself. *The Spades sure are a good-looking bunch, for there to be so many of them.*

She tilted her head and considered Luke's brothers. They were all tall, dark and very handsome, but for her money, Luke was the best-looking. She liked fair men, and Luke seemed to be the only blonde in his family.

"There you go."

Julie turned to take the plate Luke handed her, and followed as he led her to a little vine-covered trellis on the end of the patio. There were patio tables and chairs on the other side of the trellis wall, and Luke held out a chair for her.

Julie smiled at his manners, and she wasn't surprised when he reached for her hand after taking his own seat.

"Grace."

Julie bowed her head to please him as he prayed. She was beginning to get used to Luke's old-fashioned beliefs; and the more time she spent with him, the more it seemed to her that he was sincere about them.

She glanced at him over the table. His face was drawn into an earnest frown as he asked blessings on their food. His blonde bangs were falling down into his eyes, and he shook his head slightly as he murmured his prayer.

It was sweet; or at least, it looked sweet. She was still keeping a corner of her mind independent; but she could admit to herself that Luke was slowly winning her over.

"Amen," Luke said briskly, looked up, and grinned at her.

"Amen," Julie echoed in amusement, and reached for her glass of tea. She shot an admiring glance at Luke. He looked best in a simple white tee and jeans, and he was wearing them that afternoon. She remembered how thin that tee shirt had been when she was behind him on the motorcycle. How she could feel every muscle in his chest through it. Her eyes moved to his lips.

"So you grew up in Green Oak, huh?" Luke murmured. "My best friend used to live there."

Julie glanced up at him in time to see a regretful look wash over his face. She frowned. He actually looked....sad.

Not careless or smirking. *Sad.* And he'd described Trina as his friend, not his girlfriend.

"Oh?" She took a bite of potato salad.

"Yeah," he muttered, and poked at his food with his fork. "Me and her had kind of a...parting of the ways. I wish it hadn't happened."

Julie frowned at her plate. *Well, wasn't there something you could've done to stop it?* she thought. *You could've married Trina. Why didn't you?*

She looked up at him. "If you don't mind my asking—what happened?" she murmured, and watched his face.

Luke shrugged. "Aw, I guess it was my fault," he mumbled. "It still kinda stings. I'd rather not talk about it."

Julie's frown deepened. Luke looked genuinely depressed about his breakup with Trina. And he'd described her as his *friend*.

Was that how he'd thought of her, all those years?

She came back to herself. "I'm sorry. I didn't mean to pry," she replied.

His blue eyes raised to hers, and he smiled faintly. "You didn't," he assured her.

"How's your shoulder?" she asked, to change the subject. To her relief, he let her.

"Oh, lots better," he grinned, and rolled it to demonstrate.

"Did you do what the brochure said?"

He stared at her. "Huh?"

"The brochure I gave you," she replied in laughing exasperation. "The one about sports injuries?"

"Oh, oh *that* brochure!" he replied, and scratched his chin. "Well, to be honest, Julie, I didn't," he confessed.

"Why not? It would've told you what to do to feel better."

He shrugged and looked down at his plate. "Well...to tell you the truth, I don't read too well. Never have. It's hard for me to stick with most anything written up. I almost never finish it."

Julie stared at him in confusion. "But...it was just a brochure," she replied softly, and was dismayed to see him go red.

"I know. I've had that problem since I was a kid. I never did too well in school because of it."

Julie lowered her eyes, because she didn't want to make him feel embarrassed; but she thought, *That's so odd. It sounds almost like he has Attention Deficit Disorder.*

She struggled with herself, but the issue was important enough to make her override her reluctance to press him. She glanced up at him and murmured:

"Have you...have you ever been tested for Attention Deficit Disorder?"

Luke's blue eyes met hers, and the look in them was confused. "No," he murmured. "I don't even know what that is. See, me and my brothers were raised by our grandparents, and they were real old-fashioned. They didn't take us to the doctor unless we were busted up," he chuckled, and took a sip of tea.

Julie stared at him and tried to get her arms around what he'd just told her. She couldn't imagine a child trying to struggle through school, and then adulthood, with undiagnosed ADD. It would be like trying to run with a sprained ankle.

She put her hands on the table and leaned forward. "You should really look into that," she told him earnestly. "What you just told me sounds a lot like ADD. If you do have it, there are treatments that can help you."

Luke shot her a quick glance, then returned his attention to his food, and Julie closed her mouth. *I've said enough,* she thought, and watched him to see if he was offended; but Luke just took a bite of ribs and nodded.

"Thanks, Julie. I think I will. It's worth a shot, anyway."

Julie relaxed and settled into her seat. A flush of genuine pleasure bloomed across her heart, and she shook her head. *I can't help it,* she thought wryly. I *can't stop being a therapist.*

Even when I'm not sure how I feel about the patient.

The conversation trailed off into a peaceful silence, and they ate for awhile in silence. The barbecue was delicious, and Julie caught herself licking her fingers. She also caught Luke sneaking a peek at her as she licked her fingers, and she almost laughed aloud.

She glanced at Luke again, and he grinned at her. She smiled back and shook her head. It was plain she shouldn't have worried about mentioning ADD. The more time she spent with Luke, the more she saw that he wasn't a man who got offended easily, or who carried a grudge.

He's not like me, she thought with a sudden pang of conscience, and looked down at her plate. *I carry big, fat grudges. The only reason I came here in the first place was to get even with Luke. To hurt him.*

She glanced at him again. The Luke Spade sitting across the patio table had an open, sunny expression. His smiling eyes told her that he didn't have the first suspicion that she was there to hurt him.

In some ways, he was as trusting and transparent as a child. And she was taking a low, sneaking advantage of him. Julie frowned and her fork drooped down to the tablecloth.

I thought I was doing something good to get even for Trina. But I never thought it would change me like this.

I don't like the person I'm becoming.

"Is there something wrong?"

Julie blinked and looked up at Luke. He was staring at her with a faint frown of concern.

She pasted on a sickly smile. "No, why do you ask?"

Luke took a sip of tea. "You looked kinda sad, that's all."

Julie almost grimaced as her guilt deepened, and was relieved when Kate appeared behind them and put a hand on the trellis.

"The treasure hunt is about to start," she smiled. "Do you two want to join in?"

Julie rolled her eyes to Luke's with a laughing expression, and he blotted his lips with a napkin. "Why not. We're about done eating."

Julie shot him a prim glance and folded her hands in her lap. She had the feeling that Luke was going to do something to get her off someplace alone, and that suited her right down to the ground.

Kate's expression brightened. "Good! You better come back out by the pool. We're picking teams now."

Luke stood up and reached for her hand, and Julie gave it to him with a smile. She followed him out from under the pleasant shade of the trellis and into the sunny patio area around the pool. Julie scanned the crowd. There were now more people there, some of them Luke's family, but many more guests she didn't recognize. Buck Spade stood in the middle of the crowd of with his hands in the air.

"Everybody listen up! For the treasure hunt, you need at least one partner to form a team. Each team's gonna get a list of things hidden on the ranch, a map of the ranch, and directions where to find the treasure. Everybody gets five things to find, and the first one to get back here with all five, wins."

"What's the prize?" somebody shouted from the back, and Buck held up a red envelope.

"The first prize is a mystery," he called back. "You'll have to find out what it is when you win. But here's a clue: It's worth five thousand dollars!"

There were awed whistles, clapping, and laughter from the crowd as Buck held up the envelope. "The winning team has to get back here with all five things on their list, before anybody else. Choose up your partners and come get your lists!"

Luke turned to grin at her, then released her hand to shoulder through the crowd. He leaned in to grab a list, then came back to hand it to her.

Julie took it and read aloud:

1.   A plastic doll

2.   A silver dollar

3.   A newspaper

4.   An old bottle

5.   A postcard

She turned the paper over. There was a rough map of the house and the parts of the ranch closest to it, and a page of typed instructions filling the back.

Buck's voice blared out over the murmuring crowed. "All right, has everybody got a team? Let's see how many we have."

Five hands went up, and Luke grinned at her and added his own.

"All right, we got six teams! It's"—Buck checked his watch—"One o'clock. We're gonna give you three hours to find your treasures. Now the things on your lists are scattered around this ranch, but none of 'em are more than a half-mile away. We got six ATVs for everybody to use to go looking." He pointed back toward the front drive, and Julie turned. The corner of the house obscured most of the front courtyard, but she could see two ATVs from where she was.

"Is everybody ready?" Buck called and was answered by gleeful yips and yells. "All right then! Keys are in the ATVs. Ready...set...go!"

Luke grabbed her hand, and Julie laughed as he dragged her around the house and out to the ATVs. Luke slid into the nearest one, and other teams ran past them as Julie climbed into the front seat, giggling.

She grabbed the dash and braced herself as Luke cranked the motor and sent them careening out across the courtyard and into the drive.

"Quick, what do the directions say?" he yelled, and Julie flipped the page over and read:

"Molly's lost her princess doll. The princess ran away to a wishing well to ask her fairy godmother for a prince." She glanced over at Luke in confusion, but he pounded the wheel with his hand.

"That's the old well!" he yelped in excitement, and turned to her with his bangs fluttering down into his eyes. "It was here when Big Russ bought this ranch. It's down by the creek, across from the riding ring!"

He gunned the ATV, and Julie held on for dear life as he sent it careening down the driveway, then off the road and over the grassy shoulder and into a meadow. They laughed crazily as the ATV bounced them around like marbles in a box.

"Look out!" Julie shrieked, than laughed as Luke made the ATV veer away just in time to miss a tree stump. Their buggy bounced over the uneven ground, then plunged into a thick stand of pine trees and swayed back and forth to thread a path through them.

"There it is!" Luke cried, and pointed up ahead. A small well was barely visible through the trees. It was made of stone and had a small roof and a little bucket hanging from the hand crank.

Luke brought the ATV to a sudden stop at the side of the well and jumped out. Julie cried, "Look in the bucket!"

She watched as Luke skipped to the well, grabbed the bucket, and grinned at her. He held up a clear plastic bag.

"We got it!"

He came walking back and gave her the plastic bag. Julie took it and pulled a pretty princess doll out. It had long blonde hair and pretty blue ball gown.

"One down, four to go," Luke told her, and turned the wheel. "Where to next?"

Julie picked up the paper and read:

"Crazy Joe was an old man who used to live on this land. He didn't trust the banks and buried coffee cans full of silver dollars all over. Most of Crazy Joe's money has been found, but there are still a few coins left. Look for the 'X' near the big door."

Luke turned to give her a confused look. "An 'X' near a big door?" he echoed. He sat there with the motor running, and they didn't move.

"A big door sounds like it might be a barn," Julie offered, and Luke's face brightened.

"Let's look at the barn at the riding ring," he laughed, and gunned the ATV. They went roaring into a little forest of pine trees, and Julie shrieked as they weaved crazily between the trunks.

"Slow down!" she cried, and put her arms up in front of her face. A second later the ATV bounced in the air and smacked to a stop against a tree trunk.

Julie took a deep breath and looked up through her hair. The hood of the ATV had popped open and a thin stream of smoke was rising from the engine.

She looked over at Luke, and he shrugged and flashed an apologetic smile. "Must've hit a stump," he mumbled, and threw the door open. He walked around to the hood, bent down to inspect the undercarriage, and announced:

"Yeah, looks like the axle's busted. Nobody's going anywhere in this buggy today, that's for sure."

A faint frown dawned across Julie's face, and she put her hands on her hips as Luke slid back into the front seat. He turned to look at her and sighed, "May as well make ourselves comfortable. It'll be awhile before somebody finds us."

Julie raised an eyebrow, but thought: *Okay, cowboy. You want us to make out. That's all right with me!*

She turned to face him, smoothed her hair back a little, and trained a sweet, expectant look on him. Luke reached out to take her hand, and she squeezed his gently and smiled at him.

Luke looked down at her hand, and then up into her face, and said: "Julie, I was hoping we could get off someplace alone, so we could have a chance to talk. To get to know each other a little better."

A frown flicked across her brow, but Julie smiled and thought: *Well, he's winding up slow, but okay. I'm sure the pitch is coming.*

"What would you like to know?" she replied, and squelched a sigh.

Luke grinned at her and shrugged. "Well…just everything," he replied, and scooted a bit closer. "Who were your folks, and what did you want to be when you was a little girl. What you think, and what you do for fun, and what you want out of life."

Julie raised her brows. "That's a tall order," she laughed. "You want my life story?"

Luke's smile softened. "Yeah."

Julie sputtered, "Well…I was born in Green Oak, and my father was a pharmacist, and my mother was a nurse…."

She stopped suddenly, bit her lip, and shot Luke a wary look. She wasn't sure how much Trina had told Luke about her, so she should probably be careful.

"Yeah, go on."

"And, um...when I was a little girl I wanted to be a nurse like my mother," she added slowly.

Luke smiled at her. "That's sweet."

"So, um...when I got old enough I decided to be a physical therapist and went to school and got my degree."

Then, to change the subject, she added quickly: "How about you? How did you get into the rodeo?"

Luke slowly released her hand and leaned back in his seat. "Well, that feels like forever ago, now," he admitted, with a rueful laugh. "I started up when I was sixteen. We used to go see the rodeo when it came to town, and my brother Morgan told me I was good enough

with horses to try. So I started practicing at
the ranch, and then I started competing at the
local rodeos. I started winning, and so I moved
up to the bigger rodeos, and it kinda...went on
from there."

Genuine curiosity sparked in Julie's heart.
"Why do you do it?"

Luke's blue eyes looked startled, as if he
didn't understand the question. "You mean,
why do I bust broncs?" he asked in surprise.

Julie nodded, and he raised his brows and
answered, "Well...you might as well ask me why
I breathe," he muttered. "I just love it, is all."
He shook his head and smiled. "There's
nothing like the feeling of sitting on that horse,
and knowing he can kick you to the moon, and
that he wants to do it bad; and getting
launched out into the ring, and sticking with
him, no matter how hard he bucks and jerks
and twists around. It's the craziest carnival

ride in the world," he murmured, with a faraway look. "I ain't never taken drugs, but I guess it's kinda like that."

He turned to look at her. "You know?"

Julie stared at him, and affection bloomed in her. "No," she laughed. "I'll have to take your word. But aren't you afraid you might...get hurt?"

Luke looked down at his hands. "Naw," he smiled. "I don't think about that. If I did, I couldn't do it. Sure, I know guys get hurt. There was a guy last year got stomped by a bull. He's in a wheelchair now."

Julie's smile faded, and a cold hand gripped her heart. "That's awful!" she stammered.

"Yeah," Luke replied softly. "But that's the risk, and he accepted it. We all do." He looked up at her, and Julie felt her heart melting in mingled affection and fear.

"And," Luke shrugged, "if something was to happen to me, at least I've made my peace with God. If I get killed, it's all right, I'm ready to go."

He looked down again, "I ain't saying I'm a great Christian or nothing, I went for a long time there doing things I ought not," he added softly. "But if you belong to God, there's only so long you can run from him, before he ropes you, and throws you down, and makes you say uncle."

"Sounds painful," Julie drawled, and was surprised to see Luke nod and look serious.

"Yeah. Yeah, it is," he murmured, and turned to look at her.

"That's what I meant when I told you I'm trying to be a better man, Julie," he murmured. "I guess you wonder why I'm talking your ear off, instead of getting as tangled up with you as I can." His eyes moved to her hair, and he reached out briefly to stroke it.

"Well, I wouldn't mind getting all tangled up with you, Luke," Julie replied softly, and Luke pulled his hand back. He rubbed his nose and smiled.

"I wouldn't either, I promise you," he admitted. "But see, when I do that, I'm zooming right past this part." He turned to look at her. "The getting to know you part. I did that for a lotta years, and now that I see the difference, I kinda like this way, to tell you the truth.

"I kinda see why we're supposed to hold off."

Julie stared at him in confusion, but even if her mind didn't understand, her heart did. It melted in affection, and she reached for him. Luke took her in his arms, and they kissed a long, slow, sweet kiss.

Julie sighed and pulled back long enough to whisper, "If you're trying to be good, you're going about it in a funny way. Now I want to get tangled up worse than ever."

"So do I," he groaned softly, then pulled out of her arms. "Come on, Miss Julie," he told her with a determined smile. "Our buggy's busted, and we've dropped out of the hunt. We got to walk back to the house, and it's a good way."

Julie shot him a smoldering look. "You sure, cowboy?" she murmured. "I'm still right here."

Luke ran a hand through his hair and looked off into the distance. "No," he blurted. "I ain't sure at all.

"And that's why we got to go."

Chapter Forty

The next day, Julie pulled into the parking lot of the biggest grocery store in Green Oak. She'd had to force herself to go out and tend to her chores, because her heart and mind were so full of Luke that all she wanted to do was sit around and dream of him.

She was starting to scare herself.

The lot was full of cars, and its lights flicked on as she watched. The store was a black silhouette against a sunset of pink and lavender, and birds darted overhead on their way to their nests.

Julie opened the car door and slung her bag over her shoulder. She needed a gallon of milk, some frozen entrees, a bag of salad lettuce, and...

She looked up sharply as a red truck pulled up beside her. She started to walk around it, but the driver pushed the passenger door open and leaned across the seat to smile:

"Wanna ride?"

To her surprise, it was Justice Owens; and she found that she didn't particularly want to get in his truck; but on the other hand, it would be rude of her to refuse.

She smiled and pointed to the store. "I was just going shopping," she told him, and drifted closer to the truck. To her amazement, Justice leaned over and grabbed her by the wrist.

"I'm not letting you go," he told her with a smile. "You may as well get in."

Julie sighed in mingled dismay and guilt; but unless she was willing to offend him, she had no choice but to climb in. She plopped her bag on the seat, and as soon as she clambered inside, he reached across the seat to close the door and turn the truck around.

Out onto the road.

Julie licked her lips and tried to keep her tone light. "What's this all about, Justice?" she asked warily and stared at his face.

"Just a surprise." He turned to smile at her, and his eyes were glowing with what looked like happiness.

"Where are we going?" she pressed, with her eyes still on his face.

"I'm kidnapping you," he chuckled.

Julie's heart quivered in her chest. "Kidnapping me?" Her eyes moved uneasily to his face.

"That's right. I'm taking you out to dinner, so you don't need to go grocery shopping."

Julie's spurt of nervous laughter sounded weak even to her, but she was thinking: *Oh, thank God. There for a minute I was almost...scared.*

Justice turned to smile at her, and to her relief, his eyes were glowing and his tone was happy.

"I saved up for us to go to someplace real nice," he smiled. "You're gonna love it."

Julie relaxed a bit. *Okay*, she thought, *maybe I misunderstood. Maybe he's just one of those men who's awkward around women. Maybe he meant to be playful, not scary.*

He can't help it that he looks rough.

"What..what restaurant are we going to?" she asked.

He turned to smile at her again, and bounced slightly in his seat. "A real swanky place. It's in Dallas," he beamed.

Julie frowned at him. "*Dallas*—that's two hours away! Justice, I have to get up early to work tomorrow," she objected. "Why, if we were already there now, it'd take us at least an hour to eat, and two more hours to get back, and that would be after midnight!"

He shrugged. "What's more important to you, losing a little sleep, or spending time with the man you love?"

Julie's mouth dropped slightly open, and she turned slowly to stare at him. He sat there with his hands wrapped around the wheel, staring straight ahead.

She waited for him to start laughing, to tell her that he'd been joking, but he showed no signs of it.

He's crazy, Julie thought with a thrill of fear. *I'm in this truck with a crazy man.*

Justice turned to look at her, and his expression was stone cold serious; then it suddenly melted into a smile.

"Ha—had you going, didn't I?" he teased, and Julie collapsed into nervous laughter.

"You sure did," she laughed, and glanced sideways out the window.

"Don't worry, Julie. I know it's a long way off, but I'll have you back home before midnight, I promise."

Julie rolled her eyes to his, and as they turned off the main road onto the interstate, Justice showed her what he meant. He jammed his boot down on the gas, and the truck roared down the road like a bullet-shaped blur.

A little over an hour later, Justice pulled the truck up in front of an elegant brownstone in a quiet neighborhood. They were still about ten miles out of Dallas, in one of the city's affluent suburbs.

"This is it," he told her with an excited smile. "It's French. I hope you'll like it."

"I'm sure I will."

Julie glanced at the big house. There were gas lanterns sputtering outside the front doors, and as they drove up, an employee stepped out of the shadows and came to open the passenger side door.

"*Bon soir, mademoiselle,*" the man smiled, and Julie tucked a stray tendril of hair behind her ear. She'd dressed for the grocery store, not a fancy restaurant; but her jeans and tee shirt would have to do.

"*Bon soir,*" she murmured, and took the hand he offered. As she stepped down from the truck, Justice handed the keys to another man who circled around to the driver's side.

Justice walked up and extended his arm, and Julie took it with a smile, but also with misgivings. She still wasn't entirely sure that she was comfortable with Justice Owens; but she had to admit that he was spending a lot of time and money to show her a pleasant evening.

The door swung open, and the interior of the restaurant was dim, illuminated only by gas lamps and candles. But the feel was colonial, with wooden floors, paneled walls, and elegant toile wallpaper.

The greeter met them with menus in hand. "Good evening," he smiled. "If you'll please step this way."

Julie smiled at Justice as he led her through the restaurant to a cozy booth in the corner of the dining room. Julie slid into the booth and received a menu from the greeter.

"Tonight's special is cassoulet with French bread," he told them smoothly, "I recommend it with a nice red wine like Madiran or Corbières."

Justice settled in heavily beside her, and Julie perused her menu in the dim glow of the candlelight. She tried not to let her surprise show on her face, but the prices were breathtaking, and she glanced at Justice in sympathy.

"What would you like to drink tonight?" the greeter inquired.

Justice stared at this menu and scratched his nose. "I'd like a nice red wine to start," he mumbled, "and the Boeuf Bourguignon." he handed the menu to the waiter.

"What would you like, mademoiselle?"

Julie closed up the menu. "I'd like the lamb chops with the cognac dijon cream sauce," she replied, "and a glass of Chablis."

"Very good. I'll be back with your beverages."

Julie turned to Justice in surprise. "I wouldn't have guessed you were a wine drinker," she smiled.

He shrugged. "I'm not. But tonight I decided to expand my horizons. I haven't had a lot of fancy in my life. It feels good to get some of it, now and then."

Julie stared at him in sympathy. It was obvious that Justice hadn't had many of the finer things in life, and she felt ashamed of herself for suspecting him. He deserved to have a nice time. He was going out of his way, and going to a good bit of expense, to show her one, too; and so the least she could do was to be impressed.

"It's very nice of you to go to all this trouble," she told him. "You didn't have to, really."

"I wanted to," he told her. "I want us to get to know one another, Julie."

A pang of guilt flicked through her, and she was relieved when the waiter appeared with their drinks. She accepted the wine glass she was offered and took an uncomfortable sip.

Justice was taking their casual acquaintance far more seriously than she did. After their time together at the party, she was convinced that Luke was a good man after all. Her heart and her mind were full of him. There wasn't any room for Justice.

I shouldn't be encouraging him, she thought. *Now that I know how I feel about Luke, it isn't fair to keep stringing Justice along.*

She set the glass down on the table and gave him a chastened look. "Justice, I—"

He cut her off by leaning back and laughing suddenly. "Yeah, I hope nobody I know sees me going into a French restaurant," he chuckled. "They'll think old Justice's gone fancy on 'em. Become a party boy. Well, I take that back. We all partied pretty hard, on the rodeo circuit.”

Julie pricked up her ears. “Oh?” she asked, and took another sip of wine. She stared at him over the rim as he shrugged.

“Oh, sure. Maybe I shouldn’t talk about it in front of a lady, but the rodeo circuit can get pretty wild. There were lots of hard partiers, back in my salad days.”

The return of the waiter kept Julie from asking the question on her lips, and she waited until he’d set their entrees down, refilled their wine glasses, and withdrawn to murmur:

“What was that you said?”

Justice took a spoonful of stew. “Mmm?”

“About…about partying on the circuit.”

“Oh yeah,” he nodded. “Everybody did. Most of us were unmarried men, and young. In a new town all the time, all amped up.”

Julie adjusted one shoulder, then turned back to her meal. She took a small bite.

"Yeah, I don't like to tell on another man," Justice went on, "and specially not a man I knew for so long. But Luke Spade had us all beat. He sure had the system! Had those buckle bunnies lined up ten deep, every night!"

Julie felt the blood draining from her face. She reached for the wine glass.

"Luke was popular, and that was why the management put up with him, I guess. But everybody on the circuit knew he was a wild man." Justice shook his head. "Every night we all went right from the rodeo to the bars, and ol' Luke always had three or four girls hanging on his arm. He had more women in one month than most guys had in a year."

Julie looked away to hide the tears stinging her eyes, and the shocked look she was sure she was wearing. *I don't know why I'm surprised,* she thought miserably. *I know about Luke's past, he told me himself.*

Still, she made a small, strangled sound, and Justice glanced down at her. "Oh, I'm sorry, Julie," he murmured, with a regretful look. "I know that's got to be hard to hear. But it's the God's truth, and I'd hate to see a girl like you get tangled up with a guy like Luke Spade."

Justice went on: "Well, Luke was like most guys on the circuit, only more so. A lot of young guys play around. Sowing their wild oats." He took a sip of wine.

"But then me and the other guys started noticing other things about old Luke," he went on. "Nights that he lost his round at the rodeo, he'd get in a real bad mood. He'd still go with us to the bars, but the booze made him mean. I saw him backhand a girl with my own eyes once in Kansas City. The rest of us had to drag him out of there to keep the management from calling the cops."

Julie turned to frown at Justice in outrage, but he gave her a bland, level look.

It can't be true, she thought. *The man I was with yesterday was sweet and honest and kind. He'd never do anything like that.*

Would he?

The man Justice was describing was the opposite of the Luke Spade she thought she was coming to know. The Luke Spade she was starting to love.

In his place, Justice was describing a selfish, womanizing, and even violent man that no sane woman should trust.

Justice sighed gustily. "Even that ain't all," he went on. "The guys on the circuit started to notice things missing. We couldn't figure it out for a long time, but we finally found out that Luke had been swiping money and other stuff out of other guys' lockers. You'd think that a man as rich as Luke Spade wouldn't need to steal. But I guess it gave him some kind of a cheap thrill."

"Stop," Julie begged, and wiped her eyes. She couldn't hide her tears, and Justice's expression softened as he looked at her.

"I'm sorry, Julie," he murmured. "I'm sorry to bust up the idea you had of Luke in your mind. But it's better you should know what he is now, than to find it out the hard way.

"Lots of girls have."

Like Trina, Julie thought with a stricken look.

"Well, let's don't talk about him," Justice added in a sympathetic tone and reached for his wine glass. He lifted it in a toast.

"To honesty," he smiled. "And good wine."

Julie was already holding her wine glass, and it was almost empty; but she lifted it numbly and touched Justice's glass.

His twinkling eyes quizzed her over the rim. "Down the hatch, now."

Yes, Julie thought brokenly. *Down the hatch.*

"I'm going to be competing at the Fire and Fury Rodeo in Houston in a few days," Justice told her. "Why don't you come down and see me?"

Julie stared into her wine, and then lifted her eyes. "I'd love to, Justice," she replied defiantly.

"I'd enjoy that *very* much."

Chapter Forty One

By the time the red truck pulled up to Julie's condo, it was almost one o'clock. The moon was half-hidden behind a ragged veil of clouds, and the air had turned chill.

Justice flicked off the headlights, and Julie turned to him and murmured, "Thank you for a lovely evening, Justice. I had a wonderful time."

"I'll walk you in," he told her, and climbed out of the truck. He walked around to open the door for her, then helped her down, put a hand on her waist, and walked her to her own door.

Julie unlocked her front door and flicked on the foyer lights. "Would you like to come in for a minute, Justice?" she asked.

"That'd be fine," he murmured.

The big man stepped through the opening, closed the door behind him, and followed her to the kitchen. Julie tossed her handbag down on the bar and opened her fridge. "Would you like a cup of coffee to warm you up before you go home, Justice?"

"Thanks." He leaned against the counter, crossed his arms, and watched as she stuffed a coffee filter into her coffeemaker, filled it with coffee, and then with water.

The coffee started percolating, and Julie turned and asked, "How do you like your coffee, Justice—black, or with sugar or cre—"

Justice grabbed her before she had a chance to finish, and she only had time to gasp. His big fingers dug into her arms, and his breath brushed her cheek. "You're as sexy as all fire, aren't you, you little vixen?" he breathed. He yanked her to his chest without warning, crushed her to his chest, and leaned in to kiss her.

Julie raised her hands and pressed them against his chest. She learned that Justice liked to kiss hard and rough; and then, that he liked to move fast. She opened her eyes in shock as he released her arms and sent his hands wandering down her hips.

She balled her hands into fists and pushed away from him with all her strength. She laughed uncomfortably and gasped, "Whoa, whoa there cowboy!" She straightened her blouse and stepped back from him a pace. "Don't you think you're going a little fast? This is only the second time we've been out, remember." She stepped back another pace, stuck her hands on her hips, and questioned him with her eyes.

There for an instant, she wasn't sure how he was going to react; but to her relief, a sheepish look flitted across his face. "Sorry, Julie," he mumbled. His eyes flicked over her again, and he licked his lips. "You kinda make a man forget his manners."

Julie felt her face going hot, and she brushed a wayward strand of hair back from her brow. "Why don't we call it a night, *hm*?" she smiled. "It's getting late, and I have to work tomorrow."

Another, unreadable look crossed his face; but he nodded. "All right, Julie," he replied softly. "You go ahead and get your rest." He licked his lips and asked: "If I promise to mind my manners, can I kiss you good night?"

Julie glanced at him in dismay, but he added: "I promise."

Julie brushed aside her discomfort and mustered a smile. "Of course."

She stood unmoving as Justice stepped in, leaned down, and pressed a warm, firm kiss on her lips. "Good night, Julie," he murmured, and brushed her hair back from her brow softly. "I'll call you."

She smiled more naturally. "Good night, Justice."

She followed him out to the front door and watched as the big man turned and walked out to the street. He opened the door of his truck, climbed in, and drove away.

Julie sighed and turned back inside. She closed the door behind her and frowned as she drifted back to the living room. She plopped down on the couch and nibbled her thumb nail as she reviewed the evening.

The conclusion she came to was that she might've bitten off more than she could chew. She'd never meant to go out with Justice more than a time or two. She'd expected them to have a couple of pleasant evenings together, and that they'd soon go their separate ways.

Justice had approached her first, and he knew she was involved with Luke; but the fact remained that she'd only agreed to go out with him to punish Luke.

That was her plan; but of course Justice had a different one.

She blew a sprig of hair out of her eyes. She'd never known a man to get so handsy so fast, and it made her uncomfortable. Justice was at least a hundred pounds heavier than she was.

If he decided to overpower her, there'd be nothing she could do about it. The thought made her shudder, and she rubbed her arms; but it comforted her to remember that when she'd complained, he'd backed off and apologized.

He'd just got a little too revved up, that was all. Justice might be a little rough around the edges, but she was pretty sure that he meant no harm.

In that respect, he compared favorably to Luke Spade.

Her expression darkened as she remembered what Justice had told her about Luke. *It's a lucky thing I'm going out with Justice*, she thought angrily. *Otherwise I wouldn't have heard what he knew about Luke.*

Julie's frown deepened, and she bowed her head. If she was honest with herself, part of her anger was that Justice had made her wonder if the Luke she'd started to fall in love with, didn't exist.

It hurt to wonder if the sweet, gentle Luke that had won her heart was only a mask worn by the *real* Luke—a dark, selfish, manipulative man who'd weaponized his looks and his charm.

That was what she had once believed; but gradually, she'd discovered a different man.

Luke a liar, a cheat? Surely it wasn't true. It couldn't be.

Julie rubbed her arms, as if she was cold. Justice's accusations against Luke made her miserably unhappy; but as long as she was going out with Justice, she was no doubt going to go on hearing them.

Chapter Forty Two

Luke opened the door to the doctor's office and walked in nervously. He hated to go to the doctor. He hated the big, sterile hospital halls, the creepy white coats, and the needles.

Being in the doctor's office made him real glad he was healthy.

He held his hat in his hands and glanced around. The waiting room was green and brown and quiet, and it made him itch all over. There was a handful of people scattered around, all watching their cell phones or reading. They all looked as glum as if they were going to a funeral, and he glanced back at the door.

But if there was a chance he might find out what was wrong with him, he had to see this through; and so he sighed and ambled reluctantly to the front desk. The little blonde girl there was facing a computer and didn't look up at first, but she finally turned.

She looked up at him, looked again, and swiveled around with a big smile.

"Do you have an appointment, sir?" she chirped.

Luke rubbed the back of his neck. "Yeah. Luke Spade, three o' clock, Dr. Peterson."

"Spade," the girl echoed, and consulted a chart. "Yes, I have you down." She handed him a clipboard and nodded toward the sofa. "Fill this out and bring it back to me along with your identification and your health insurance card." She dimpled at him again, and Luke nodded to her.

"Yes, ma'am."

He took the clipboard, walked over to the sofa, and plopped down with a sigh. He pulled a pen out of the clipboard clasp and began to fill out the boxes; but then he paused.

The questions were about *feelings*, and *thoughts*, and all the stuff he'd never talk about to strangers, and he frowned and crossed his legs, and then uncrossed them.

Sure do get up in your business, he grumbled under his breath, as he scratched out his answers. *I ain't even talked to my family about this stuff.*

He finished up, then reached for his wallet to pull out his driver's licence and insurance card. He glanced at the blonde girl at the front desk, and she met his eyes and smiled again.

Guess she's gonna see this, too, he thought glumly; but he had no choice but to get up and go over to hand the clipboard to her. He watched as she made copies of his cards, and tucked them back into his wallet when she handed them back.

"We'll call you back when the doctor's ready to see you," she told him, and he stifled a sigh, but nodded.

"Thanks."

"You're welcome," she dimpled, and Luke glanced back at her before he walked to his seat.

He sat down on the couch with a gusty sigh, stuck his legs out, and crossed them at the ankle. He pulled his hat down over his eyes, laced his fingers together over his chest, and settled down for a nap.

He figured he was going to have time for one.

He drifted off, and woke only when a nurse at the far door called out in a voice like a trumpet.

"*Spade*! Luke *Spade*!"

Luke roused up with a start and pulled his hat off his eyes. *Well, I guess I'm up,* he thought, and stood up slowly. He walked across the room to the far door, where a heavy, middle-aged woman with large glasses and spotted blue scrubs greeted him.

"Follow me, Mr. Spade."

Luke followed her slowly. She stopped in the middle of the hall and nodded toward a scale. "Please step up on the scale, Mr. Spade."

Luke stepped up on the scale, and the nurse leaned in. "Two hundred fifteen pounds," she murmured, and scribbled it down on her clipboard. "If you'll follow me."

She stood to one side of room number three, and Luke walked in reluctantly. The room looked tiny to him. Made him feel like a big dog in a little kennel.

Hardly enough room to turn around.

"If you'll sit down on the table, Mr. Spade, I'll take your blood pressure."

Luke climbed up on the table and stuck out his arm. The nurse rolled up his sleeve and wrapped the cuff around it, and Luke sat there patiently as she took the reading.

"Your blood pressure's normal," she told him with a smile. "Even a little on the low side."

"Good," Luke muttered fervently. He reached up and loosened his collar with his free hand.

"The doctor will be in to see you in a minute," she told him, and breezed out. The door closed with a snap, and Luke was left alone with his thoughts. He scratched his arm and sighed.

What am I doing here, he thought uncomfortably. *I'm not sick, and this place makes me...*

The door opened suddenly, and a man wearing a white coat breezed in. "Good afternoon, Mr. Spade," he smiled, and extended his hand. Luke shook it, and the doctor sat down behind a computer console and consulted the screen.

"I'm Dr. Peterson. You're here for an ADD consultation today, is that it?"

Luke adjusted one shoulder and looked away. "Yeah."

"Why do you think you might have it?" the doctor asked, and turned to face him with his fingers laced over his knee.

"Well, I..." Luke swallowed and looked down, then away. "I never am able to finish anything," he finally grumbled. "I have a hard time bearing down on a job, or reading something to the end."

The doctor nodded. "Well, that's a start. Has anyone else in your life suggested that you might have it—your parents, your siblings, maybe your kids?"

Luke looked away again. "My—girlfriend told me I should go to a doctor to see if I have it," he replied.

"I see. Well, an ADD diagnosis isn't a one and done," the doctor told him briskly. "It's a process. ADD is a developmental disorder, not an illness. The first thing we usually do is have you fill out a special questionnaire about yourself." He unclipped a few papers and handed them to Luke.

"There are about eighteen questions on this questionnaire," the doctor told him. "I want you to indicate how often each one is true for you: never, rarely, sometimes, often, or very often."

Luke glanced down at the paper with a frown.

"I'm going to step out for about twenty minutes to give you a chance to fill it out," the doctor went on. "I want you to consider each question carefully. When I return, we'll discuss your answers."

The doctor clapped him on the shoulder and walked out of the room. Luke glanced after him as the door swung shut, then looked down at the questions.

Problems remembering appointments.

Procrastinate.

Trouble concentrating.

Restless.

He frowned at the words, and they slowly faded away. In their place, he was seeing his old third-grade classroom, and his teacher's irritated face. The other kids were giggling.

"Try again, Luke," she sighed, and crossed her arms. "From the beginning."

He closed his eyes as the shame he'd felt washed over him again. He struggled to focus on the words, struggled to get them out of his mouth.

"The...black h-horse..."

"Yes, yes, the black horse," the teacher prompted. "Go on."

"The...the..the bl-black..."

"Go on. Don't keep repeating."

"Black...the..the black..."

"Luke's a dummy!"another boy sniggered, and the teacher snapped, "All right, never mind Luke, we'll move on to someone else. Peggy, *you* read the sentence."

He sighed, and slowly the classroom faded back into his memory. He looked down at the questionnaire and lifted the pen in a trembling hand and began to check the boxes.

Often.

Very often.

Very often.

Often.

He stared at the questions, and the page slowly blurred out again. He saw Buck standing in front of him with his hands on his hips, saw him shake his head. "Luke, what in the world am I gonna do with you? I asked you to brush down these horses three hours ago. There they stand, just the same as when I left."

He saw himself shuffle his feet. "Sorry, Buck. I just got sidetracked doing something else and...forgot."

He bowed his head. The scene shifted in his memory, and Trina's tearful face formed in his mind, and he saw her eyes full of hurt as she stared up at him.

"You mean you don't remember what day this is?"

Her words had gripped him like an icy hand, because he could see by her face that he should know. But he didn't have a clue, so he'd had no choice but to shake his head and brace himself.

"It's our *anniversary*, Luke," she'd told him in a quavering voice. "You forgot again, didn't you?"

"I'm sorry, Trina..."

Luke was still seeing Trina's face when the door opened, and the doctor walked in. Luke looked at him as he sat down again in front of the computer. "Well, let's see how you answered," he said, and reached for the clipboard.

Luke handed it over with a racing heartbeat. He watched as the doctor's eyes flicked over it, then inhaled and looked up at him.

"I'd say that based on these responses, we'd be justified to move on to the next step," the doctor replied. "That's a physical exam, because sometimes physical conditions can mimic the symptoms of ADD. If we don't find anything there, the next step is for me to talk to your family members. People who knew you well as a child. If they verify these answers, then we can move on to a diagnosis of ADD.

"Once we have a diagnosis, we can start thinking about treatment," he went on. "Most people with ADD have a combination of treatments: drugs, lifestyle changes, sometimes therapy. We'll try different things to see what works best for you."

Luke stared at him with painful intensity. "Doc, tell me...is this ADD thing something I'm doing, or is it...is it like being sick, where you can't help it?"

The doctor's expression softened and he leaned over to touch his arm briefly.

"ADD is not your fault," he said slowly and clearly. "It's a medical condition. You didn't choose it, and you can't help it. But I'm optimistic that we can improve your quality of life. Maybe a great deal, with the right treatment."

Luke stared at him, and for the first time in his life, his secret guilt and shame lifted off his shoulders like a huge rock being rolled away. His brothers had never really seen what he'd been dealing with: but the rock had been there, just the same.

It's not my fault.

It's not my fault.

The doctor stood up and patted him on the back. "You need to make an appointment at the front desk for your physical exam, and we'll go from there." He extended his hand, and Luke shook it numbly.

The door closed, and Luke sat on the exam table staring into space; then his golden head slowly drooped, and he put a hand to his eyes as his shoulders shook with years of pent-up grief.

Thank you Lord, Luke wept, and shook his head. *Maybe I can finally get shut of this thing.*

Maybe now I can stop letting everybody down. I'd give anything for that.

I'm grateful.

Luke exhaled with a long, deep breath, wiped his eyes. He squared his shoulders, pulled his hat down low over his eyes, then pushed off the table and walked out of the room.

Chapter Forty Three

"Hey, Julie!"

Luke's sunny voice reached out for her through the speakerphone, and Julie stiffened and crossed her arms as she remembered what Justice had told her about Luke.

That Luke was a liar, a thief, and a woman beater. She didn't want to believe it, but she couldn't forget it, either.

"Hello, Luke," she replied coolly.

"I don't know if I told you before, but I'm going down to Houston in a few days to ride in the Fire and Fury Rodeo," Luke murmured. "I was wondering if you'd like come down to see me ride."

Julie frowned and hesitated. After what Justice had told her about Luke, she shouldn't want to go anywhere to see him; but she still did, in spite of everything.

She bit her lip. "...All right."

Luke's tone brightened. "That's great! I have to go down early, but my family's going down to Houston to see it. You could go with them if you want to."

Julie glanced away in conflicting irritation and guilt, but replied, "Oh, I'd love to, but I have something else going on that night, and I'm afraid I'd make them late. I'll come down in my own car, though."

She thought, *If you flirt with more buckle bunnies at that rodeo, and we fight about it, I don't think I'll want to come back home with your family.*

"Well, that works, too," Luke agreed. "I sure am glad you can make it down. I'm looking forward to seeing you there," he confessed.

"Oh, I'll be there, all right."

"Great! It's at the Houston Stadium, and it starts at seven, but my event starts at ten," Luke told her, then added more softly:

"I'll be thinking of you when I'm in that ring."

I hope you will, Julie thought; but the tender tone in Luke's voice was already making her weaken, making her ashamed of her distrust. She closed her eyes and tried to hold onto her suspicions, but they were slipping away. She wanted to believe that Luke meant what he said, that he wasn't the thief and liar Justice had made him out to be.

"I've been thinking of you a lot, Julie," Luke went on, and his tone sounded warm and sincere. She could almost see his smiling, sky-blue eyes.

Julie bit her lip and struggled to stay mad, but Luke wasn't helping her. He wasn't acting at all like the liar and cheat Justice had described.

She remembered the times she'd been in Luke's arms. He'd shown self-control when she herself had wanted him to give in to temptation.

When she'd asked him why he didn't, he'd told her that he was trying to be a better man. Maybe he had been a wild man in the past, but he wasn't acting like one any more.

And it *was* true that Justice was jealous of Luke. Justice hated Luke, she'd seen that right away. Maybe he'd painted Luke much worse than he'd really been. Maybe he'd lied outright. He might just be trying to drive a wedge between her and Luke.

Julie closed her eyes and frowned as she murmured: "That's sweet, Luke."

"I mean it," he replied softly, and Julie frowned and thought: *I want to believe that.*

"I went to the doctor, like you said," he went on. "He told me that I might have ADD, sure enough. He gave me a long list of questions about myself. He said that my answers showed we need to go on to the next step."

Julie's anger evaporated, and she felt instantly chastened. A wave of sympathy and tenderness washed over her.

"*Oh.*"

Julie felt her face going hot, and she thought, *Look at me, scheming to make this man miserable, when he's probably been struggling with a chronic illness all his life. His symptoms may even have been the reason he and Trina broke up. She wouldn't have known why he was so unfocused.*

What's wrong with me?

"Yeah," Luke sighed, "I have to go back for a physical exam, and then he says he's gonna call my family in to answer questions about me when I was a kid." He chuckled, "He'll get an earful, that's for sure."

"I...I'm glad you're having it checked out," she mumbled, and ran a hand through her hair in distraction.

"Yeah. I just want to thank you for telling me about it, Julie," he told her warmly. "The doc says that if I have ADD, he can help me with it. But it's worth more to me, just to know that I'm not crazy."

Tears stung Julie's eyes, and she murmured, "No, you're not crazy, Luke. I'm glad I was able to...help."

Luke's voice went as low and soft as a whisper in her ear, and the sound sent tingling all down her neck.

"I appreciate it, Julie. I can't tell you how much." There was a long pause, and he added: "I'm really looking forward to seeing you down in Houston. I hope you wait for me after the rodeo. I'd like us to go out someplace after."

Julie grabbed for the last shreds of her anger, but they slipped out of her grasp and blew away for the last time. And as soon as they were gone, another emotion, far stronger and twice as certain, came flooding in. The reason she couldn't believe Justice was that...

I'm in love with Luke.

"I'd like that, Luke," she whispered.

"I'm real glad, Julie," he murmured softly. "I'll see you there, then," he told her. "Bye, darlin'."

"Bye, Luke."

Chapter Forty Four

The next day was her day off, and Julie spent a few hours shopping in town. She dropped by a little boutique full of cowgirl clothes, because she wanted just the right outfit for the big rodeo in Houston.

She wanted to knock Luke's eyes out, and she came out of the store with two bags and one box: one bag filled with a solid turquoise-colored cowgirl shirt, another filled with a pair of Wranglers that fit her like a glove, and brand-new turquoise cowgirl boots covered in wine-red flowers.

She was in a happy mood when she turned into her condo complex; but when she turned onto her street, she saw Justice's red truck parked outside her house, and her heart gave sickly thump. Justice was beginning to make her a bit nervous.

She hadn't counted on him taking such a shine to her; or maybe that was just what she told herself to feel less guilty for stringing him along.

She wanted to tell him that she wasn't interested in him anymore, but she hadn't been able to bring herself to do it so far. She wanted to choose the right time.

She had the feeling that Justice might not take it well.

Julie pulled the little VW into the driveway, but stopped short of going into the garage. She stepped out and walked to meet Justice, who was already halfway down the drive.

"Well, I didn't expect to see you here, Justice," she smiled.

"I got to go back down to Houston today," he replied, "so I thought I'd come and say goodbye before I lit out."

A wave of relief washed over her, and she slung her purse strap over her shoulder. "Well, why don't you come in," she invited. "Have a snack before you go."

"That sounds real fine," he smiled, and put his hand on her arm as she led him up the walkway and into the condo.

A prickle of something like fear crawled across her neck as she led him into the kitchen. "I have some sandwiches and tea," she told him. "A little wine, if you want something stronger."

Justice propped himself up against the counter and crossed his arms. "Surprise me," he smiled.

Julie busied herself with making sandwiches, and Justice watched her as she pulled cheese and mayonnaise out of the fridge.

"I'll be riding in the Fire and Fury Rodeo this weekend," he told her. "Why don't you come down to Houston with me?"

Julie shot him a quick glance, then shrugged and smiled apologetically. "Oh, I have a conflict," she murmured, "thanks anyway. Maybe we can make it some other time."

He frowned at her. "You told me you wanted to go," he objected.

"I'm a woman," she replied jokingly, and shrugged. "It's a woman's prerogative to change her mind."

His eyes narrowed. "This wouldn't have anything to do with the fact that you've been seeing Luke Spade, would it?" he demanded.

Julie glanced up at him quickly. *Why, he's been stalking me,* she thought in shock; but replied, somewhat tartly: "It's none of your business who I see, Justice. And I don't like the thought of you spying on—"

His expression hardened, and he grabbed her by the arm. "Look here," he growled, "don't you tell yourself that you're going to use me to get to Luke. Don't you even *think* about doing that. If there's anything I hate in this world, it's a lying woman."

Julie struggled angrily against his clutching fingers. "Let go of me!" she spat.

"I know what you're thinking, I can see it on your face," Justice added and narrowed his eyes. "You think you can play the two of us against one another. You think that's a funny game to play, do you?"

Rage surged up in Julie's chest, and she stared at him in wide-eyed fury. "Get your hands off me!" she snarled, and snatched her arm out of his grip. She danced back from him and held her throbbing arm resentfully.

Justice stared at her, and to her astonishment, a look of shame played over his face, like the shadow of a cloud flitting over a hill. He glanced down at the floor, then up at her again.

"I...I'm sorry, Julie," he muttered. "I shouldn't have got so wound up. It's just that...it's hard to see you with another man when I care about you so much."

"You have a funny way of showing it," she panted and stared down at her arm. There were four red marks where his fingers had clamped her skin.

"I'm a rough man, Julie," he told her in a deep, mournful voice. "I've had a hard life. But I had no call to let that...touch you."

Julie glanced up at him angrily, and he nodded silently, turned, and walked to the door. He paused there with his hand on the knob for a long moment, then looked back at her regretfully.

"I can't be nice and polite about you seeing another man, because...I think I'm falling in love with you."

He put on his hat, walked out, and closed the door behind him. Julie stood there staring after him in shock; but as soon as she'd gathered her wits, she hurried to the door to watch as he walked out to his truck, climbed in, and drove away.

I'm certainly not going out with you again, she thought to herself resentfully, and rubbed her throbbing arm. *Who do you think you are?*

I don't care how rough your life is, Justice Owens. You don't get to clamp my arm so hard that...

She glanced at the door and wondered what she would've done if that six-foot-tall rodeo tough hadn't backed off when she'd gotten angry.

If he'd just…kept coming.

The thought was so unsettling that Julie hurried back to the door and locked the deadbolt with a *snap*.

Well, at least now he isn't a problem for me, she thought and scanned the empty street beyond her drive. *I'll just tell him not to call me anymore.*

This is more than enough reason to tell him to shove off!

Julie looked down at her arm. The initial redness was slowly giving way to the first faint signs of a bruise.

Anger whisked up in her again, and she went to the refrigerator for ice. As she pressed a bag of frozen blueberries to her arm, her flare of anger slowly ebbed.

Justice *had* apologized for his outburst. He'd let her go. And she couldn't stop seeing the vulnerable look that had flicked across his eyes just before he left.

I think I'm falling in love with you.

She glanced back at the kitchen door and wondered if he'd meant it. Justice Owens didn't strike her as the kind of man who fell in love easily or lightly, and for an instant she felt almost sorry for him.

But the throbbing in her arm quickly reminded her that she'd do better to feel sorry for herself; and she grumbled as she pressed the frozen bag to her bruised skin.

Chapter Forty Five

The big football stadium was lit up like Friday night for the Fire and Fury Rodeo, and Julie shouldered through the crowd on her way up the stadium aisle. The Spade family had bought out a whole row in Section A; high enough to get a bird's eye view, and low enough to be close to the action.

Julie looked up and caught Kate's eye. The redheaded beauty raised her arm and waved, and Julie smiled and juggled her beer and pretzels as she climbed up to join Luke's family.

"Welcome folks, to the twentieth Fire and Fury Rodeo!" a warm male voice cried over the loudspeakers. "We hope you all have a nice time tonight. We've got an all-star lineup of ropers, riders, racers and wrestlers for you, and a corral full of the biggest, meanest, strongest, and fastest animals in Texas. If it can be rid, roped, thrown down, or tied up, it's here tonight!"

Julie settled onto the rodeo bleachers beside Kate Spade. She set her beer and her bag of pretzels down on the concrete floor and leaned out to wave at Buck, and Heather and Morgan, and Donna and Carson, who were further down the row.

Kate turned to her with a smile. "I'm glad you were able to come down to Houston," she murmured. "The rodeo's always fun, but it must be specially exciting to have a boyfriend competing," she added with a twinkle.

Julie sighed, but smiled and nodded. "Y-es," she agreed, and Kate laughed at her expression and patted her arm.

"No need to worry. Luke's an old hand at this. He knows what he's doing."

Julie nodded and looked away, then straightened up. Luke was climbing up the bleachers two steps at a time, and she jumped up and hurried to meet him in the aisle.

The Spade clan called out to him, and he raised a hand and grinned as they called; but he stayed in the aisle until she reached his side. Luke slid a hand around her waist and leaned in to kiss her. Julie received that kiss enthusiastically, but to her disappointment, he pulled away.

"I wanted to come and get a good luck kiss before I go back to get ready," he said softly, and brushed her cheek with his fingers.

Julie raised an eyebrow and twined her arms around his neck. "That was hardly even a real hello," she teased. "I can do better than that."

Luke bit his lip, but shook his head. "I'd love to stay and let you," he murmured, "but I got to go. Wait for me after the competition. I want us to go out after."

"I will," she smiled and brushed his unruly shock of hair back from his brow. He leaned in to give her another quick peck, then he smiled, put on his hat, and tipped it to her.

"Adios."

"Be careful," she told him. He grinned and sauntered off in the way a cowboy always did when he knew a young woman was watching him go.

Julie watched his broad back slowly disappear into the crowd and sighed. She returned to her seat, a bit crestfallen; and Kate patted her arm.

The announcer intoned, "Folks, we'll kick off tonight's rodeo with the National Anthem. Will everybody please stand."

A pair of riders burst out into the arena carrying billowing American flags, and the crowd stood up as the strains of the national anthem echoed through the stadium.

Buck leaned over and told Kate something, and Kate turned to her and took her arm.

"Julie, Buck says he meant to give Luke a lucky penny for his ride tonight," she smiled, and pressed a shiny penny into her hand. "Would you run down and take it to him? He's in the staging area at this end of the arena."

She nodded toward the end of the stadium, beyond where the goal posts would be at a football game, and Julie nodded.

"Sure, Kate," she smiled. "I want Luke to have all the luck he can get."

Kate beamed at her, and Julie stood up, pocketed the penny, and made her way to the big corridor behind the stands. She slipped through the crowd, passed snack vendors and restroom areas, making for the staging area where the riders waited to be called up.

The crowd thinned out as she approached the far end of the corridor. That area was more for the riders and rodeo workers, and at the moment at least, it was empty.

Julie turned to leave the big corridor and descend the bleachers, then gasped as a hand clamped down on her arm and yanked her sideways into a utility closet. She shrieked once, and another hand clamped over her mouth.

She rolled terrified eyes up to a huge shadow looming over her. The last sliver of light in the little utility closet revealed a shock of red hair, and two hard, dark eyes staring down at her. The door slammed shut, and the room went dark.

Julie's heart jumped in her chest. *It was Justice. Justice had caught her.*

He shook her shoulders. "I saw you coming in with that gang of Spades," he hissed. "Did you think I wouldn't see it? Did you think I wouldn't know why you're here?"

Julie shrank to hear the violent emotion in his trembling voice. *He's crazy,* she thought in terror. *Why didn't I see it before?*

Oh God, she prayed, *don't let me end up like Penny!*

He paused, then suddenly ducked his head to kiss her. His hand lifted from her face to be replaced instantly by his lips. Julie sputtered and struggled as he smashed his mouth against hers and dug his fingers into her arms.

She turned her head and shrieked again, and he smiled down at her and panted, "I can't trust you for nothing, you little black cat. You're always sneaking out, aren't you? Always looking for that old yellow tom cat out there.

Well, I'm going to take care of him," he growled, and kissed her again.

Julie frowned and turned her face away with a sob, and Justice shook her until her hair fell down over her eyes. "When there's no more yellow tom, they'll be nobody left for you to sneak out to," he nodded. "That's right, isn't it? *Isn't it?*

"I'm going to fix him," he muttered, and let her go. Julie fell back against a rack of soap and brushes, then stiffened in terror as she heard a faint, metallic ring. Something gleamed in the faint light coming in under the door.

She crouched there, watching in wide-eyed horror, waiting for Justice to kill her; but there was a smile in his voice as he muttered,

"Oh no missy, this ain't for you. This is for ol' Luke. Yes, sir. He's gonna look real good face down in the dirt. He's gonna look just fine with a broken neck, when his cinch straps break!"

Julie stared at the tall shadow in open-mouthed horror, and when he turned for the door she threw herself on him and clawed at his back.

"No, no!" she screamed, "*Help*, somebody! *He—*"

The next thing she knew, something smacked her face so hard that she spun around, crashed against a metal rack, and fell to the floor. She looked up through her hair to see Justice's dark silhouette against the open door. He stared down at her for an instant, and the roar of the crowd outside poured in through the open door. Then he closed it tight, and the room went black again.

Julie was seized by blind panic. She scrambled up again and grabbed for the doorknob. It was locked tight from the outside, and no matter how hard she shook it, she couldn't force it open.

She thought of Luke, sobbed, and beat against the door. "Help!" she screamed. "Help, somebody let me out!"

The crowd roared outside, and she heard a male voice announce: "Houston, put your hands together for our next contestant, a Texas boy, Luke Spade. In a few minutes Luke'll be riding in the Fire and Fury Rodeo for the first time in five years. Tonight he's riding a real tornado, the local legend, Busthead!"

There was another roar, and Julie pounded on the door. "Let me out, somebody please let me out!"

The crowd died down, and Julie beat on the door until it shook. Her head snapped up when a puzzled voice called from the other side of the door.

"Is somebody in there?" it called.

"Yes!" Julie shrieked. *"Let me out!"*

The knob turned, and she burst out. She pushed her rescuer aside and rushed down the wide corridor toward the staging area, shrieking, "Stop, stop! Somebody stop the ride!"

"And...here he comes!"

Julie reached the end of the stadium and went flying down the bleacher steps toward the chutes just as fast as she could run. She shoved people out of her way, screaming warnings that were drowned by the roar of the crowds.

Chapter Forty Six

Luke shouldered into his safety vest and grinned at his fellow competitor, Rusty, who'd been holding it up for him.

"Thanks."

"Good luck on that monster," Rusty told him and slapped his shoulder. Luke raised his hand as his friend walked off to go to the observation deck. He inhaled, shook his arms out, took a minute to get into the zone, and then sauntered up to the chute. Busthead was a big, muscular chestnut with a black mane and tail, and it greeted his arrival by kicking the metal rails until they rang.

Bang. Bang bang bang bang.

Luke paused to wait for the bronc to calm down. He inhaled, and was about to climb up the rails, when a familiar voice stopped him in his tracks.

"Hey, Luke! Long time no see."

Luke turned his head. It was Justice Owens. Justice stuck his hand out, and he shook it with a puzzled look.

"I just wanted to say good luck and welcome back to Houston," Justice smiled. "It's good to see one of the guys in our old crew!"

Luke raised his brows, but answered, "Well...thanks Justice." He shook his head and thought, *Well, what do you know.*

Busthead snorted and kicked the chute until it rang like a bell: *Bang bang bang bang.*

"He's a hot one," Justice observed, as he watched the bronc rattle the metal cage. "Here, let me help you. The other spotters are busy down the way, and you're up next. You need to have somebody help you in the chute. Go ahead and climb up."

"Thanks."

Luke grabbed the rails, climbed up to the top of the chute, and positioned himself to drop down slow and easy into the saddle. Justice was on the other side, and he nodded, "Go ahead. I'll spot you."

Luke exhaled and lowered himself gingerly into the saddle. Busthead bucked hard, and Justice shot an arm out to keep him from pitching forward and hitting the horse's neck.

Luke glanced at him gratefully. "Thanks."

"You all in?" Justice asked.

"Yeah. Just give me a second." Luke gripped the thick neck rope and prepared himself for the release. He glanced over, but Justice was bending down, as if he'd seen something wrong with the saddle.

"Is there something wrong?" he frowned.

"No," Justice called, and climbed off the rails. "I thought there might be, but you're ready to go. Ride 'em, cowboy!"

Luke glanced out into the huge ring over his left shoulder. Every face in the stands was turned toward him, and he leaned back, gripped the rope tight with one hand, raised the other, and nodded once.

The gate swung open, and Busthead exploded from the chute like a tornado. The horse went airborne and Luke leaned back, trying to match the bronc's jolting rhythm as it jumped and landed and jumped again. The coliseum lights streaked past like bright streamers and the roar of the crowd filled his ears.

It was just like always, just like old times, and the old adrenalin rush surged through his veins, put him on the top of the world. He raked his heels against the horse's flanks, and was getting into a smooth rhythm, when something suddenly snapped.

Luke frowned as his saddle slid to one side, dragging him with it, and he grabbed the rope with both hands. Busthead screamed and did a corkscrew twist, and he was launched into the air.

Luke twisted, fell, and hit the ground hard and face down. It knocked the wind out of him, but he rolled over quick to try to scramble up.

He raised his eyes, and all he saw was the bronc rearing to the sky right over his head. He saw his pickup men come swooping in, saw them grab for the halter; but the next thing he felt was the horse's hooves crushing his chest and his arm.

Searing pain burned his lungs. He gasped and tried to roll free, and the pickup men turned the bronc, but not before it kicked him again. Luke shouted in agony, and the next second a half-dozen faces were bending down over him. One of them yelled:

"Call the ambulance!"

Luke rolled his eyes up. The last thing he heard, before the world went black, was the screams and gasps of the crowd.

Oh Lord, he prayed.

Oh Julie.

Chapter Forty Seven

"Luke!"

Julie clawed through the crowd, gripped the metal fence with both hands, and was struck speechless to see a dozen cowboys kneeling down in the center of the ring.

Oh no, she moaned inwardly, *I'm too late!*

One of the men moved away, and Julie screamed to see Luke lying face down on the ground surrounded by EMTs. She grabbed the rails and scrambled over, but a rodeo clown ran up and took her arm.

"You can't come into the arena!" he told her, and dragged her back to the fence. "It isn't safe!"

"But that's my boyfriend!" she sobbed. *"Luke!"*

He shot her a sympathetic glance, but pushed her back up onto the fence. "He's getting medical help right now," he told her. "You don't want to get in the way, honey."

Julie half-fell over the fence and twisted around. As she watched in horror, the EMTs strapped Luke onto a plastic board, lifted him up, and carried him to an ambulance that had just pulled up to the big gate.

"Where are they taking him?" she demanded.

"Harris Methodist," he told her.

"Can I ride in the ambulance?" she begged, but to her dismay, the man shook his head.

Julie turned on the words and rushed toward the exit. Her car was parked out in the lot, and she ran out of the arena and across the brightly-lit blacktop. She dodged through rows of parked cars and trucks, praying breathlessly as she ran.

Oh, God, don't let him die!

She spotted her car and dived through two rows of cars to reach it. She dug in her jeans pocket, pulled out the key, and snapped the lock open.

Julie wept as she slid into the seat and gunned the motor to life. She sent the VW roaring out of the lot with its tires squealing, and flipped the GPS on.

"Harris Methodist," she gasped, and the little screen pulled up a local map.

Fifteen minutes later Julie swooped into the hospital parking space, switched off the engine, yanked out the keys, and burst out of the car. She crossed the emergency parking lot at a run, swept through the automatic doors, and rushed to the ER admissions desk. She almost crashed into it.

"I'm here to see Luke Spade," she gasped. "He was just brought in."

The nurse swiveled around slowly in her chair and glanced at her. "Are you family?"

Julie's hopes drooped. "No. I'm his...I'm his girlfriend." Panic seized her, and she leaned over the plastic counter. "I have to see him!"

The nurse swiveled back around to her computer and tapped through a few screens. "Luke....Spade," she murmured, then shook her head. "I'm sorry, miss. Mr. Spade was taken straight in to surgery. No one is going to be able to see him."

Fear and frustration erupted in Julie's chest like molten lava; but she knew it would be useless to take it out on the nurse.

"But..."

The nurse nodded toward the waiting room. "You can wait here, if you like. But it may be hours before we have any news."

"You will tell me when Luke gets out of surgery?" Julie pressed in a quivering voice. "You'll tell me how...how he did?"

The nurse glanced up at her again with a flick of sympathy in her eyes. "If you like."

"Yes, please. As soon as you have any news at all!"

The nurse nodded once, then turned back to her computer, and Julie hugged herself unhappily and drifted into the emergency waiting room. The big room was cold and mostly empty that night, with only a few people huddled in corner chairs. A big television was mounted on the wall, and a talk show host laughed soundlessly and turned to his celebrity guests.

Julie moved across the room aimlessly. Everything felt unreal...even her own body. She couldn't feel her hands or feet. She felt like she was floating above the room and only looking down at it.

I must be in shock, she thought numbly, and put a hand to her brow. *I should sit down.*

She moved to a far corner of the room, just beside the window, and curled up miserably in the last chair. *Hours,* the nurse had said. *Hours* to find out if Luke was going to live or die.

Julie put a hand to her eyes and turned her face to the window, away from passersby. As soon as she closed her eyes, her mind showed her Luke's broken body lying there in the dirt of the rodeo ring. It showed her the rodeo clowns, frozen in the air as they sprinted toward him, showed her the open mouths of onlookers, frozen in screams of dismay.

All because of her.

Her shoulders convulsed with a sudden burst of sobs, and she clapped a hand over her mouth to keep from screaming aloud. *Oh my darling,* she mourned. *My sweet Luke!*

She shook her head bitterly. *This is my fault. All my fault!*

If Luke hadn't been trying to impress me, he never would've signed up for this rodeo. If I hadn't been trifling with Justice, he never would've tried to hurt Luke.

He was right. I was playing them against one another. And not even for love.

For revenge.

I did all of this!

She squeezed her eyes shut and bent down in the chair with silent sobs. The sound of the busy ER went on around her: the faint mumbling of the television, the soft patter of nurses and visitors walking past her, the occasional squawk of the hospital PA.

Doctor Levin to the Emergency Room.

Housekeeping to Nurse Station Three.

Someone sent a heavy piece of equipment rattling past, and Julie turned her face toward the windows to shut out the rude, careless sound. It was horrible that Luke could be dying a few rooms away and no one seemed to notice or care.

But then, how could she be angry, when she hadn't cared? She'd played her little game right to the end. She'd wanted to hurt Luke, and she'd succeeded beyond her wildest dreams.

Julie hunched over, wracked by fresh grief. *I'll never forgive myself if Luke dies. How can I go on, knowing that I killed the man I love?*

The main doors slid apart on the other side of the room, and a blast of new air rushed in. Julie heard a strong male voice announce, "We're the Spade family. Our brother Luke was just brought in on an ambulance."

The nurse's voice replied softly, "Your brother's in surgery right now, Mr. Spade."

Julie raised her head and rolled tear-stained eyes to the entrance. Twenty people were standing in it, and they were all facing the check-in nurse. Buck was staring down at the nurse, and Morgan and Carson were at his elbow. Two other men who looked related were just behind them, and Kate and Heather came walking in as she watched.

"You can wait for news here, if you like," the nurse told Buck. "We'll let you know as soon as he gets out."

Julie hunched a shoulder and shriveled up inside in shame. She could expect no sympathy from Luke's family, because she deserved none. She turned her face to the window and hoped that none of them noticed her, but she couldn't leave.

She had to know what would happen to Luke.

She listened as the family slowly fanned out across the big waiting room. She heard them settle down into chairs, murmur questions to one another, fidget and sigh.

Slowly the waiting room settled down again, with the same soft sounds of nurses walking to and fro, occasional announcements, and the *whoosh* of the front door opening and closing.

The time seemed to crawl. Julie turned this way and that in the hard chair, but there was no way to get comfortable. The room was cold, and there was a constant draft.

But in spite of all those things, she finally drifted into a gray twilight in which she could still dimly hear the mumbling and shuffling of the waiting room, and yet floated on the threshold of sleep.

A soft touch on her arm made her rouse up with a start. "What happened?" she yelped and rolled wild eyes.

There was a redheaded woman staring down at her. Julie frowned, and gradually realized that it was Kate Spade.

She glanced away in shame, but Kate sank down into the chair beside her, leaned over, and gave her a long, warm hug. Julie sat stiff and motionless in her arms, but Kate murmured, "I just noticed that you were here. I'm sorry we didn't see you before, Julie."

Julie couldn't meet her eyes, but couldn't keep from asking: "Is there any news?"

"Not yet," Kate murmured, with a look of overflowing pity. "Why don't you come over and sit with us? There's a couch over there. You could stretch out on it and get a little sleep while we're waiting."

Julie shook her head. "I can't sleep."

Kate scanned her face in sympathy. "Come over and sit with us anyway. You'll feel better."

Julie kept her eyes on her lap. "No, thank you," she murmured in a tiny voice. "It's kind of you to offer."

Kate squeezed her hand. "Is there anything I can get you from the snack machine then? A bottle of water, some crackers maybe?"

Julie glanced away. "I couldn't eat."

Kate looked at her for a moment, then rose. "I'll ask for the nurse to bring you a blanket," she murmured. "If you need anything, just ask."

Julie huddled down into her chair as Kate's soft footsteps faded. She kept her eyes open just long enough to glance at the clock. It was three a.m. in the morning, now. Luke had been in surgery for four hours.

Panic clawed at Julie's throat as the implications of that sank in. Four hours meant that they were fighting for his life, and that they were having trouble. She rolled her head against the back of her chair and closed her eyes. Even if Luke survived his injuries, he could come out paralyzed, maimed, brain damaged.

Because of her.

Guilt rose up like a black wave in her heart, and there was no escaping it. It fell on her again and again until she was lying face down and motionless on the floor of her own mind.

The weight of it was unbearable. It threatened to crush out the last embers of hope in her heart—even her will to live.

Oh God, Julie prayed in despair, *God help me. Please, please don't let Luke die! Oh, please spare him!*

A dry sob shook her. *I know this is my fault, and I'm so sorry...please forgive me. If only I could take it all back!*

Please guide the doctors. Help them save his life!

Another wave, a wave of exhaustion, rolled over her. Her head sank down onto her shoulder, and as she sat there, someone walked up and draped a warm blanket over her shoulders. She snuggled into it thankfully, and she gradually slipped back into the gray twilight between waking and sleeping. Time passed.

Dr. Evans to Trauma.

Julie frowned and tried to get comfortable in the chair. She heard, or imagined she heard, soft voices talking nearby.

I found her there thirty minutes after we arrived. She's devastated, of course. No, don't rouse her.

She'll want to know.

I'll tell her when she wakes up.

There was a faint draft, and the voices faded back into the twilight. Julie drifted there for an endless time, or maybe a short one; but her mind wasn't completely drugged with sleep. It showed Luke splayed on the dirt floor of the rodeo ring with his bangs covering his eyes. She was there again, desperate, clawing and shoving to get to him through the crowd.

All my fault.

Please, God!

A soft voice at her ear made her eyelids flutter open, then close again.

"Julie."

She frowned and turned her face into the blanket.

"*Julie.*"

A touch on her shoulder roused her. She looked up sleepily to see Kate and Heather Spade standing over her. Their sad faces sent terror branching through her like electricity.

She sat up and clutched the blanket in her hands.

"What's wrong?" she gasped.

Kate patted her shoulder. "Nothing's wrong," she replied softly. "Luke's out of surgery now."

Julie stared at her. "Is he…"

"He's in intensive care," Kate murmured. "He's stable. The doctor said that the surgeries were successful, but they just have to wait and see how he does now."

Julie set her mouth, because it was trembling. "Can I see him?"

Kate's eyes were sad. "They won't let anyone but family see him now. They're letting us stand outside his bay, but only two or three at a time. We can't go in, and he isn't conscious anyway."

Julie sank back into her chair, and her tiny flare of hope flickered out.

Heather sat down beside her. "Why don't you go home, Julie," she murmured. "There's nothing you can do, and Luke isn't conscious. We'll call you as soon as we get news."

Julie shook her head. "No. I want to be here in case he wakes up. When will they let me see him?"

The two women exchanged a look, and Kate patted her shoulder again.

"Honey, he isn't going to be conscious for awhile," she replied gently. "Luke could be in intensive care for days, maybe. You should go home and try to get some sleep."

"It doesn't matter," Julie mumbled, and turned her face back into the blanket. "I wouldn't sleep any better there."

The two women looked at each other again, and Heather rose to stand beside Kate.

"You can come back to the ranch house with us if you want," she murmured. "We're going there now, and there's plenty of room."

Julie's mouth twisted underneath the blanket, and she glanced up at them over it. "Thank you, but I want to stay," she murmured in a trembling voice.

Kate touched her arm one last time, and the two of them withdrew. Julie huddled deeper into her blanket, and the sounds of their footsteps slowly faded into silence.

Chapter Forty Eight

The sound of buzzing intruded into Julie's mind. It was faint, but it underscored the throbbing headache between her eyes. She turned over on her pillow and tried to shut it out, but it droned on just on the edge of consciousness.

She opened one eye. She was in her bed at home, and her phone was ringing. Slowly the previous day came back to her, and she gasped, sat bolt upright, and grabbed for the phone. She flicked it on and clapped it to her ear.

"Yes?"

Kate Spade's soft voice answered. "Julie, this is Kate. Luke's doctor came by. He told us that Luke is stable and recovering from his surgeries."

"Is he all right? Can I see him?"

There was a momentary pause. "I'm afraid not," she replied softly. "He's still in the ICU. The doctor said that they've done all they can for him. We can only wait now.

"He says that the next few days will be critical."

Julie turned her face into her pillow.

"Julie?"

Julie inhaled and turned back to the phone. "Thank you for calling," she murmured. "Please let me know if...anything changes."

"I promise. Are you okay?"

Julie frowned, but replied, "As okay as I can be."

"I wish you'd reconsider coming out to the ranch," Kate replied softly. "I know Luke would want that."

"I...I might later. Thank you."

"Call us if you need anything."

"I will."

Julie hung up and pulled her hands over her face. A black curtain of despair fell down over her, blotting out all light. There was nothing she wanted to do, nothing she could do, but lie there and pray.

Only God could help Luke now; but He had little reason to listen to her prayers. Still, she had no choice but to pray; so she closed her eyes and tried again—for the thousandth time.

God, please, she moaned in despair. *I know this is my fault, I admit it all. I've been a monster, I deserve to suffer. But Luke doesn't. Please don't let him die!*

They say you're supposed to be merciful, and Luke needs mercy.

I'm begging you!

She rolled her face into the pillow and clutched the coverlet in wordless desperation. She'd lingered all night in the ER waiting room, and when she'd finally been forced to give up and go home, she'd been too weak and groggy to drive. Her car was still in the hospital parking lot, because she had to call a cab to get home safely.

She hadn't eaten and felt lightheaded and weak; but she had no appetite.

God, please. Only make Luke well and I'll do anything you say, anything at all!

If you want money, I'll donate money to the church. If you want me to go and work at a homeless shelter, I will.

I'll become a missionary, if that's what you want!

What do you want me to do? Tell me!

She beat her fists against her pillow in wordless frustration, but it was no use. It was no wonder she felt no answer to her prayers, no wonder that the sky seemed made of bronze. She'd never gone to church, not even as a child. Trina had invited her to Vacation Bible School one summer, but her parents hadn't let her go.

And when she'd gotten older, her teachers had told her that religion was a tool to control people, and to crush them with false guilt.

The result was that she'd heard of the Bible, but she'd never read it. She'd seen paintings of Jesus, but she'd dismissed him as a myth.

And now that science had done all it could for someone she loved, now that she needed a miracle, there was no one to call.

God didn't know her, so why would he pick up the phone?

Her phone suddenly trilled again, and Julie jumped up and grabbed for it.

"Hello?"

Trina's sad voice replied, "Julie? Kate Spade just called me and said that Luke's been in an accident."

Oh no, Julie thought in stricken dismay, *Trina. I didn't even think about her!*

She stammered, "T-that's right, Trina." She swallowed. "Luke's been in a—a horrible rodeo accident."

She could hear tears in her friend's voice. "Kate said that—he was in the ICU."

Julie closed her eyes in a futile effort to block out that mental image, and her voice quavered as she replied, "Yes."

There was a long, heavy pause. Finally Trina murmured: "Is he going to die, Jules? Kate wouldn't answer, but I know *you'll* tell me the truth. I have to know!"

Julie rolled her eyes to the ceiling and tried to justify her best friend's faith in her. To tell her the whole, awful truth. To admit that she'd caused this disaster.

Julie opened her mouth to confess, but the words died on her lips. She just couldn't bring herself to make her best friend hate her.

So she just shook her head. "We don't know, Trina," she answered brokenly. 'They've done all they can for him. We have to wait and...and see."

Trina's voice was barely audible. "*Oh.*"

Julie tried to focus and mumbled, "If you want to come down to the hospital, Trina, you can stay with me as long as you like."

Trina's voice trembled as she murmured, "Is Luke able to have visitors?"

Julie cringed inside, but she answered, "Not yet. They're not letting anybody see him now."

"I guess I'll wait then. Until he...he can talk." Trina inhaled sharply and added, "I...I have to run, Jules, there's somebody at the door."

"Bye," Julie murmured, but the line was already dead. She set the phone down and stared at it.

There was nobody at Trina's door.

Julie hugged herself unhappily. She'd forgotten all about Trina, and what Luke's accident would mean to her. If Luke died, Trina would be brokenhearted, and...

Trina's baby would lose its father.

Julie's eyes widened with the awful certainty that she'd ruined, not just Luke's life, but Trina's life. The howling storm of guilt inside her heart finally pushed her under. Julie collapsed on the bed, and blackness filled her whole soul.

This is my fault.

Chapter Forty Nine

Julie rolled her head on her pillow and opened her eyes. The ceiling of her bedroom was mottled with shifting moonlight. She turned to look at the window. The wind was moving the branches of the trees outside, and the beam of silver light streaming through the pane danced with light and shadow.

Time had passed, but she didn't know what day it was. The days and nights had melted into one another, one long, dark tunnel of misery. No word had come about Luke, good or bad. Trina hadn't called her, and Julie guessed that her friend was face down on her bed crying. Her own candle of hope was flickering out.

The only thing she was absolutely sure of, was that she'd ruined her own life, and the lives of the two people she loved most in the world.

She stared dully at the moonlit room. *What good does it do for me to go on with my life now,* she wondered. *Even if Luke lives, I can't escape this.*

No one else knows what I did, but I know. I'll never be free of that.

It'll follow me like my shadow. It'll haunt me to my dying day!

She rolled over into the pillow, and despair bent over her in the silence of the deep night.

Why go on like this? it whispered. *Why not follow Luke?*

You saw what he looked like, face down in the dirt.

You know in your heart he won't make it.

Why not atone for the hideous thing you did?

Then you can be free.

Julie squeezed her eyes shut, but there were no tears left in her, no hope left, no excuses to hide behind.

There was nothing left in her but one last gasp, one fading prayer.

Oh, God.

The words trickled out silently in her mind, and her despair lessened a bit. Julie dug her fingers into the pillow and abandoned her pride.

God, things can hardly get much worse. I have nothing to lose now.

If you're there, show me.

She waited, breathing into her pillow, but nothing happened. The silence of her room was deep and unbroken.

She turned over and pushed her hair out of her eyes.

Please forgive me.

Please help me to forgive myself!

She lay there, waiting in the darkness; and slowly she became aware of a new presence in the room. With it came a wave of warmth and love that rushed into her heart like the sea into a china cup. She saw nothing with her eyes, but this new presence was Jesus.

She knew it instantly, without having to ask; and she was amazed that He didn't seem angry about what she had done. She sensed no blame.

She sat up slowly and faced the foot of her bed. There was nothing there but moonlight, yet He was also there.

And the love and the warmth wrapped around her like a soft, luxurious blanket. Suddenly there was nothing wrong, nothing to worry about.

She even sensed a flick of amusement in the newcomer's smile.

Julie smiled in return; then her mouth crumpled up, and she bowed her head and wept, because she knew she was forgiven.

Luke will be all right, she heard in her mind. *Go confess to him.*

When she raised her head again, to her dismay, she was once again alone in the bedroom. The presence of Jesus was gone; but the afterglow of His love and warmth still filled her heart. She bowed her head and wept again. Her heart was broken, but joy was pouring through its every fracture.

Luke was going to live; and she was forgiven.

Chapter Fifty

The sound of the phone ringing woke Julie the next morning. She mumbled and turned her head, then opened her eyes. The phone went on ringing and she suddenly gasped, sat up, and snatched it off the nightstand.

"Hello?"

Kate's voice replied. "Julie, it's Kate. I'm sorry I haven't called you until now, but we didn't want to disturb you until we had the green light from Luke's doctors." She paused, and there was a big smile in her voice as she added: "Luke's out of the ICU and in his own room now, Room 302. He's conscious and able to talk with us.

"He's been asking for you."

Julie slapped her feet on the floor and was halfway to the bathroom before she gasped, "I'll be right down. Tell him I'm on my way!"

"I'll tell him," Kate laughed softly. "We'll see you soon."

Julie hung up the phone as she entered the bathroom, then paused as she remembered what had happened the night before. She raised her eyes to look at herself in the mirror.

She raised a hand to her face. *I don't look any different*, she thought in wonder.

But she was; and Jesus had told her, not just that Luke would be all right, but that she had to confess to him.

The implications of that were just beginning to hit her; but she had to do it, even if she was afraid to do it.

She showered and dressed quickly, and within fifteen minutes the cab she'd called pulled up to her condo. She skipped out to slide into the back seat of the car, and it whisked her off to the hospital.

When the cabbie deposited her at the front entrance of the hospital, Julie paid him and hurried inside. She breezed past the front desk to the main bank of elevators and pressed the 'up' button.

When the gleaming doors slid open, Julie rushed inside. As the doors closed again and the car began to rise, she closed her eyes and took a deep breath. She'd focused on getting ready and getting to the hospital, she hadn't allowed herself to think about what she was doing.

Until that moment; and it was just settling down on her, what confessing to Luke would mean.

If she told him the truth, if she confessed that she'd hated him and done her best to punish him, that she'd encouraged Justice just to spite him and was the reason Justice had tried to kill him, he'd surely...hate her.

He'd most likely tell her to get out and never come back.

Julie closed her eyes and struggled with herself as the elevator rose.

I don't know if I can do this.

I don't need to do this. There's not a living soul who knows what I did, not even Trina. I don't have to confess.

I don't have to risk losing Luke's love.

What would I do, if he rejected me for it? I'd never get over losing him.

But a countering thought formed in her mind, one that she couldn't deny, even if it frightened her.

Jesus had told her to do it; and she owed Luke the truth, even if it made him hate her.

She blinked back tears. Yes, it would certainly make him despise her. He'd have to be more than human, not to hate her for what she'd done to him. He was going to tell her what she was. He was going to throw her out of his room. He might even scream at her as she fled.

She deserved those things, and she was just going to have to endure them.

She was going to face the music.

The elevator chimed softly, and the doors slid open. Julie walked out and moved down the hall slowly and reluctantly. She walked to Room 302, put her hand on the door handle, and paused. The soft stirrings of the hall behind her were the only background to her internal struggle: the muted murmur of a television four rooms down, the chatter in the nurse's station, the faint *ding* of the elevator at the end of the corridor.

Julie closed her eyes and breathed, *God help me. Help me to do what I came to do. Help me get the words out of my mouth.*

She turned the handle and nudged the door open. She swallowed a gasp as the bed inched into view. Luke was propped up in a sitting position, and his eyes were closed, as if he was asleep. But his face was badly bruised, and there were a dozen stitches across an ugly gash on his brow. Her eyes moved down. Luke's chest was covered in wires, his left arm was in a cast, his right leg was in a cast. His bare right arm was hooked up to a drip tube.

Julie pulled her mouth down like a child. She stood in the doorway and struggled to control herself; then she inhaled, squared her shoulders, and walked softly to his bedside. Her first strangled whisper was so soft she hardly heard it herself.

"Luke?"

He lay there, silent and unmoving, and she swallowed and stammered the words out a bit louder.

"Luke, it's Julie."

His eyelids fluttered open. He turned his head slowly, and his face lit up in a beautiful smile. He reached out to her with his free hand.

"You're a sight for sore eyes," he breathed, and Julie mustered a crooked smile as he took her hand.

"How are you...how are you feeling?" she murmured, and his face blurred. She blinked it back into focus and sank down into a chair beside the bed.

"A lot better," he murmured. "They got me whacked up on some kinda horse tranquilizer," he laughed weakly. "It makes me awful goofy, but it cuts the pain right in half."

Julie bowed her head and wept in spite of herself, and Luke's brows crept together. "Ain't no need for that," he told her, and squeezed her hand. "They tell me I'm gonna be all right. Course, I'd love to get out of here, but I'm on the mend."

Julie shook her head and sobbed. This was the happy ending she'd prayed for. Luke was going to live, he was going to recover, and at that moment at least, he still loved her.

She wanted to hold onto that love, to the look in his eyes, to the warmth of his fingers curled around hers. If she kept her promise to God, it was going to be the last time.

"You don't have to cry, Julie honey," he told her softly. "Just you being here makes me feel better than all the drugs in the world."

Julie raised her head slowly and looked at him through swimming eyes. The next words she spoke would determine which of two very different futures she would live; and she opened her mouth, closed it, and opened it again.

"Luke, I...."

She bowed her head, struggled fiercely with herself, and blinked back tears as she continued, "I wanted to be with you. I tried to be. But they wouldn't let me anywhere near you."

Luke tightened his hand around hers. "I know it, honey. They told me."

She hung her head and forced herself to go on. "Luke, I love you with all my heart."

His thumb caressed her hand. "I know that too, darling."

She kept her eyes on the floor as she faltered, "But there's something else you don't know, Luke. When I came back from the emergency room, when I didn't know if you were going to live or die, I prayed to God that you'd make it. I prayed all day and all night, and I finally...did that thing you talked about, Luke. I don't know the right name for it. I gave up and told God...*uncle*."

The bed creaked, and Julie looked up to see Luke trying to turn toward her, slowly and with difficulty. His blue eyes were glistening.

"Don't try to move," she told him, but he gripped her hand, gripped it again.

"There's nothing you could tell me that would make me any happier," he whispered. "Not a thing in this world."

Julie looked up helplessly at the joy in his eyes and forced herself to go on.

"I felt like God was telling me something, Luke," she told him in dull resignation. "He told me that you were going to get better. But he said that I had to tell you the...truth."

Luke's brows rose slightly. He lay there, looking at her, as she struggled to get the words out of her mouth.

"I...I haven't been honest with you, Luke," she told him in a small, pained voice. "I didn't sign up for that riding class because I wanted to learn how to ride. I know how." She looked away and added miserably, "I...I signed up because I'm Trina's best friend and I hated you for hurting her."

She bowed her head and wept, "I saw how crushed she was, and I blamed you for it. I thought it was all your fault, and I...I swore I was going to get even for her. I swore I'd show you how it felt to fall in love with someone and have them break your heart!"

Her own heart broke as Luke's fingers slowly uncurled and his hand dropped away from hers; but she took a deep breath and made herself go on.

"Trina didn't know. I never told her," she whispered. "She never held a grudge against you, Luke, I know that. It was my secret, all my own idea.

"I thought you were a monster. I wanted to hurt you. But...the more I got to know you, the more confused I was. You didn't act like a monster. You were sweet, and caring, and...nothing but a gentleman, from first to last." She shook her head. "Bit by bit, I found out that I'd been wrong about you, Luke."

She raised her eyes to his. "I fell in love with you."

Luke sat unmoving, staring straight ahead. He didn't speak or meet her eyes, and Julie looked down at her lap in despair.

"I only went out with Justice to spite you. I used him to make you jealous, but it backfired," she wept. "It made him jealous instead. He told me that he loved me, and...he threatened me, told me not to play him.

"The night of the rodeo I came down to the gate to see you, but Justice caught me," she quavered. "He pulled me off into a little storage room and accused me of lying to him." She shook her head bitterly.

"He told me he was going to cut the cinch on your saddle," she wept, "that he wouldn't stand for me to be sneaking off to see you. I tried to get out, I tried to warn you, but Justice locked me in there until it was too late. I had to beat on the door and scream until somebody let me out!"

Luke slowly turned his head to look at her, and Julie dropped her gaze in shame. "So you...you see, this is my fault, Luke. I wish to God I could take it all back. I'd take your place if I could, but the damage has been done. I've ruined you. This is all my fault, and I don't blame you if you hate me.

"I'm so sorry!"

Her voice broke, and she dissolved into tears. There was a long, heavy silence, and as that silence stretched out, it made Luke's response clear to her. He wasn't going to answer. He was going to say the kindest thing possible.

Nothing.

Julie nodded in despair. *It's over,* she thought hopelessly. *I did what I came to do. I may as well go home now.*

She wiped her eyes and prepared to stand, but her heart jumped into her throat when Luke turned to her.

"Sit down, Julie."

She stared at him in dismay. *Here it comes,* she thought. *He's going to rip me.*

He nodded toward the chair. "Please."

She sank down into her chair, bowed her head, and clasped her hands in her lap. *Well, I owe him this,* she thought dully. *After what I did to him, the least Luke deserves is the satisfaction of telling me off.*

She waited in miserable suspense, heart pounding; and the touch of Luke's hand on hers shocked her like a live wire.

She looked up at him in shame; but to her surprise, his expression was calm and his eyes were clear and free of anger. His fingers curled around hers again.

"I don't blame you, Julie," he murmured, and squeezed her hand. "You didn't cut the cinch on my saddle. Justice did, and it don't surprise me one bit. He's always had that in him, and he's always hated me. If you hadn't never met him, he would've found another excuse to do what he did. No, you didn't do this to me, Julie."

Julie's eyes teared up as he looked at her and went on, "I don't blame you for being mad at me about Trina, either. I was mad at myself." He sighed and looked up the ceiling.

"I love Trina," he murmured. "Always have. But I would've been happier if we'd just stayed friends, cause that was the way I always saw her. But she kinda...put me up on a pedestal," he sighed. "Made me out to be some kinda knight in shining armor, and I couldn't live up to that. But I couldn't bring myself to break her heart, either, and the longer we were together, the harder it was to disappoint her." He shook her head.

"I put it off and put it off, until she finally had to do what I should've, years before. I'd give anything if I could go back and change what I did, but I can't."

He glanced up at her, and the thoughtful look in his eyes deepened. "You gave me a big gift, Julie. I never understood why I couldn't never finish anything. Why I felt so itchy and restless half the time, why I could hardly finish a simple job. You told me why. It was because I had ADD. It all makes sense now, and I can't tell you what it means to me, to understand that it wasn't...something wrong inside me. Something that was my fault."

Julie's mouth crumpled up in sympathy, but she didn't dare to press him, didn't dare to reach out. She sat there, holding his hand, marveling that he could be kind to her.

He turned toward her, and this time his clear eyes glistened. His hand curled tight around hers, squeezed it.

"You just don't understand, Julie. I could never hate you," he murmured "Even if you'd really hurt me, instead of just thinking you did. I couldn't do it.

"I've loved you from the first time I laid eyes on you," he whispered. "I couldn't stop if I wanted to."

"Oh, Luke!"

Julie bowed her head and wept, and he sighed and rubbed her palm with his thumb. "I wish I wasn't trussed up like a Christmas turkey," he sighed. "I'd show you what I mean. But maybe it's better like this. It forces me to tell you that I love you, instead of...well, the other way."

"I wish you weren't in that cast, either," she whispered fervently. "You're the sweetest, kindest man I've ever met!"

They stared at one another for a long, pregnant moment; then Julie suddenly bent over him and lowered her lips to his with her hands in the air. She brushed his lips as gently as she could, then kissed them, then kissed them again.

Luke looked up at her with longing in his eyes. "You better sit down," he groaned. "You make me feel too good, I'm like to hurt myself."

She uttered a spurt of joyous laughter, then sank back down into her chair and took his hand. Her heart was glowing, bursting with the surprise of one miracle piled on top of another: Luke was going to be all right, and somehow, he still loved her.

She couldn't believe it.

Luke pulled his hand and hers back up onto the edge of the bed. He looked over at her, and his eyes were serious.

"Julie, there's something I haven't told you, too," he murmured. "I had big plans for after the rodeo. If things had gone like they were supposed to, I was gonna take you out to a nice restaurant when I'd finished the competition."

Julie leaned against the bed rail and smiled at him. "That sounds wonderful. We can go there when you get better."

Luke gazed at her and lifted his hand to graze her cheek. "There was more to it than that," he whispered. "I had a big old diamond ring in my back pocket that night, and I was gonna give it to you at that restaurant. When we were sitting there in the candlelight, at some nice little corner table all tucked away from everybody else."

Julie's mouth dropped open slightly, and she searched his eyes. "Luke..."

"I don't have it here with me now," he went on, "but I can pretend like I got it." He smiled at her with a flicker of his old good humor and took her hand. He lifted her ring finger and slid his hand over it.

"Pretend I'm doing it now, Julie. That I'm asking you to marry me." His smiled faded, and he looked at her in appeal.

"Cause I am."

Julie frowned at the floor, and her eyes teared up again. "Are you sure you want to marry a woman who's caused you so much trouble?" she whispered brokenly. "I don't deserve your forgiveness, Luke, much less your...love."

He released her hand to put his fingers under her chin. He gently raised it until she had to meet his eyes.

"Julie, the reason I never married Trina, was because I didn't feel anything for her but friendship. I wanted my bride to be sweet, all right, and Trina was sweet; but I wanted the woman I married to hit me right between the eyes, too. I wanted her to make me feel hot and cold at the same time, to keep me awake at night dreaming of her. I've met a lot of women over the years, but not one of them did that for me.

"Until I met you. You're smart, and sweet as sugar; but you hit me like a hammer that first day, and I ain't never gonna be the same again," he smiled. "I ain't doing you any favors here, darling. You'd be doing me one, if you said yes.

"Do...*do* you say yes?"

Julie laughed and cried together, and nodded, and sputtered in frustration. "Of course I do," she wept. "I love you with all my heart, Luke Spade." She bit her lip and added softly, "I wish I could show you!"

Luke grinned and reached out to caress her hair. "You save it up for me," he murmured.

The door opened behind her, and Julie was disappointed to see a nurse bustle in. "Well, I hope you've had a nice visit," she smiled, as she pulled a wheeled machine into the room.

Julie released Luke's hand as the nurse pushed the machine up to the bed. As much as she hated to leave, she knew that the nurse was giving her a not-so-subtle message; and so she turned to him with a smile.

"I'll come back tomorrow," she murmured.

"Yes ma'am," he grinned, and kissed her hand.

Chapter Fifty One

Morgan pulled his wife's tiny hand through his arm and squired her down the hospital corridor. Her other arm was filled with a big gift basket full of goodies for Luke.

He glanced down at her as they neared Luke's room. Heather had a soft heart, and he didn't like to take her too often to see Luke, because it busted her up. She was all smiles while she was there with him, but when they got out of earshot, she always cried a bit.

She hated to see anybody hurting, and she knew Luke was, even though he never let on.

He slowed down as they got closer. "Now Heather," he told her gently, "just remember that this isn't Luke's first...well, it ain't the first time he's got busted up. He's tough, and they're giving him enough painkiller to knock out a horse."

She glanced up at him and smiled, and the yellow cellophane on the basket made a crinkling sound. "I know. I'm all right."

"All right then," he rumbled, and patted her hand; and they walked to Luke's room together. The sound of giggling drifted from inside, and Morgan frowned and exchanged a puzzled look with Heather as they stood there.

Morgan rapped lightly on the door with his knuckles. "Luke, it's Morgan and Heather. Can we come in?"

Luke's voice was faint, but sounded cheerful. "Come on in!"

Morgan nudged the door open and peeked around, and to his astonishment, he caught Julie pulling back from planting a kiss on Luke's lips. She glanced back at them, cleared her throat, and sank back down into her bedside chair.

Him and Heather exchanged a look, and then walked in. "Glad to see you, Julie," he nodded, and the Luke's dark-haired girlfriend looked down and smiled primly.

Heather smiled and walked over to the bed. "This is for you, Luke," she murmured, and held the basket out so he could see it. "We had it made specially for you. It's got jerky and summer sausage and cheese and a few bottles of beer, when you can have it."

"Oh, I can have it now," Luke told her earnestly, and turned his head to give her a pleading look.

"That's not true," Julie amended, and took the basket into her lap, and Morgan caught himself laughing under his breath. It looked like Luke's new girlfriend was riding herd on him.

It was good to see.

"Aw, come on Julie," Luke pled. "I haven't had a beer in two weeks."

"You'll have to keep him honest, Julie," Heather laughed; but then her eyes widened and her mouth dropped slightly open. Morgan frowned and followed the direction of her gaze, but he couldn't see anything new.

Just Julie's hand.

Heather gasped and reached for Julie's hand. "You're *engaged!*" she shrieked, and Morgan felt his own mouth dropping open.

Morgan glanced at Julie's hand. Luke had gotten his girlfriend a chunk of ice, all right.

Heather laughed and held Julie's hand up to the light. "How could I miss that gorgeous ring!"

Julie's cheeks went pink, but she reached for Luke's hand and smiled; and Morgan stepped in to lean down over the bed and shake Luke by his shoulder.

"Congratulations, boy!" he laughed, and it warmed his heart to see how Luke's face shone. His little brother looked happier than he'd ever seen him.

Heather pushed him aside to throw her arms around Julie's shoulders. "Welcome to the family," she whispered, and gave Julie's cheek a kiss. "I'm so happy for you! Have you two chosen a date for the wedding?"

Luke glanced at Julie. "Well, I'll have to get out of here first," he grinned, "and they tell me I'll have to get a lot of rehab. But lucky for me, I got my own physical therapist."

Morgan raised his bushy brows and rubbed his nose, and Heather folded her hands and looked down into her lap.

Julie turned to tell them, "We're thinking a late fall or maybe a winter wedding. It depends on how Luke does, of course; but his doctors say he should be much better by then."

Heather looked up at him and reached for his hand, and he took it. "Morgan and I had a winter wedding," she murmured happily. "It was so beautiful. Maybe I can help you. Give you some ideas."

Julie's expression softened, and she smiled. "That's very sweet of you," she replied quietly. "We'll have to put our heads together when Luke gets better."

Luke struggled to sit up straighter. "They tell me I'm getting out of here in a few days."

"How did we miss that news?" Morgan wondered aloud. "We've been asking them for a solid week."

"They just told us today," Julie replied.

Morgan reached for Heather, and she snuggled against him as he put his arm around her shoulders."Well now, that calls for a real celebration," he smiled. "We'll have to throw you a big old welcome home party."

"I can't wait," Luke muttered. "The doctors and nurses have been real great to me, but a hospital's no place to live. I'd walk out of here on my hands if I could!"

Morgan chuckled, but he noticed that Luke reclined back into his pillow, as if the conversation was tiring him. He turned to Heather and murmured, "We need to go. We don't want to wear him out."

Heather reached out to touch Julie's shoulder and smiled, "Is it all right with you two if we tell the family you're engaged?"

Julie and Luke exchanged a glance, and Luke grinned, "I don't see why not."

"Good," Heather beamed. "Because I don't think I could've kept it to myself!"

Morgan leaned down to murmur in her ear. "Let's run, darlin.'" He raised a hand in farewell. "You rest up, Luke. You do what Julie tells you."

'You are coming back, ain't you?" Luke asked with a frown, and Morgan nodded.

"Don't worry, we'll be back. So will everybody else once we tell them your news," he laughed, and waved again. "We'll see you tomorrow."

"Bye Morg. Bye Heather," Luke called, and Morgan walked out with his arm around Heather. But as he pulled the door shut behind them, he noticed that Julie's smile faded, and that Luke lifted his good arm to let her lean against him.

She looked like she was overcome with emotion.

Heather glanced up at him in frowning concern. "What's that about?" she whispered, but he put a finger to his lips and closed the door.

"That's between them, sweetheart."

Chapter Fifty Two

"Here they come!"

Kate giggled and scurried away from the front door. She joined the throng of people gathered under the big banner hanging across the big atrium of the ranch house. The banner read *Welcome Home Luke and Julie* in multicolored letters.

Buck was standing at the door, and he opened it wide to let Jesse push Luke's wheelchair into the house. The first appearance of his toes sticking out from his leg cast was greeted by a shout of welcome and a babble of laughing voices.

Luke's face lit up as he looked up and saw his family gathered there, and most of his friends from town and the rodeo. He was mobbed before his wheelchair rolled all the way into the house, and a dozen hands slapped his uninjured arm and his head.

"Looking good, dog!"

"Welcome home, Luke!"

"Get you a beer, buddy?"

Kate stepped back from the knot of people clustered around Luke's wheelchair, and she noticed as Julie slipped in behind him, smiling but for the moment, unnoticed. She walked up and quietly slipped an arm around her waist.

"Welcome home, Julie," she smiled. "We're so glad you're going to be a part of our family."

She noticed tears in Julie's eyes and hugged her closer. "Don't worry. Luke's going to be all right."

Julie looked up at her and nodded. "That's right," she whispered. "Thank God."

Kate took her hand. "Come on, let's leave this rooster party for awhile. We've got a surprise for you."

Julie gave her a curious glance as she led the way through the crowded house, past the main staircase, and into the back hall.

Julie followed her into the dining room and stopped in the doorway as she saw balloons and a pink confection of a cake in the middle of the table. The cake was surrounded by presents wrapped in pastel paper and frilly bows.

"Welcome to your wedding shower," Kate told her, and Julie stared in speechless surprise. Tears welled up in her eyes.

"Would you like some cake?" Kate offered, and Julie nodded and wiped her eyes. She glanced around the table. Heather and Donna smiled at her, and Miss Ada walked in and set down a silver coffee pot.

Julie sank down into the center chair at the table and watched as the housekeeper placed a luscious slice of yellow cake in front of her. Kate smiled as she watched Julie swipe off a bit of the pink buttercream frosting she'd slathered on.

Julie took a taste, then looked up at her, and then at her other future sisters in law.

"I...I don't know how to thank you," she mumbled.

"We're glad to do it," Kate assured her, as she sat down beside her. "Miss Ada, can we get a cup of coffee for our guest of honor? That cake is going to be delicious with a nice cup of Kona."

The housekeeper leaned over the table to pour coffee into the china cups, and Julie took a forkful of cake. "*Mmm,*" she mumbled, "It's heavenly!"

"Open my gift first," Heather urged, and presented a pretty, pale yellow box with a powder blue bow on top. Julie smiled, put her fork down, and took the box. When she lifted off the lid and pushed away the tissue, there was a smaller wrapped box inside. She smiled uncertainly and looked a question.

"Open it," Heather urged.

Julie opened the box and pulled out a glittering silver gift card. It wore the logo of the most expensive spa in Dallas, and it was for a breathtaking amount. She raised her eyes in amazement.

Heather beamed at her. "You've been working so hard, helping Luke with his physical therapy and going back and forth to the hospital. Morgan and I thought you both could use a little pampering."

Julie shook her head. "I don't know what to say," she stammered. "This is...*so* generous."

"Mine next," Donna murmured, and handed her a box wrapped in pink and silver stripes with a shiny silver bow. Julie shot her a grateful-looking glance and lifted the top.

She raised a perfect crystal champagne glass, one of a set. The stem was made of gold and studded with an array of glittering pavé diamonds. Julie gasped and turned the glass in her hand, but something inside sparkled as she twirled it.

She raised startled eyes to Donna's smiling ones as she reached in and pulled out a dazzling tennis bracelet of brilliant-cut diamonds.

"Oh, Donna," she gasped, "thank you!"

Donna nodded and murmured, "For your honeymoon. The bracelet can be the first piece of your trousseau."

Kate smiled and leaned toward her. "Here, let me fasten it," she offered, and secured the clasp. Julie held her wrist out, and the diamond bracelet and her engagement ring glittered on her hand like a constellation of stars.

"It's beautiful," Kate approved, and added, with a twinkle in her eye: "Now it's my turn." She picked up a pale green present with a white bow and gave it to Julie.

Julie looked down at it. "You've all really gone overboard," she murmured. "I can't even..." She paused for a long moment, then slowly lifted the lid.

She reached in, and there was nothing in the mound of tissue but a business card. It read:

Pamela Wooten

Travel Agent

Dallas Destinations

Kate's eyes twinkled. "That's the business card of your travel agent," she smiled. "Your account is already funded. All you and Luke have to do now is decide where you want to go for your honeymoon."

Julie put a hand to her mouth and lifted brimming eyes to Kate's. She struggled to speak, failed, and shook her head.

"I don't know what to say."

"Say thank you," Kate told her, and Julie sputtered with tearful laughter.

"Thank you. All of you," she added fervently, and turned to Heather and Donna. "I'm just...speechless."

"We have one last present for you," Kate added, and reached for a large, rectangular package oddly wrapped in pale blue paper. She placed it carefully on Julie's lap.

"It's from all three of us. It's more of a practical present."

Julie shook her head and slowly opened the package. Kate winked at her sisters-in law as they watched Julie pull out a toy tennis racket made of red plastic.

"That's for when Luke gets out of line," Kate told her with dancing eyes. "We can all guarantee you that these Spade men are stubborn and rambunctious.

"They all need to be threatened with a thwack now and then."

Julie laughed out loud, and her future sisters in law joined in with her as she set the racket aside. She shook her head again.

"Thank you. I never expected anything so..." her words trailed off and she waved her hands.

Kate reached over and hugged her. "You're family now," she murmured. "And you've been so good for Luke. He told us that you helped him get his ADD diagnosed, and he's had it since he was a child. Buck says Luke's like a different man now.

"And of course, that's not even counting how happy you make him," she added softly. "We can all see that."

Julie pulled her mouth down like a child and hugged her, and Kate laughed and smiled at Heather and Donna over her shoulder.

"Well, now that Julie's opened her presents, let's enjoy our cake before one of the men folk come in here and see it," she told them, and soft giggling filled the room.

"I know that's right."

"Pass me a plate."

Chapter Fifty Three

A few days later, Julie set her coffee cup down on the patio table and gave Luke a rueful glance. She'd been staying in the guest room at the ranch house, but she was about to leave.

Luke reached out across the table and took her hand in his. "Are you sure you want to do this alone?" he asked softly, and rubbed her fingers. His blue eyes were full of sympathy, and Julie knew he'd come with her if she let him; but she shook her head.

"You're sweet, but no," she murmured. "I have to do this by myself, and the sooner the better. I've been dreading it, and I've put it off for too long."

"I still think I should come with you," he muttered. 'This is my mess."

Julie gave him an affectionate glance. "No, this mess is mine," she whispered. "And I'm going to face the music. Wish me luck," she added wistfully, and Luke leaned over to kiss her.

"I'll be praying for you," he whispered against her cheek. "Call me when you get there."

"I will."

Julie stood up, slung her bag over her shoulder, and leaned down to give Luke one last goodbye kiss before walking across the patio to the courtyard in front of the ranch house.

It was still early morning, and a thick fog still hovered over the green swell of the shallow hills beyond the house. Julie walked over to her VW, opened the door, and slid in.

She sat there for a moment, then bowed her head in prayer.

Lord, she prayed, *I'm scared.*

I know how I'd feel.

Please don't let her hate me.

Please.

She sighed, opened her eyes, and cranked the car. It was a long drive to Oklahoma City, and there was a real chance that when Trina heard what she had to say, she might have to come straight back.

But she had no choice. She and Luke were getting married, and she couldn't let her best friend find that out from anyone but her.

Julie flicked on the radio as she sent her car down the long drive. She was trying to distract herself, but a few minutes of jangling music made her so nervous that she had to snap it off again.

She'd gamed out every possible scenario in her head; but she couldn't deny that Trina's most likely reaction was going to be that she'd feel betrayed.

She'd been telling Trina that she sympathized, that she hoped she and Luke would get back together, at least at first. Then, she'd told Trina that Luke was responsible for their baby, that she needed to force him to do right by her.

And now, Trina couldn't be blamed if she questioned her sincerity. If she wondered if her best friend had been romancing her ex behind her back...all along.

Julie slapped the steering wheel in frustration. She could see herself telling Trina: *I know it sounds crazy, but I was going after Luke to get revenge.*

For you.

I didn't tell you at the time because I knew you wouldn't approve.

And my plan just...went a little sideways.

It sounded like a lie, she knew that, but she had to convince Trina it was true, because it *was* true. She wasn't going to lose her best friend.

She couldn't.

But even *that* wasn't the only near-impossible task on her plate. Assuming Trina didn't throw her out, and assuming Trina forgave her for snagging the man she wanted more than anything else in the world, she had to convince Trina to tell Luke she was pregnant.

It had been *so hard* not to tell him herself.

Julie stopped at the big ranch gate, closed her eyes, and imagined Luke's face when he found out that she'd known about his baby, and hadn't told him.

But she'd promised Trina she'd keep her secret, and she couldn't bring herself to break that promise.

She owed Trina at least that much.

Oh Lord, she prayed, *help me.*

She popped her sunglasses on and turned out onto the road. She'd turned it over and over in her mind until her head ached; but in the end, all she could do was tell Trina the truth and hope that their long friendship would survive the shock.

Julie pulled the VW into Trina's apartment complex just before lunchtime. It was Saturday, and Trina was expecting her. Trina's little sedan was parked on the curb, and Julie licked her lips nervously as she pulled the VW up behind it.

She pulled her sunglasses off and glanced at the little apartment door. *Well, this is it,* she told herself in dread.

As she watched, the door opened and Trina's smiling face appeared in it. She was wearing the little yellow duck smock top and white slacks, and her face was pink and glowing. Julie smiled back and climbed out of the car as Trina walked to meet her.

"Julie, I've missed you so bad," Trina murmured, and held out her arms. Julie went into them and hugged her, but stared over her shoulder in dread.

"Come in. I have *so* much to tell you," Trina smiled, and took her hand.

"I...I have something to tell you, too," Julie mumbled uncomfortably, as Trina pulled her along.

Trina laughed as she ushered her inside and closed the door behind her. "Good! We'll get all caught up. Come and sit down," she invited. "Let me get you something to drink. Are you hungry?"

Julie sank down into a chair by the door and clasped her hands in her lap. "Maybe we should talk before we eat."

Trina disappeared into the little kitchen, and the sound of clinking glasses drifted out. "Tea or coffee, Jules?"

"Tea," Julie replied tonelessly.

Julie came back out carrying two glasses of tea. Julie took one from her and took a fortifying jolt of caffeine.

Trina sat down on the sofa and set the glass on the coffee table. "Jules, I went to the doctor a few days ago," she confided. "I had an ultrasound, and the doctor said that my baby's a *girl*."

Joy jumped up in Julie's heart. "Oh, Trina!" she cried gladly, and Trina nodded. "I was praying it would be a girl," she smiled, but her smile faded as she added, "I'm still worried about how I'm going to manage with a baby," she added. "I hardly make enough money to support myself." She looked up at smiled. "But you've been so sweet, Jules. I almost feel like I can make it when you're here to help me!"

Julie frowned in pain to think that she'd probably lost her chance to do that. She'd so looked forward to helping Trina raise her baby, and now it looked as if that wasn't going to happen.

Julie smiled at her in wistful love. "That's wonderful, Trina," she murmured. "I'm so happy for you."

Trina took a sip of tea, then set it down and faced her expectantly. "Well, that's my news. Now I want to hear yours!"

Julie licked her lips. "Well, um...Trina...what I'm about to tell you is hard for me," she confessed, and gave her friend a pleading look. "It's a strange story, but I swear to you that it's true. Will you promise to hear me out?"

Trina's look of happy expectation faded into a puzzled look. "Of course, Jules," she murmured.

Julie stared at her earnestly. "We've been friends all our lives, Trina," she went on softly. "Have I ever lied to you?"

Trina's puzzled look deepened into a confused frown. "Never," she replied. "Is there something wrong, Julie? You can tell me. No matter what it is, I promise I'll understand."

Julie closed her eyes and mouthed a silent prayer, then ventured: "Trina, you remember when you first told me about breaking up with Luke Spade. You were crying, and upset, and it was terrible for you."

Trina's frown deepened. "Yes, I remember."

"Well, I got...*really* angry at Luke Spade," Julie confessed, and lowered her eyes. "I got mad because I saw how badly he'd hurt you. I blamed him for everything you went through."

Trina cocked her head to one side, like a bird. "But...I was the one who chose to leave, Jules," she pointed out softly.

Julie nodded miserably. "Yes, I know, but I blamed him anyway," she replied. "I thought he'd just used you, and strung you along, and taken advantage of you."

Trina shook her head. "No, Jules, that wasn't what happened," she replied earnestly. "Luke is a sweet man. He'd never do that."

"I know," Julie nodded. "I know now, but I didn't know then. I really kind of...hated him."

The troubled look on her friend's face gradually changed to worry. "What are you trying to tell me, Jules?" she asked slowly.

Julie glanced away, then down at her feet. "I wanted to get even for you, Trina," she blurted.

"Get *even*? What do you mean?"

Julie looked up at her miserably. "I got this idea in my mind that I needed to punish Luke Spade," she sighed. "I wanted to do the same thing to him that he did to you. To show him how it felt to be used."

Trina's mouth dropped slightly open as Julie added: "I decided to...to make him fall in love with me, and then break his heart. Just like he did to you."

Trina shook her head. "But he didn't do that to me," she objected. "And if you were going to try such a thing, why on earth didn't you tell me about it *then*?"

Julie looked away in frustration. "I knew you'd never agree to it, Trina, you're too nice," she explained. "I wish I had told you, now."

Trina stared at her in dismay as she went on, "So...Luke was teaching a riding class at the Seven Ranch, and I signed up as an excuse to meet him. And I...I got him to ask me out, and...I...did my best to...to..."

Trina's eyes flashed. "To seduce him!" she exclaimed indignantly.

"No," Julie blurted out, with a pleading look. "Well, yes, but it didn't completely work. He kept telling me he was trying to turn over a new leaf, that he'd made a promise to God to be a better man. I think that you breaking up with him made him see he needed, to, Trina," she added softly, and Trina lowered her eyes.

"Anyway, he liked me all right, but he..." Julie shrugged and waved her hands in the air. "He kept popping the brakes on. Not that I minded," she hurried to add. "I was very mean to him for your sake Trina, I tortured him in all kinds of ways. Except that," she added forlornly, "the more time I spent with Luke, and the better I got to know him, the more I wondered if I...might be wrong about him." She lifted her eyes to Trina's in appeal.

Dawning comprehension spread across Trina's freckled face. "You fell in *love* with him," she gasped. "*That*'s what you're trying to tell me, isn't it, Julie?"

Julie nodded wretchedly and lowered her eyes. "Yes."

Trina jumped up from the couch and paced back and forth across the little room. "I can't believe it!" she cried, and stared down at Julie as she passed.

"I didn't plan for it to happen," Julie moaned, and pulled her hands down her face. "The last time I was up here with you I hated his guts, I swear! But...he's just such a sweet man, Trina," she murmured, and looked up at her friend. "Just like you said. The better I got to know him, the more I couldn't hate him."

She shook her head unhappily. "And things just...went downhill from there."

Trina stopped pacing and stared down at her, and the angry look on her face faded a bit. "Well," she sighed at last, "I guess I can't really blame you for falling in love with Luke. Everybody does, sooner or later." She walked back to the couch and sank down onto it.

Julie closed her eyes and forced herself to press on. "Trina, there's more." She licked her lips and gave her friend a pained glance. "When Luke had his accident at the rodeo, we'd been dating for a little while, but seeing him so hurt, and not knowing if he was going to live or die, just...flushed me right out of the bushes." She gestured helplessly.

Trina sat up in alarm. "He's all right, isn't he?"

Julie gave her a startled look. "Oh yes, he's fine now! The doctor says he's going to make a full recovery."

Trina leaned back into the couch and exhaled, and Julie went on, "I've never been so miserable in my life, as the first days Luke was in that hospital." She shook her head. "I prayed to God for his life. Imagine—me praying!"

Trina glanced up at her sharply, and there was an odd, eager expression in her gray eyes. She waited as Julie added, "I didn't want to live any more, if Luke died. As the days passed without any word, I got this black, dark depression over me. I got so low that I stopped begging God for Luke's life, and...started begging for my own."

A heavy silence fell, and Julie stared at the floor, remembering it. "I don't know anything about religion. I didn't even know how to pray," she said at last. "But I told God that if He existed, to show me. And He did.

"I got this...*knowing*," she murmured. "I can't explain it, but this warmth came over me, this love," she stammered. "And it had a name. It was Jesus. The strange thing was that He wasn't at all like I thought He'd be," she thought aloud. "He was so relaxed. He had this sense of humor, even, I could feel it. This love."

"I wanted that. I told Him so, and...the depression just lifted off me like a blanket, Trina. I still didn't know if Luke was going to live, but I didn't want to die any more. I knew that no matter what happened, it was going to be all right.

"I guess I'm a Christian now," Julie sputtered and shook her head. "Who would've thought."

Trina stood up slowly and came over to kneel down beside her. She looked up into her eyes and smiled.

"I'm so glad for you, Jules," she whispered, and a tear slipped down her cheek. "I haven't been the best Christian in the world, I know. I've made a lot of mistakes. But I've been praying for you to do this since I was eight years old." Her mouth crumpled up and her eyes filled with tears, and Julie felt answering tears sting her own eyes.

She reached out for her friend, and Trina leaned in to hug her tight. "I'm so happy right now I can't be mad," she whispered. "This is the best news in the *world* to me, Julie!"

Julie closed her eyes and let herself bask in Trina's forgiveness for a few luxurious moments. *Please, God,* she prayed, *please help her forgive me for what I'm going to tell her next.*

It's the hardest part of all.

She glanced sidelong at her friend and gently pressed her out at arm's length. She stared sorrowfully into Trina's eyes and forced herself to murmur, "Trina, I...I went to Luke's hospital room, when he was well enough to see me. I told him everything I'd done. I told him that I was your best friend and that everything I did, I did for revenge. I told him you didn't know," she added quickly, as Trina's brows rushed together in dismay, "I told him you had no idea! But I also told him what I just told you," she whispered. "That I fell in love with him in spite of myself. And you know what he did, Trina? He forgave me...*everything*."

Her own eyes blurred as she went on, "He told me he loved me, too. He asked me...to marry him."

She raised her eyes as Trina's face went blank with shock. Her friend slowly stood up and walked back to the sofa. She sank back down onto it and hugged herself.

There was a heavy silence, and at last Julie murmured, "I didn't want you to hear it from someone else, Trina."

The silence fell again, stretched out. Julie waited in wretched suspense as Trina processed this news. Finally she looked at Trina's frowning face and pled, "Trina, *please* say something. Yell at me, cuss me out, I don't care. But I can't stand to see you sit there and cry!"

At that, Trina finally roused up. "I'm not crying," she said softly. "I did that a long time ago."

She sighed and looked up at the ceiling. "I won't lie, when I first came up here I dreamed that Luke would come running after me. That he'd find me somehow, that he'd tell me he loved me and wanted to get married." She picked at the nubby fabric of the couch. "But when the days passed, and there was no word, I had to let the last little shreds of that dream go.

"I held out for a long time. I kept Luke with me for years, and I was happy. But I began to see that he wasn't," Trina sighed. "That I was being selfish. Oh, I gave him one last chance to change his mind about marrying me," she laughed shakily, "but when you love someone, you have to do what's best for them, not what's best for you."

Julie's heart melted in sorrow. She stood up and went to sit on the couch beside Trina and took her friend in her arms. To her overwhelming relief, Trina slipped an arm around her.

"Come back home with me, Trina," she whispered. "You can stay with me for the weekend. Tell Luke about the baby. He still doesn't know he's a father."

She pulled back to give her friend a pleading look. "Don't you think he should?"

Trina glanced at her, then down at her hands. "I guess it's time," she nodded. Julie closed her eyes, and a weight like a boulder lifted off of her shoulders and rolled away.

Thank you, she prayed, and hugged Trina tight.

"Luke and I will be with you every step of the way," she promised fervently, and squeezed her eyes shut. "You don't have to worry about the baby. You don't have to worry about anything, Trina.

"Not a thing in this world!"

Chapter Fifty Four

Julie walked to the glass wall of the guest room at the Seven Ranch and gazed down on the rolling meadows below. A flurry of fall leaves danced past the window and blew away.

It had been four months since Luke had come out of the hospital; four months of intense physical therapy. Luke had fought for every tiny gain, and his grit and determination had amazed her. He'd fought like a champion to be where he was.

He'd quickly moved from a wheelchair, to a walker, to a cane, to normal movement again. A few weeks before, against her wishes and her advice, he'd gotten back up on a horse again.

To prepare for their wedding.

Julie glanced down at the world beneath her window. A huge white tent had been erected in the flat, grassy meadow below, and a corral full of saddled horses flanked it to the north.

Luke was a rodeo star, after all; and when he'd told her, sheepishly, that he'd like to be married horseback, she didn't have the heart to refuse.

As far as she was concerned, anything Luke wanted, Luke was going to get.

She turned back to check once last time in the mirror before she left the room. Her inky hair was swept up on top of her head and spangled with crystals that glittered there like stars in the night sky.

Her dress was a custom-made gown, created by one of her designer friends in Los Angeles. Julie gave herself a critical glance in the mirror.

The shoulders of her gown were sheer netting spangled with crystals. The bodice was made of ivory-colored silk and hugged her like a second skin; and the glorious skirt was made of a hundred layers of floating ivory tulle that belled out magnificently from her hips and swept the ground three feet from her body.

Julie's hand crept to her face. She was wearing Luke's wedding present, a fabulous pair of diamond earrings, and her diamond bracelet and wedding ring glittered on her left hand.

Her only departure from haute couture were the sensible ivory-colored granny boots hidden beneath her massive skirt. She'd longed for elegant silk pumps, but finally had to concede that she'd never get up onto a horse in three-inch heels.

A soft knock at the door made her turn her head. Heather's smiling voice murmured: "Julie, are you ready?"

Julie walked to the door with her skirts swishing loudly around her, and she opened it to see her sister in law's beaming face.

"I'm ready," she smiled.

Heather took her arm lightly and led the way to the little elevator at the back of the hall. Julie glanced at the stairs ruefully. She'd never get down them alive in her massive skirts, and she moved gratefully into the little car.

Heather pressed the button and arranged the bouquet of ivory-colored roses that she was holding for her. She murmured, "You look like an angel, Julie. You're a gorgeous bride!"

Julie murmured her thanks, but she was thinking: *I haven't acted like an angel. But I've been treated like one anyway.*

I guess that's what Luke means when he talks about God giving us what we don't deserve.

The doors opened, and Julie followed Heather through the side room, and out to the atrium of the house. Luke's burly brother Jesse held the big front door open for her, and she walked out into the courtyard.

Three horses were standing in the yard. A big, gleaming, coal-black horse was ready and waiting for her. It was fitted with a brand-new sidesaddle, and a big, sturdy set of wooden mounting steps had been pushed up to the horse's side.

Heather helped her walk out to the horse as she prepared to climb up onto the horse's back; then Jesse walked up to hold the horse's head.

He nodded toward her. "Go ahead and mount up," he mumbled.

Julie lifted her skirts and climbed the steps slowly and carefully. She grabbed the pommel and hopped up into the saddle, and Julie handed her the bouquet, helped to arrange her skirts, then stepped back, smiled, and lifted her cell phone to take a picture.

Jesse grumbled, "Go ahead and get on your horse, Heather. I'll be behind you."

Heather lifted up the pale yellow skirts of her bridesmaid gown, climbed the mounting steps, and hopped onto the sidesaddle. She turned the horse's head and brought it up behind Julie's, and Jesse walked to his horse, mounted, and pulled up to the rear.

Julie nudged her horse, and it began walking down the drive, slowly and with stately beauty. The path to the tent was roped off and festooned with white roses, and as she entered it, she passed a double row of cowboys on horses: Luke's rodeo friends, all wearing

Stetsons and suits. They grinned and removed their hats as she slowly passed, and Julie glanced down to hide her smile.

As she passed under a flower-decked arch, and into the tent, the guests rose from their seats and turned to watch as she rode past. Julie's eyes moved across the crowd and found Trina's shining face, and her eyes blurred with tears as she remembered how Luke had received the news that he was a father.

He'd accepted that news humbly and with happiness; and his reconciliation with Trina had healed Julie's own heart.

Julie's eyes moved to the front of the tent, and her heart leaped with joy to see Luke mounted on his own black horse, waiting for her. He'd taken off his black hat, and his hair shone like gold under the lights as their eyes met. Julie smiled and mouthed the words *I love you,* and almost laughed to see his face go red.

Her eyes moved to four of Luke's brothers, all mounted on horses beside him; and to her own sisters in law, whose willingness to act as her bridesmaids, on horses, she could never repay.

She sent her horse down the aisle, and on to stand beside Luke's; and she reached out to take the hand Luke extended to her.

They turned to face the mounted rodeo chaplain that Luke had chosen for their wedding, a cowboy with a bushy hair, a bushy brown moustache, and round, tiny glasses.

"Dearly beloved," he began in a gravelly voice; and Julie listened as the familiar words of a traditional wedding service flowed over them.

It was so wildly unlikely that it felt almost like a dream: the fact that she loved, and was marrying, a man she'd once hated; but it was true.

She glanced over at Luke's face, and the love shining out of his eyes confirmed for her that she'd been blessed beyond her deserts and her wildest dreams. She was marrying the sweetest, most loving man she'd ever met, and her heart burst with joy, then overflowed with gratitude.

I'm new at this, Lord, she prayed as she watched Luke pull out her wedding ring and slip it onto her hand. *But I love you, for giving me Luke alone. Not even counting that you saved my life that awful night, that you forgave me and helped me forgive myself.*

That you helped me stop hating, and taught me how to love.

I love you, and I can never repay you.

Except maybe by doing my best to love this man, and Trina, and all my new family.

I'll do my best, I promise you that.

She came back to the present in time to hear the chaplain intone, "Place the ring on Luke's finger and repeat after me."

Julie took Luke's hand with a smile and slid a solid gold band onto his brown finger, then gazed into his eyes and thought: *Yes, with all my heart.*

"I, Julie Parker, take you, Luke Spade to be my lawfully wedded husband. To have and to hold from this day forward, for better or worse, for richer, or poorer, in sickness and in health, for as long as we both shall live.

"So help me, God."

Chapter Fifty Five

Buck flopped down onto the big leather couch in the ranch house atrium, loosened his collar, and stuck his feet up on the coffee table.

"Well, it was a fine hitching," he sighed, and poured himself a celebratory glass of whiskey. "Everything went off pretty good. No horses spooked, no pies on the floor, and we saw Luke and Julie off to the airport."

Carson sank down onto the couch beside him and poured out his own glass of whiskey. "Jackson Hole's beautiful this time of year," he muttered. "Pretty decent place for a honeymoon."

He glanced at Buck's big boots planted on the table, and frowned. "You've got your feet on the mail," he muttered, and knocked Buck's feet off the table. He lifted up a sheaf of letters.

"What'd we get?" Buck mumbled, as he took a sip.

"Nothing interesting," Carson mumbled, then frowned. "Well, it looks like I spoke too soon. Where's Jesse? He got a letter from somebody in..." He frowned and added, "the Polanco Colonia, Mexico City. Huh. Pricey address." He lifted his bright eyes to Buck's.

"Do you read Spanish?"

"Fair," Buck mumbled.

Carson's mouth curved up. "Let's open his letter."

Buck sat up and snatched it out of his hand. "You need some kind of transplant," he sputtered, and tapped his chest. "In *here*! I guess now that Luke's gone, and you two can't torture each other any more, you're setting your sights on Jesse. Well, watch out," he laughed. "Luke didn't care, but Jesse'll beat your eyes together."

Their brother's frowning face appeared at the door. "Why am I going to beat his eyes together?" Jesse demanded, and turned suspicious eyes to Carson's face.

Buck tossed the letter through the air, and Jesse reached out and caught it. "You better pay attention to your mail," Buck drawled, and nodded toward Carson.

Jesse shot Carson a warning frown and opened the letter. He ran his eyes down the first sheet of paper, and then another one, grunted, and tossed the letter down.

He shouldered out of his dress jacket on the way to the kitchen. "I'm getting a bite to eat, then I'm going home," he called over his shoulder.

"Night, Jesse," Buck called, and took another sip; but Carson went to gather up the discarded papers and brought them back to the couch. He handed them to Buck with a smile.

"Read it."

Buck turned to look at him. "Don't you have anything better to do?" he demanded.

"I'm curious. And he doesn't care, he just threw it down for anyone to read."

Buck sighed and held his hand out, and Carson grinned and gave him the letter.

Buck pulled a pair of glasses out of his jacket and adjusted them on his nose. He read:

"Dear Mr. Spade:

My name is Isabella Lucia Armenteros y Sedano."

Buck paused and rubbed his nose. "That's a mouthful." He sighed and went on, "Your name has been recommended to me as a man who can tame difficult horses. This report has been verified to me by many, and I would like to retain you to help me with my family's thoroughbred horse, Tequila Chaser."

"Poor girl," Chase laughed, and lifted his glass to his lips. "Nobody must've told her that Jesse's kind of a horse himself."

"I will be coming to your country this week," Buck read, "and I will bring my stallion with me to your home."

Buck stared at the letter in frowning concern, and Carson threw his head back and laughed. "I'm going to stick around," he chuckled. "This should be funny."

Buck turned to the next page, then tossed both down on the table. "Somebody should write to that girl and tell her not to come," he muttered. "Jesse's going to send her right back to Mexico. He hardly coaches anybody with their horses unless the mood hits him right. And he don't look like he's in too good a mood."

"The letter probably wouldn't get to her in time," Carson observed. "She said this week. She may already be on her way," he laughed.

Buck sighed, drained his glass, and stood up. "Well, I'm not gonna get involved," he muttered, and put his glasses back in his pocket. "That's Jesse's business, and he'll handle it." He stretched big and yawned. "All that party food made me sleepy. I'm going upstairs."

"Night Buck," Carson called absently, as he picked the letters up off the table.

"Night."

He was no sooner gone, than Donna drifted into the house. She caught sight of her husband sitting on the leather couch, and she walked over to perch on the arm beside him.

"What mischief are you up to?" she demanded with a smile. "You look like a cat with feathers in its mouth."

Carson raised his eyes to hers and smiled. "I'm not involved at all," he told her. "I'm just going to watch." He drained his glass and walked to the stairs, leaving his wife to frown and trail after him.

"Involved in what?" she asked in a puzzled tone. "What are you going to watch?

"Carson?"

www.ingramcontent.com/pod-product-compliance
Lightning Source LLC
Chambersburg PA
CBHW061922220726
48287CB00018B/25